WATERSPOUT

WATERSPOUT

A Pink Sheep Novel

TROY FORD

Waterspout

Sweet Flag Books

EBOOK ISBN: 979-8-9926138-2-7
PAPERBACK ISBN: 979-8-9926138-3-4

Cover Design: Design for Writers

To Leo, always

The Pink Sheep Novels

Lamb
Waterspout

PROLOGUE

[Excerpts of the following appear in the Fiftieth Anniversary Edition of *Bonfire Magazine*.]

You can imagine our mixed feelings as we gathered that autumn evening in Paul Allenson's Upper East Sixties apartment to celebrate his birthday two months after his funeral. Paul had thrown himself a party every year since 1981, through his rise (and precipitous fall), but before putting the family home on the market, the younger Allensons decided to raise one last glass to his memory. Paul Jr., flown in from London, and Blair, recently pregnant, hosted this last pageant of colleagues, friends, ex-lovers, and notable acquaintance, and now that any formal mourning period could safely be said to have passed, rumors could be examined and discussed in more (and less) discrete tones. Paul had been an insatiable gossip, and would have been the first to hold forth. Everyone agreed there were worse ways to go.

One person elicited an intrigued buzz among even that illustrious bunch.

"But did you see who's in the library?"

Diminutive, dressed all in pearl gray alone near Paul's storied portrait, the artist himself, James Traywick, stood like a docent on hand to explain the infamy of his own painting.

Being close to their age, I had bonded in friendship with the kids of my mentor and former fling. Unlike Paul, tall and fair, they had inherited the darker, almost Eastern features of their late mother. We three huddled behind an august fiddle leaf fig to survey the gradual unleashing of tongues—these parties had been an annual cafe society bacchanal for a company which fancied itself a new Vicious Circle. Paul Jr. admitted he had not seen his father for over two years, what with the demands of work, the legal drama, and the never forgiven insult of his childhood bedroom's sacrifice to a new staircase connecting their downstairs apartment with the still gutted upstairs Paul had purchased for an expansion into a duplex. "Project Showcase" must now fall on someone else's shoulders.

"It's a shame—the old place never looked so good." He examined a recent update, the tooled, topaz leather wall upholstery in the lounge conjuring a smoky men's club vibe. I mentioned the material was a flawless vinyl imitation installed by a craftsman who owed Paul a favor.

"He always was a sucker for veneers." Paul Jr. caressed the figured embossing. "Swank."

Late to the party, I asked about the pale specter in the library, and Blair whispered with glittering eyes, "Oh! That's the guy who did the portrait! The guy! You should introduce yourself."

The portrait had been an unsettling fixture over the fireplace during that last awkward chapter of Paul's life. His clear blue eyes contained small flecks of emerald green—I had noticed them early on, struck by their brilliance across the breakfast table as Paul faced a sunny window. The painting captured not only those famously jewel-bright eyes, but also the force of his charisma, fanned to heroic effect. Since receiving the sad if unsurprising news, I had forgotten about the mysterious artist who unwittingly provided the gasoline which burned Paul Allenson's life to the ground.

Were it not for the conspicuous reticence of the other guests to enter the library, I might have dismissed him at a glance. Blair's urging reminded me of the tragedy attached to his name. New York society had barely registered the second-page news from California at the time, but the scandal embroiling Paul had been cocktail party fodder for years before his lurid demise. With Paul's death reigniting interest in his troubles, here was an untold story mooning around like a lone wildebeest in tall grasses.

I approached him in the paneled library and introduced myself. "James, is it?"

"Actually I go by Jimmy." He turned to face me and I nearly gasped in startled recognition of his impairment; I'd only seen him so far in profile. I knew the story—why was I taken off guard? Jimmy searched my face as though expecting the reaction I had barely managed to stifle. His gaze shifted and he noticed the awards wall over my shoulder by the door.

"Look at all those—I didn't know he'd won so many—oh. These are all his—"

"Wife's," I confirmed. "Pulitzer. National Book Award. Honorary doctorate. Those are Paul's." I pointed out the trio of local journalism awards. "She didn't marry him for his writing creds."

"Or his fidelity."

"Oh, they had an arrangement of course. I mean, she had a name and family money—but you know how charming Paul was. I guess she was a bit reserved—she needed his chutzpah. They were quite the power couple back in the day."

Claire Hopper had been struck down by breast cancer at the height of her writing career fifteen years earlier. Paul had nursed her devotedly with the help of a full-time nurse and a cocaine habit.

I asked Jimmy if he would like to see upstairs—to break the ice, to get him alone, and to discuss an idea Paul himself had proposed not long before he keeled over of a heart attack at a hotel with a rentboy from the Bronx. He nodded eagerly.

By annexing Paul Jr.'s former small bedroom, the new staircase joined the two apartments in their entry halls. Other than the stairs, however, the transformation of the addition had been stalled for over a decade. The purchase and demolition ate up much of Paul's share of the trust within a year of his wife's death, and the whole upper story remained open and empty from one end to the other. An exact duplicate of the downstairs apartment, Paul had wanted to double the modest square footage of their three bed/three bath half a block off the Park. Another perk was the view over the shorter building next door. While their living room downstairs only had windows onto the street, the upstairs also had windows on the parkside wall. Jimmy spotted these right away and walked over to see. The empty space contained little more than steel columns, dangling wires, and the scarred original floors filmed with plaster dust and footprints.

Up the stairwell came the jangle of a dropped glass and a scream—Paul's friend, Sandrine (No last name? French? Algerian?) prone to smashing things for dramatic effect on screen and in life. I hovered along the street-side windows, observing Jimmy, so slight he almost seemed a child from a distance. Someone so short could get lost in a crowd, might prefer to hold himself apart from teeming crushes. Such a person could be excused for wearing a shock of color. I knew a dozen adorable imps who got away with loud prints, blasts of red, orange, peacock blue without looking ridiculous. Jimmy's gray-on-gray, while not unfashionable, begged you to overlook him.

"He's practically an idiot savant," Paul had told me during the initial excitement of his debut. "I mean, he's not a retard obviously, but he's got no formal education." Paul never minced words. "Where he got his talent is anyone's guess. Real shame about his face though—my god, he was a beauty— bona fide ten, and I do mean 'bone'—I was half hoping to double-down and get him a modeling contract out here. You've seen the pictures."

I had, a set taken months before his first show. Without the context of his petiteness in person, you might picture him on a billboard towering over Times Square in a pair of white briefs, a blond Olympian stopping traffic. Whatever luster he once had, here was an altogether changed person. Sipping sparkling apple juice, for one thing—Paul had said he was a drinker.

"This would have been his new master bedroom, I guess," Jimmy said, his voice so soft I had to bend closer. "He told me it was going to have a view of the Park."

I knew Paul sometimes came upstairs at night to gaze through those windows at the green, suffering from a cocaine-fueled insomnia. "He thought the lamplight in the trees looked like a magical realm, some wonderland in the city like a dandelion in cracked asphalt."

Jimmy whispered in reply too quietly for me to catch what he said.

We stood side-by-side looking out. Time to get to the point, now or never.

"You know I'm a journalist, right?" He did—Paul had mentioned me, he said. For obvious reasons, Paul's article from four years before had focused on Ramon Castro, and left Jimmy's part vague, but Paul had thought it might be time to tell his story. He had refused most interviews as his star had risen, an enigma some speculated was intentional. Now he had a new dealer and a new show selling respectably, well-reviewed if perplexing—his recent work was a complete departure from his debut. He was not a recluse, he insisted, just preferred to remain behind the firewall of agent and gallery. Meeting him in person, I understood why he had also avoided being photographed.

"Do you think it's time to set the record straight?" I asked, thrilled he was all but suggesting the story.

Jimmy sighed and peered at me again with his singular stare.

"I got sober after that whole mess," he said, almost apologetically, "and there is one person I'll never be able to make amends to—Oscar—how I handled him is my biggest regret. So yeah, maybe I do owe it to him. I have been thinking it's time."

He agreed that evening to an interview about the events five years earlier, and we talked in a series of calls over the next month.

ONE

This is a California story, a Western story, not unlike the story of America itself.

The people in it are chasing something or leaving something behind. Like many tales of the West, there are different ways to arrive at the end of the line—no next stop, no further frontier. No one really leaves America for greener pastures.

Once upon a time, tales of the West let you outpace your troubles, one step ahead, welcome to your Destiny. If you follow that fateful road all the way to the Coast, in a Rush or otherwise, that's the edge. No going back, no going forward.

This is a story of people drowning in troubled waters.

—From "The Blood-Dimmed Tide" – Paul Allenson, 2016

Overwrought by Thursday morning Bay Bridge traffic though he was, Jimmy rolled his eyes to heaven when he found a parking spot right in front of Coffee Lab. A weathered woman in a gold lamé halter, as though waiting for his arrival, stood and ushered him into the space with a deep bow before careening amiably down the sidewalk, good deed accomplished. Tourists and businesspeople alike parted in cautious waves before her, oblivious to her charms. Spitting distance from Union Square, the night shift punched out and sailed off.

This was the second time in a week Jimmy had rented a moving van, and he couldn't even afford the insurance offered at the agency. Between losing his job, the deposit on his new studio and other costs, his checking account balance had dipped below three digits for the first time in—well, not that long, really, but still. And now he had to remove his paintings from the cafe, not three days after leaving his Mission apartment for exile across the Bay.

Connor, Coffee Lab's manager, had sent a terse email giving Jimmy forty-eight hours to clear out. Connor had grown exasperated by the picayune details of lining up unknown artists hoping for an exhibition credit on their artist bio. He had commissioned a permanent art installation, a mural by his Persian girlfriend in long, minimalist panels based on a Fibonacci sequence to go with the clinical, all-white scheme of the place.

When Jimmy called, Connor had been unyielding. "I know we're cutting it short, but it's not like you've sold anything."

"It's supposed to be a six-month show."

"I'd hardly call it a show, we just needed something to hang on the walls."

Behind the spot where Jimmy parked the van, a dumpster squatted for a few other light renovations Connor was undertaking "including the disposal of any and all artwork not removed in a timely manner" his impatient reminder email had warned.

Jimmy brought his own hammer this time. When he'd arrived for the installation, the sullen barista had taken fifteen minutes to locate theirs, hiding in plain sight as a paperweight under the Carrara marble counter. He had hung the paintings a foot higher than normal because Connor warned patrons would lean their greasy heads on them. Easy enough to pull them down, but he would need a ladder for the hooks.

But if he was expected, why now was the stepladder missing? That same saturnine barista now hung on the arm of the espresso machine squinting at Jimmy.

"You are not gonna make a scene, little man. I'm here by myself—I've got the morning rush." She glowered with a raised eyebrow ring, nodding toward the only patron, a pale stranger sitting at a table reading The New York Times. "And Connor said I didn't have to help you take your shit down."

"I'm not asking you to help me, I just need a ladder. You had a ladder two months ago," he said, voice shaking. Did she hiss at him just then, or was that the machine?

He understood any further conversation with her would be making a scene, his mother's voice ringing in his ear: "James Christopher Traywick, do not make a scene, or I swear to god..." But Bitch Barista had pushed some new forthright button of his ire. He would make a scene!

"How about we call Connor?"

"How about you call Connor, you little fudge packer." Her head swiveled dangerously on her shoulders. "Your stuff sucks anyway."

Jimmy froze, a knot of pounding blood. "Girl, I am literally holding a hammer—"

As he brandished it to show her what's what, New York Times-guy appeared suddenly beside him and snatched the hammer away.

"Careful, sport—here let me hold that for you. Why don't you step out for some air while I have a word with this young"—he cast a disdainful gaze at the barista and gave Jimmy a wink—"lady."

Flustered, Jimmy grabbed the nearest painting, a self-portrait. A softly drawn-out *sssss* whispered behind him. This time, the girl was nowhere near the espresso machine. Glaring at him, arms folded, she twisted her tongue piercing between her teeth. Bitch did hiss! Perhaps he would take a moment and go unlock the rental van before he did something rash. He carried the painting out the door, off the curb and into the street behind the van, the swish of charging traffic just one step further.

No wonder so many pedestrians got run over in San Francisco: these one-way streets were practically freeways.

Beside him sat the van on one hand, and on the other the dumpster. Strong gusts of air and acrid exhaust threatened to knock the painting against grimy metal on either side. His slender wrists creaked trying to steady it. He stepped back, set the canvas on the pavement, noticed too late the used condom lying in wait to gum itself to the bottom edge of the frame. It had poo on it. Jesus Fucking Christ. The TenderNob—of course, that old verge where Snob Hill and the Tenderloin flowed together into the gutter.

He could have laughed, or screamed. Breathless, weightless, Jimmy would not have been too concerned if he'd lifted off and floated straight out of the atmosphere.

Did he give a shit about the rest of the paintings still hanging? For half a second he considered just leaving them all and driving off. Maybe, at last, time to say fuck it all—fuck art, fuck goth chicks and their fucking festering piercings, fuck getting laid off, and landlords and their illegal sublets—fuck San Francisco for that matter—fuck EVERYTHING and EVERYONE, FUCK!

As he struggled to calm down, he caught his own forlorn reflection in the plate-glass window of the cafe and stood transfixed. Maybe it was the light, maybe the adrenaline, but the pale ghost now staring back seemed washed-out, and today, washed-out felt one step away from roadkill. And there at his feet, as if mocking his mortification, his self-portrait gazed up, still fresh. Poor kid. That sweeter Jimmy, that younger, naiver Jimmy, smiling in a field of orange poppies and still believing kindly art teachers grew on trees.

New York Times-guy walked out, his brow knit. Perhaps he guessed all that was in Jimmy's mind.

"How you feeling, Kindercamp?"

The question took him off guard until he remembered he wore his beloved threadbare t-shirt—"KINDERCAMP" it read, with finger-painted stick kids and stick animals, a relic from a summer camp job back in Fresno. A size too small, he had grown out of it but saved this piece of his increasingly distant childhood.

Jimmy sighed, his pique spent. "I'm alright. What'd you say to her?"

The guy shrugged. "I told her when she plays with her piercing it looks like she's picking her nose." Jimmy laughed in spite of himself. "But you know, just now I had this strange feeling you were about to make another mistake out here. May I?" He lifted the self-portrait as Jimmy trapped the dirty rubber with his sneaker in a rare moment of quick thinking.

"This is good." He praised the balanced composition, the confident brush strokes, precise details, perspective, color scheme. "Really well done." In the painting, obviously a selfie, Jimmy had shown his own arm holding a cell phone in the bronzed tones of a similar Ralph Lauren ad he'd used as a color reference. "It would be a real shame for you to give up because some nobody in a tired cafe gave you a hard time."

"No, I wasn't—I ... I've just been at this for so long, and they shut me down."

"C'mon kiddo—are you even old enough to drink?"

"I'm twenty-four," Jimmy admitted.

"Alright, well seriously, I've known artists who took twenty years to get noticed, and here I am, noticing you—you're very good. I'm Paul, Paul Allenson. I'm visiting from New York."

"Jimmy Jimmy Traywick."

Paul didn't acknowledge the joke. "I'm a writer but I do a little scouting for dealers, nothing formal—I keep my eyes peeled, make introductions. You've got real talent." He mentioned the other painting which had caught his eye through the window the day before, the reason he had stopped in—the landscape with a dilapidated adobe bungalow and a dead oak shriveled as a burnt matchstick. The house looked worn away by poverty as much as time and weather. Haunting. He'd read about Santa Ana winds somewhere—where was that? Jimmy shrugged.

"But this is a very good likeness. How much do you charge? I've been thinking about a portrait for a while, but nobody does it the old-fashioned way—everyone and their mother is a goddamn photographer now."

The price was marked on the wall, Jimmy figured he had definitely seen. He stepped back up onto the sidewalk, still a head shorter than the New Yorker. After a moment's hesitation only a gambler would have noticed, he quoted twice the listed price, "for commissions."

Paul shrugged. "Reasonable. You have a studio?"

Yes, a fantastic new space across the Bay, just moved in

Monday, not even unpacked.

"Albany? Over by the track—that's where you live?"

The track?

"Golden Gate Fields. What are you doing tomorrow morning?"

Jimmy was free, as it happened, his new job started the next weekend.

"Tell you what: I'll help you take your paintings down, but you have to wear that shirt again tomorrow."

Back inside, Jimmy moved one of the plastic chairs into position to reach a hook.

"Are your shoes clean?" the barista yelled. She waved her hand limply as though powered by hot air. "Those are designer chairs. Also, if you fall, we're not responsible."

Paul addressed the girl warmly. "My dear, I'm worried. You should go to a doctor, the holes in your head look infected."

TWO

Of all people, it was Marlys who had introduced her son to vodka martinis, because of her admiration for, of all people, 007. Marlys Traywick adored Roger Moore.

"I adore Roger Moore," she'd always say. The only cocktail she ever drank was a vodka martini, shaken not stirred. She taught Jimmy how to make one on his twenty-first birthday while explaining the ins and outs of the Bond franchise, at least as far as it concerned her.

"Roger Moore—of course, he was The Saint first, oh, he was handsome, oh, that cute little car, if I ever gave up the Landau it would be for a vintage Volvo, white of course, just like my Roger." Behind her back, Jimmy called her butter-yellow Ford LTD "Landau" the Banana Boat due to its color, spongy ride, and ponderous length.

For Jimmy's special birthday, Marlys had fished out the old martini shaker, unused since James Sr. had died, and polished up its silver-plated finish as Jimmy slouched at the kitchen counter.

"No vermouth, I can't stand that Spanish nonsense, too sweet. The vodka knocks the corners off the ice, the ice takes the edge off the vodka." She shook it good and hard until the silver frosted, an old pro. "Truth is I prefer an onion—that's a gibson—but an olive is traditional, you can have mine."

She served herself and Jimmy from a mirrored tray on the patio, lit a Parliament, and held up her glass for a toast. "To Roger Moore!" She didn't bother to wait for Jimmy to clink her glass and took a deep sip. "Oof. Perfection. Oh, and to you too, dear, happy birthday. But Sean Connery, I mean, I suppose he was more manly, but he hated women, you could just tell he enjoyed slapping them around, he was your father's favorite of course, but I could not abide him."

And so it became a tradition: a shaker full of martinis for their twice weekly chats, though mostly Marlys could not be bothered and drank her rosé instead. She took great pains to keep track of Jimmy's calls though—Marlys always kept score—missing a call to his mother came with a high price. Today she just wanted to check in to see how he was settling into his new place and spent the obligatory half hour describing the state of her grout.

"Four hundred dollars he wants, just to clean it. Not even to redo it, actually chunk it out and redo it, no, four hundred dollars just to clean it! But I don't think it even can be cleaned, I've tried everything: Magic Eraser, the grout attachment on my steam cleaner, bleach! I blame your father, of course, he should have made them rip out all the tile when they first redid it, I told him then, I said, 'It's too close together, there's hardly any room for the grout to get in there, it's just going to crack and fall apart and be a mess within a year,' and of course I was right..."

"Mother. Mother! I gotta get going." Jimmy endured the offended pause. Her sapphire enamel lighter snapped as she lit another cigarette and settled in with a long, calming exhale. Marlys would now keep her son on the phone as long as she liked—she kept a tally of such slights, too. Also, she might have something juicy to tell.

"James, there is no need to shout. I meant to tell you—I hope you're sitting down—Maryann died."

"Oh my god! That's awful—when? What happened?"

"Well, I only heard about it on Tuesday when Julio came."

"Julio? Who's Julio?"

"The gardener, James—you remember Julio, he's been working on our yard since before your father died."

"I thought his name was Juan." Actually he knew it was Juan—he had sucked Juan's dick.

"Is it? No. It's definitely Julio. Anyway, his brother Roberto is—was—Maryann's gardener, and he told Julio, and Julio told me when he came on Tuesday."

"Jesus, that's terrible—but how?"

"He didn't say."

"Didn't you ask?"

"Oh, his English is terrible, I hate talking to him."

"But did you go over—did you talk to—what's her husband's name?"

"Steve. No, I didn't go over, I mean, it happened two weeks ago—it's not like he bothered to come over to tell me, her best friend. No, if he wants to, he can walk two houses down and say something."

"But what about the funeral?"

"I assume that's all over with by now—gracious, James, you can't leave a dead body hanging around for two weeks. Think."

"No, I mean, wouldn't you have gone to the funeral if you'd known?"

"Of course! Probably. I mean, if they'd had a service at the house, certainly—at least then I might have had a chance to find my punch bowl she borrowed and never gave back, the one Gramma gave me, the one with the owls. I guess I'll never get it back now."

"Well, Jeez, I'm sorry mother."

"Oh, you know—that's life—it's not like I've used it much the last few years. Anyway, like I say, live and learn—don't lend people things you want back because you never know when they'll stiff you—Oh! I mean—I didn't mean it like that. Anyway, I meant to tell you they're having another one of those gun exchanges down at the Sheriff's Department—they're giving away raffle tickets for a new car, that's something, huh?"

"Yeah. Something. I thought you already turned in Grandpa's old service revolver."

"I did! And they weren't even giving anything away then, stupid me. But no, I was thinking of your father's hunting rifle you took with you last time—if you brought it back, I could turn it in and we'd get I don't remember how many tickets they said, not as many for a rifle, those gang bangers don't like carrying around rifles of course, they can't hide them in their droopy pants, and the whole point is to get them to turn in their pistols."

"I know all about what the gang bangers of Fresno are hiding in their pants, mother." Long pause. Jimmy snapped open the clasp on the old cedar trunk next to his mattress, still lying in the middle of the floor where he had dumped it on arrival.

"What was that?" Marlys cried.

"Just the trunk, mother, I keep the rifle locked up in it." He took the weapon out and checked the chamber for the millionth time. It was a handsome gun, with brass fittings and a rich wood grain, slender for a child's use and barely touched.

"Well, anyway, if you want me to turn it in we could win a car."

"That's like the only thing I have of his, besides his ring. I don't really think I want to give it away." He was still unclear as to whether this particular gun had been given to his father by his own father, or whether he had purchased it for Jimmy and never gone through with the gifting out of some vague presentiment that his son was not that kind of boy. "And I can't have a car up here anyway, there's no parking, and I can't afford insurance and all that. You don't need a car—you've got the Landau."

"True, but then I'd have a second car for you when you came to visit and you wouldn't have to drive mine all over town—it hasn't stayed in pristine condition cruising all over Fresno willy-nilly." She had sold James Sr.'s Oldsmobile after Jimmy moved to San Francisco—if only she knew what Jimmy had got up to in the Landau the few times he had been down to visit and she had deigned to let him drive it.

"I think I'd rather keep it—he never took me hunting, but it does have some sentimental value."

Big sigh. "Alright James, well I'm just going to remind you that the vast majority of gun deaths are owners with their own guns, and while I know you would never intentionally hurt me by committing suicide, you practically live in Oakland now. What if someone breaks in? What if someone uses it against you?"

"Albany is very safe, mother—I don't even have any bullets. Trust me, Oakland gangbangers have even less room to hide guns in their pants than the ones down in Fresno."

"James Christopher! I don't like that kind of talk about pants and your gay stuff. It's disgusting."

Jimmy's turn to sigh. "Yes, mother." He turned the rifle around, put the barrel in his mouth and pulled the trigger. Click!

"What was that?' Marlys cried again.

"The clasp of the trunk, mother. Again."

"Don't patronize me, James. You might also consider that if we won the car, we could sell it and split the money so I'll just plant that bug in your ear. It's already almost killed someone—remember the time you and David snuck in the house in the middle of the night and your father thought you were a burglar?"

"How could I forget?"

"Food for thought. How is David doing? I saw his mother the other day at the grocery store—oh my, has she aged. Completely let herself go. I feel like sending her an anonymous note, someone should tell her to slap on a little lipstick at least."

"Dee is fine—he's doing a show in the city tonight, I'm going over later."

"Give him my best. Have a nice time."

"My mom says 'Hi.' Did you add Matt to the guest list?"

"Oh. Fister Matt? Was I supposed to?"

"Yes, I texted you. I already told him he was on the guest list, Dee..."

"OK, settle down—I'll call Dan. What time will you be there? Ish...?"

"Probably ten-thirty, maybe..."

"You're keeping the van for tonight?"

"Yeah, I tried to return it early for a refund, but they weren't having it."

"Good. I'm banned from Uber on account of glitter. I'm getting a ride down, but you're my ride home."

"Alright."

"And my show is at eleven thirty, don't be late."

"Alright! Jesus. See you later—call Dan now."

"Dan?"

"To add Matt to the guest list! Oh my god..."

"Ha! Just fucking with you, bitch! See ya!"

With a disco nap and a shower, Jimmy sobered up from his afternoon martinis and headed back to the City. He was meeting Matt at ten before heading to The Stallion, half hoping he might want a quick pump and dump in the van—might as well get his money's worth since he didn't have to return it until the next morning. Matt, maybe boyfriend or maybe just the guy he had been fisting in exchange for dick, liked things almost as dirty as Jimmy. They hadn't talked specifically about feelings aside from a surreptitious "I love you" while shooting a load.

A Happy Meal at the SOMA McDonald's was a favorite trick to avoid filling up his stomach before hitting the clubs. He had been casually collecting the toys for years, lots of Star Wars characters, a fair few Hot Wheels Barbies, My Little Ponies, and Teenage Mutant Ninja Turtles.

"Aren't you a little old for a Happy Meal?" the girl at the counter asked.

"Bless you," he said.

She popped her gum. "Bless me why?"

"It's for my kid brother, he's in the car."

"By himself...?"

Jimmy sat at the picnic table in the city-sized McPlayPlace—a couple of bouncy horses on springs, a teeter-totter, and a slide regurgitated from Ronald McDonald's mouth behind a yellow picket fence—practically a sandbox compared to the suburbs, urban space at a premium and all. City kids had such low expectations. Cars stopped at the intersection as he dumped the contents of his bag, SpongeBob tumbling out. Excellent. Cars pulled away as he ignored the sandwich and ate the fries—aw, good and hot. Could happiness be bought so easily? Yes, if it came with a side of fries.

"Where's your Daddy, little boy?" Matt had snuck up from behind.

"He's getting a blowjob in the bathroom," Jimmy said, mouth full.

"Without his boy? It's almost like he wants you to get into someone's van."

"Already got the van, I just need the perv."

Matt often said out loud the acerbic comments others might keep to themselves. ("Jesus, woman! Put some back into it! This isn't a knitting circle—punch my hole!") But he was Jimmy's favorite type: dark, bearded, stocky, belly—every inch the hipster lumberjack in plaid shirt, jeans, and horn-rimmed glasses. True, maybe more of a lust connection than love, but thanks to the incessant talking, Jimmy felt no need to step out of his quietly aloof comfort zone.

("He's just like me, quiet!" Marlys once declared to a concerned guidance counselor, to which James Sr. growled, "Marlys, you don't know what you're fucking talking about.")

Jimmy motioned to the plastic bench seat. "Sit, or do you wanna grab a bite?"

Matt sat, sheepishly. "I'm good, I already ate. I thought you'd be here—your little ritual. Who did you get?"

Jimmy wagged SpongeBob and made him dance on the table.

"I'm sure he'll keep you good company." Matt pretended distraction watching a Tesla pull out of the drive-thru. "So listen, I was hoping I might catch you here rather than have to go into the bar." Jimmy stopped chewing—not much of an appetite in the first place, the fries now turned to wood pulp in his mouth.

"I'm sober," Matt said, "one month chip yesterday."

"Oh really."

"Yeah, you know, after the last time you came over, I went on a bender, started posting ads for all comers—"

"There's worse things..." Jimmy offered an indulgent smile.

Matt pursed his lips. "Yeah, only I ended up partying on tina for three days—started hallucinating—it wasn't pretty..."

"Oh. Wow, scary. I mostly steer clear." Jimmy had had his encounters with meth and was grateful never to have clicked with any tweakers, the learning curve for tina was fast and straight down. But he sensed an announcement.

"Anyway—I think I need us to chill, you know, with me getting sober and you moving to the East Bay, maybe this is a good time to take a break—it's not like either of us has a car, and BARTing back and forth for playdates—really?"

"Playdates, right..." Jimmy said. Was this twinge regret? Because someone was taking away a toy—or because he had feelings for the toy?

"I mean we had some fun." Bringing things to a swift close. "We could still get together once in a while—you've got great hands..." Keeping options open. "Anyway—I thought the big boy thing would be to talk in person. I've been going to AA meetings every day—I'm not even sure how to get fisted sober, people keep telling me I've gotta give up poppers too and I'm like 'Nooooo!'"

Jimmy sighed. "I get it," he said, "and you're right—BART would get old fast—and doing it sober for your sake probably would kill the mood."

There came a moment when everything stopped. For three full breaths, no cars passed, no customers inside—the staff was out of sight behind the counter—even Matt could find nothing to add. They were completely alone, no witnesses: If a bear dumps a twink under the golden arches, and nobody hears...?

Jimmy huffed and nodded. "So good luck with all that."

Matt stood up, hesitated. "What about you? Ever thought about AA?"

Stop right there.

"Let's not," Jimmy said. "Let's just call it a night."

"Fine. The shit of it is—I actually like you better when you're drunk."

Jimmy chucked his half-eaten food at the overflowing trash, missed, picked it up and crushed it onto the top. He handed SpongeBob to Matt. "Company—for your meetings," he said with a quick peck on the lips before walking away.

At the corner waiting for the light, he glanced back just as Matt threw the toy hard at the garbage can. It bounced off the side, and he stalked off. Jimmy returned to retrieve SpongeBob from the pile of trash on the ground. Not broken—sponges were resilient. Seized again as earlier by that same breathless floating—adrift now between the vastness of starless city sky and stone-cold streets—Jimmy sat back on the bench and regarded Bob. Oh, to be a simple sponge anchored to bedrock in wondrous depths and not some unfriended flotsam. Under and past the freeway, Matt's receding figure turned left toward the Mission and disappeared, no looking back. Time to get wet, then—it was past eleven and Dee was expecting him.

Half a block too late, Jimmy muttered aloud his perfect rejoinder, too good to keep to himself.

Fuck sake. Obviously: "I like you better when I'm drunk, too."

THREE

"Dan, you big stud—vodka tonic. Please." Jimmy sat at the end of the bar closest to the door so he could see when Dee arrived. Dan poured him an extra strong cocktail but waved away his money.

"No need, baby—DeeDee's got you covered. She did say you were only supposed to be drinking beer tonight though."

"Rough night." Jimmy shrugged, tossed the straw on the bar and slurped. He loved dive bars best, the hollow, pants-optional places with clothes checks where he could while away an evening with a blurry romp wearing just his shoes and an adorable grin. Blacked out in the back room, the sweetest ass in the City would let you blow a load up in him—no need for lube, someone else's wad already greasing the gears. Some of the older bartenders loved little Jimmy—just like the old days, good for business.

The Stallion, where Dee performed his regular Thursday night gig, lacked the tang and dark corners of his favorite drinking holes though the alley out back was legendary. The bar was so long they needed five bartenders to cover. A model train outfitted with a coach and horses instead of an engine ran on tracks suspended from the ceiling, in perpetual motion over the top shelf of liquor bottles and winding around the dance floor through year-round garlands of Christmas lights.

Jimmy dangled his legs off the barstool, feet not reaching the floor. He was even shorter if he stood, eye-level to nipples. As he looked into the crowd of guys jockeying for drinks, the crowd looked back, looked away, snuck appraising glances. Jimmy knew for every "hot boy" aimed at him, there was another "What the fuck is that kid doing in here?" He was accustomed to the perplexed double-takes.

Jimmy could teach a class: Beta Males—Love and Lust for Runts.

Step One: Station yourself at the end of the bar or in a lonely corner—don't get lost in the crowd—outlying prey are alluring to hunters.

Step Two: You are a bottom, relax.

Step Three: A squeaky clean asshole is the key to repeat business.

Step Four: Quantity over quality—beggars can't be choosers. No matter how cute, a pocket gay in a city full of bottoms ranked somewhere below drag queens with big dicks.

But hey, with a couple three drinks in you, any old port in a storm would do. Down the length of the bar, he watched the Tetris shuffle of breeding stock—grass-fed, organic, free-range, Angus, Omaha, Kobe, Hamburger Helper—all yelling in each other's ears over the pounding music. He had tricked with that tall, big-eared doofus last year, but the guy refused to look at him now. That one further on had a great beard and a six pack, even if his eyes were crossed. Another dude was thinning on top, but he had a great smile thanks to several thousand dollars' worth of veneers, Dee had told him.

What were they all saying? What did people talk about in bars? Their boring retail gigs? Favorite kinks? Dental work? "Cute kid, but I need a man not a leprechaun"?

How to choose? Why choose? If you would all line up, please, all deposits will be accepted in a timely fashion, thank you. No talking.

Where to start? When in doubt—guy or guys flirting with possibly maybe making eye contact—when Jimmy froze, shrank into his seat, never knew what to say or do next, he could always turn to the bartender and say, "Vodka tonic, please."

Once, on an early morning 14-Mission bus, almost empty but for a handful of single men arranged at a wary distance from each other, Jimmy took his usual place near the back. Next stop, a short Asian lady stumbled onto the bus, she could be someone's mother. Clearly in a state of half capacity, she leaned spaghetti-legged against the ticket machine, tore her bus pass while stuffing it back in her pocket, did not notice the half that fell to the floor. Poor thing.

The doors of the bus closed, the driver stomped on the gas, probably on purpose. The lady careened into the man sitting closest to the front. She fell right into him, not even raising a hand to stop herself. He squawked and pushed her away. The driver laughed. No apologies, she grabbed a post, leaned in and squinted at the grumbling man. She spoke to him but he ignored her and she continued down the aisle to the next rider. Rinse, repeat. As she got nearer he could see her puffy, beet-red face, no make-up, dowdy, pudgy, mom-jeans. Shit-faced. She was plastered, at six o-clock in the morning!

She approached the next guy, and this time Jimmy heard what she was asking.

"Wanna fuck?" Jesus Christ. She was making her unflappable way through the entire bus with this solicitation. She had her sea legs by then, took the rolling bounces and swerves in stride. "Wanna fuck?" Half a dozen men on the bus, no women, and she was going to ask every one of them until she scared up some dick. You go, girl.

She approached the old black man two seats up from Jimmy, but he hollered at her before she could utter her proposition. "You steppin' too close you squash-colored banana bitch!" Unfazed, she lurched past. She regarded Jimmy in his turn with the most unfocused, bloodshot eyes he had ever seen, and then she passed, saying nothing.

He turned and watched as she came to the next dude pulling a hoodie down past woodgrain Wayfarers, shrinking away from her with a scowl. "Wanna fuck?"

Bitch.

Jimmy nodded at Dan and tapped his empty glass. "One more? I just got dumped."

Dan had that sexy, rundown Dad look about him. Hung like a horse, too. He was one of the owners as well as a bartender—Jimmy rarely bought his own drinks at The Stallion.

"Aw, poor boy. Maybe you need Daddy to take your mind off it."

"Great minds, Mister." He clinked his fresh glass against the beer Dan swilled. "I gotta say 'Hi' to Dee at least."

"Drink up then, she's here."

Like a Macy's Thanksgiving Day balloon floating into view—towering and gas-filled—Dusty Davenport the Banjo Queen loomed in a titanic platinum bouffant with no fewer than two dozen pink bows glued askew. His enormous beginghamed bosoms slapped, smacked, and poked into faces and eyes along his merry way to the bar. Double-D, the Singing Harlot, DeeDee to his friends, just Dee to his mom, his older sister—to whom his musical repertoire owed an immeasurable debt—and Jimmy. As he approached, Dan popped a straw into a bottle of water and handed it across the bar for Dee to sip.

"Jimmy Jimmy, serial slut—what the fuck are you drinking? Dan! What did I tell you?"

"It's a good stiff seltzer, bitch." Jimmy downed the cocktail in a gulp and pushed the glass at Dan who swept it away behind the counter. "What's it to ya?"

From behind Dee's enormity and banjo case, four puppies in full playgear emerged, hoods, suits, collars, the works.

"Dan, Jimmy—this is the new crew: Humper, Thumper, Spanky and Sue. Puppettes—this is Dan, our host—and this is Ladybug, you guys, I was telling you about him."

"She was—nice to meet you, Ladybug—this isn't my usual gig, just sayin'," Sue said in a husky but unmistakably girl's voice, putting out a leather paw to shake. "You forgot Bitz," she said to Dee.

"Shit! Mr. Bitz! How could I forget? Bitz plays the washboard." A guy in a pig snout and pink onesie stepped forward and saluted.

"Call me 'Jimmy.'"

"Oh! And Vic! Say 'Hello' Vic! Where the hell is Vic? What happened to Vic?" Dee looked up, down, and sideways before the friend Jimmy had spoken to on the phone but never met popped up. Dark hair, dreamy eyes, Vic was thicker and taller than Jimmy. And young.

"Jimmy!" They leaned in for a hug. When Jimmy got laid off from ArtHaus, Dee had hooked him up with his non-binary friend Vic who worked at another art store across the Bay. "Nice to meet you in person finally!"

"At least you're on time," Dee said, "did you go to Mickey D's already? What'd you get?"

"Dumped."

"Oh shit! Fister Matt?"

"Who else?"

"Yeah, I saw him at a meeting—I figured that was coming, sorry pumpkin…"

Jimmy feigned irritation. "And you said nothing?"

"Hi—hi—oh, hi handsome," Dee cooed to knots of admirers. "And spoil your surprise? You're not going to tell me you actually like that big dummy? I mean, cute in a nice warm mitten kind of way, but you said yourself you were only playing at the red hanky game…"

"I know. I know! Whatever, let's not talk about it. What're you singing?"

"John Denver—'Grandpa's Leather Sling.'" Jimmy made a face. "It's hot—they'll love it." Dee signaled to the Puppettes. "Drink up, on stage in two! But you—" He turned back to Jimmy. "Don't get fucked up, dammit! Is the van a stick? I can't drive a stick."

"Automatic."

"Like your ass. Good. Fine. Whatever, I don't care—that van is my ride home tonight with or without you, whore—give me the keys—where's it parked?"

"Backside of McDonald's." Jimmy handed over the keys and they disappeared into a plastic cleavage.

"Story of your life. With or without you! Puppettes! Vamos!" They disappeared into the crowd. Vic stayed behind.

"Women!" Jimmy said. "Welcome—want a drink?"

The kid hesitated. "Well..."

"Dan! What you got for innocent kids who wander into dark alleys?" Three shot glasses appeared on the counter and quickly filled with tequila. Vic might look like a baby bunny, but they picked up a glass and knocked it back with no problem.

"You've done this before," Jimmy smirked, feeling large now. "Aren't you cute. Aren't they cute, Dan?"

"Sure." Dan wandered off.

Vic pressed in close so as not to shout. "I'm not actually twenty-one yet, don't tell— DeeDee got me in."

"Ha! That's cool, I usually feel like the youngest one in the room, nice to know I'm not for a change. Hey, thanks again for the reference at Albany Art—I think it's going to be great! Remind me how you know Dee?"

"I've been doing his graphics."

"Right! The party flyers and stuff. Nice, I thought they took a big step up recently."

Vic smiled shyly. "And you're from Fresno—artist—painter."

"Art store hustler, barfly, hole in the wa—" Jimmy stopped himself—the kid was going to be a coworker after all—and pointed toward the stage. "I think they're starting."

"You wanna get closer? I've never been to one of his shows before."

Jimmy shook his head. "Nah, I'll stay here—you go."

Vic kissed him on the lips, not a friendly peck but pillowy soft and lingering, their breath cool and sweet. "Dee said you were cute, but, wow! See you later?" They squirmed and slid away before Jimmy could answer.

Dee's music was eclectic to say the least—"maniacal" easily serving as a unifying theme. The John Denver parody of "Grandma's Feather Bed" had the Puppettes arrayed around

Dee on the stage, hands behind their backs, Bitz down in front on the washboard, clickety-clack. Hoots and whistles filled the bar. Dan wandered over while everyone's back was turned and poured them two more quick shots.

As Dee blasted off, banjo screeching, the pups brought forth two hand puppets each— thrift-store Cabbage Patch dolls, a paw stuffed up the ass of each one. As they performed their demented patty-cakes, Jimmy wondered if Grandma knew what Grandpa had got up to with the boys.

The Puppettes danced their little dance—do-si-dos and spankings—there were dildos, and a squirt gun, and something about "not much sleep but smokin' lots of meth." Magic. Silly lyrics and ridiculous choreography were Dee's calling card. "The Muppets on Molly" one columnist had dubbed Dee's last Christmas Extravaganza. ("I don't know what drugs this queen is on but go see her show quick before she drops dead.")

Then Dee started in with his "Marlene Dietrich Sings Patsy Cline" shtick—a bit of Disney, and Schoolhouse Rock—lots of banjo riffs and saucy banter, Scorpions, and then a nice Gaga medley to juice up the crowd. Green Acres and other sitcom nonsense—Jimmy had heard all this before.

Dan poured one more shot for Jimmy and nodded toward the back door. "Sneak out back?"

Showtime. "Let's go."

Dan signaled one of the other bartenders as Jimmy ducked under the bar flap. Out the back door, the narrow alley known as The Trough was deserted but for a dumpster and recycling bins full of empty bottles giving off their musky fume. On the cinder-block wall, a chalkboard still noted the scores of pigs servicing last Sunday's T-dance.

"On your knees, boy." Dan was bouncing in his boots, squeezing his crotch urgently. He unzipped and his half-hard cock flopped out.

Suddenly slow-mo and unsteady, Jimmy hesitated. "Come on, Dad—I mean Dan!—just a quick pump and dump?"

"Fuck you, boy, you got about eight drinks off my top shelf, and I've been holding in this piss for an hour."

"Five." That much Jimmy remembered.

"They were doubles!"

Jimmy relented when Dan laid an importunate hand on his shoulder to push him to the ground. He sighed, took off his clothes and threw them over the side of the dumpster. He knelt over the rusted drain in the asphalt, grit pricking his knees.

"Awright, fucker—show me what you got."

FOUR

"Wake up, bitch!" Dee poked Jimmy with the toe of his pump none too gently. "Time to go!"

Jimmy startled awake and sent an empty beer bottle clattering across the alley. Had he drunk that, too? A thank you gift from Dan, he guessed. Somehow Jimmy had put his clothes on before passing out against the wall next to the dumpster, but his shirt was back side front and his underwear missing.

He slouched in the back door, trailing Dee past the bar. The music thumped, boys danced, but Dan was too busy pouring drinks to do more than nod. Aha—Jimmy's briefs hung around Dan's neck, a trophy. The other bartender, a brawny Latin stud Jimmy had lusted after, hooted and rang a bell over the bar. Dee twinkled and waved goodbye as they passed, but Jimmy knew what the "Walk of Shame Bell" really meant—one of the bartenders had screwed a boy in The Trough mid-shift.

"A triumph!" Outside on the sidewalk, Dee punched the sky. "They loved it! But how would you know, my little cum bucket? Jesus, you stink! You smell like something washed up on a beach. Thank god we're not driving my car. You're taking a shower the minute we get home, but I'm starving. We have to stop at the Volga Hut."

Still drunk but squinting out of his blackout, Jimmy watched the City slip by, an amber-toned film reel unspooling. San

Francisco had never felt like home, had always somehow held him at arm's length—he could not even keep track of the shortcuts Dee took, the twists and turns swirling his head into a spin that thankfully righted itself after a moment. No spins tonight, no thank you. Of course, he usually rode the bus with eyes glued to his phone, but he should at least recognize these street corners and buildings, the swooping views down hills into the Bay. Jimmy had only spent three nights in the new Albany apartment, but already the City felt like a cousin not seen for a decade—changed, remote, an adult now with more mature concerns. He leaned his cheek against the cool glass of the window and shut his eyes.

Never a gentle wakener when he was irritated, Dee slammed the van door. Jimmy almost vomited. At least he recognized the neighborhood off Lombard. "I thought we were stopping for food."

"We are—we're here, it's across the street from my house, you've walked past it dozens of times." Jimmy closed one eye to read the sidewalk sandwich board. "Volga Restaurant" with a black bear in a tutu and party hat riding a unicycle. He had missed it, dozens of times apparently. "You're coming in with me. I guess you don't smell too bad—here—" Dee sprayed him with a pocket-sized breath freshener. "Minty."

One o'clock, and a few diners still lingered over drinks and dessert in the modest space. Volga accepted no reservations—first come, first served, authentic Russian cuisine, burgers and fries for the kids if they were picky. Its ten tables were spread incongruously with red-and-white checked tablecloths and candles plugged in drippy chianti bottles, inherited from the former Italian owner, cuisine changed but the decor still serviceable. Behind the bar, a newer mural involving gold-leafed onion domes hovered over a pack of older gentlemen in tracksuits smoking cigars by a 'No Smoking' sign. A rash-faced waiter rushed forward with alarm, and an accent.

"Madame! Sir, uh ... Madame. We are closing very soon, very soon..." Dee pushed past him with a great sweep of wig and plunked down at the bar, waving to the cigar smokers. They laughed and whistled like they knew him.

"We won't be staying—we'll take our food to go." He jabbed at the order pad as the kid fumbled. "Write this down—I want a chicken breast, rare—a potato—and a side of Russian dressing, hold the salad. Got it?" The boy did not write, only gaped. "I said write that down, child—oh, just go tell the cook—you're new here, aren't you? Run along."

He did, in fact, run. Not half a minute went by, long enough for Dee to apply some lipstick and blow kisses to the cigar smokers, before a great voice boomed out from the back.

"DeeDee!"

A startled woman dropped her fork.

A giant of a man, a great dark beast, stalked out to the dining room, and though Jimmy was far too drunk to be truly afraid, he stepped behind Dee anyway. Here was the largest man he had ever seen—six-six at least—four hundred pounds, easy. He had the biggest, bushiest, blackest beard, a bald head, and a huge smile with a front tooth missing. Jimmy couldn't take his eyes away from the gap. Snappy black pants, black shoes, black shirt—all black, including the thicket of chest hair frothing out his open collar.

"What are you doing here so late, my sweet?" He stooped to deliver the gentlest kiss on each of Dee's cheeks, clearly familiar with the famous "Zone of Beauty" and all of its proscriptions.

"Looking good, handsome! And smelling good too—not cooking tonight?"

"Cousin Ludmila here tonight—she's much better cook than me—I tend bar."

"Cool, cool—Jimmy. Where the hell did you go? Jimmy!" Dee reached around and wrenched him out from behind. "Jimmy, this is Feo, our proprietor. Feo, I'd like you to meet Jimmy, my oldest friend."

Feo's embrace was like being hugged by the forest, pine-scented and everything. He sniffed Jimmy and gave a knowing grin. "Ah, Jimmy—you've been having some fun tonight, eh?" He winked. "Good clean fun, eh, DeeDee? You do this to little cricket?"

Dee groaned in horror. "Are you crazy? This walking gutter is practically my sister! A thousand times no! This is Jimmy! Remember? 'Ladybug Picnic', your favorite! He's the one who came up with the idea of just four ladybugs with two puppets each—he was in my first show! A loveliness of puppets! Genius!"

"No!"

"Yes! Imagine jamming the stage with twelve whole ladybugs! What was I thinking? Where would my wig go? I built my whole act around hand puppets thanks to this little lush. Oh, the possibilities! But no—he was out working the alley tonight instead of watching my show."

"Working?"

Dee rolled his eyes. "James is in the service sector."

"Many happy customers?" Feo smiled down at Jimmy. "Is late, we close soon. Ludmila makes you a burger, yes? Yes. Too late for a little song, maybe?"

Dee already had his banjo out of the case. "My darling, I thought you'd never ask." He plucked a few notes for attention. "One two three—four five six—seven eight nine—ten eleven twelve—ladybugs came to the ladybug's picnic..."

Thankfully, it was a short ditty and like most of his covers, Dee played double time. The other patrons turned in their seats, aghast but indulgent. Feo leaned over on the bar close by Jimmy, his warm breath not unpleasant in his ear.

"DeeDee sure funny, huh? So silly—Ladybug Picnic."

Yes, he agreed, Dee was fun alright—no alcohol required.

"But what about you, cricket, something to eat?"

Jimmy clung to the bar and focused on the one thing he knew he should not: the missing tooth. "Nothing..." he whispered.

"Oh no—you have burger, huh? Nice coleslaw, nothing fancy."

Even without the shirtless fireman and the kazoos, Dee's jazzy version elicited cheers and whistles from the cigar smokers, slightly more polite clapping from the others as he wrapped up his song.

"Ah! DeeDee's right, my favorite!" Feo lumbered back to the kitchen.

The remaining diners slowly headed out the door, two tracksuits helping a wobbly third off his barstool as the waiter wiped tables. Dee turned his full attention on Jimmy for the first time all night.

"Wow—you're a wreck! What happened to just a few beers?"

Jimmy shrugged and fought the urge to belch fire. "I got an early start—some 'tinis in the afternoon, and Dan liquored me up to get me out back."

Dee sighed. "Goddamn Dan, I gotta talk to him—again—but you know what, you're a big boy, and who the fuck am I? The help! You gotta start helping yourself, sister. Whatever. He's a whopper, huh?"

"Who?"

"Feo. I bet he's got a monster cock." This perked up Jimmy's attention.

"What's with the tooth?"

"I dunno—it must have just happened—it's kinda cute—positively pugilist."

It did give him a rough and tumble look, Jimmy admitted.

"I think he likes you, though—I've seen some of the trade he's got coming over at night, I mean, of the blond and by the hour persuasion..."

"Say what?"

"He lives in my building—downstairs—I think he hires hookers—young, blond, and kinky—that's half the reason I brought you with. I think he's loaded, by the way—he owns half this restaurant. Honestly, James, ketchup."

There was a spark, yes, a definite one, Jimmy began to think—Dee could sell a side of beef to a vegan. Real work not to stare at that missing tooth, though—once noticed, impossible to not.

"By the way, guess who I ran into? Bob!" Dee spit out as Feo returned with a to-go bag. "Oh, Feo—you great big bear of a hunk of a man you! Say 'Thank you' Jimmy. How much do we owe you?"

Feo shook his head. "Two more songs, another night."

Jimmy could barely speak. The mention of Bob and the smell of burgers turned his stomach. He smiled weakly as Feo grabbed him by the shoulder for an affectionate shake, the jostling almost knocking him over.

"My DeeDee—you take care of our little cricket, here—make sure he eats now before he goes to sleep, yes? Yes." Another quick air peck on each cheek, and Dee corralled Jimmy ahead of him out the door and across the street.

"What did he say?"

"Who?" Dee foisted the bag and banjo case on Jimmy as he unlocked his building door.

"Bob!"

"Oh! Bob—yeah I ran into him, where? In front of the pet store. Yes, I was just coming out with Trix and ran right into him, like, almost literally, and there really was no avoiding him or vice versa, much as we both might wish, so..." They rode the elevator up, and heard the familiar frantic clicking and snuffling behind the door as Dee fiddled with the keys. "I told him you died!"

"No!"

"Yes! I said 'Did you hear? Jimmy got shot up the ass by a cop who was fucking him with a gun!"

"You did not!"

"I did! Haha! Because I wanted to embarrass him for what he did to you, and then I said they read the will and you left him a bequest."

"Dee, for fuck sake..."

"I said 'Jimmy left you four hundred dollars!' He got so mad, it was a hoot! Trixie B. Davis, as I live and breathe!" Dee squealed and fell on the hall floor in a heap of crinoline to greet the English bulldog with kisses. "You give Mama some sugar, my precious pumpkinhead. Who's my squishy face? You're my squishy face...!"

FIVE

Vic: ***hey jimmy, you ok? you disappeared after the show***

Friday morning, Dee's famous Strawberry Surprise Smoothie in a to-go cup and the van returned, Jimmy took stock before this Paul guy arrived at his studio. Strange to survey his little life in so few boxes, the new apartment still a blank canvas. He was tempted to really go for it, more work, less live—just do it, make a decision: painter first, boy toy second. Maybe all he had been missing so far was a real commitment. Yes, that must be his problem.

Upstairs in the loft, he sorted canvases against the walls. Most of the oversized ones he hadn't bothered to wrap in the move—packing materials weren't cheap. These he leaned against the long, far wall, earliest to latest work, trying to catch a glimpse of the same spark Paul had seemed to notice at the cafe.

Jimmy's community college art teacher had urged her students to accept that most of their earlier paintings would never be sold, just studies, practice, experiments not meant to be seen unless by some wild accident a masterpiece should emerge. ("You never know! Haha!") Some artists destroyed their failures, but that seemed a terrible waste. Gesso was cheap. Slather on a layer of white, and you were good to go with a fresh blank.

Mrs. Stacey had once set them a collage assignment to produce a new work entirely constructed out of previous attempts. They could use anything— drawings, sketches, photographs, paintings—as long as it was all their own original work. Some students grumbled about destroying their precious oeuvre.

"Yes," she replied, "this will also be a lesson in humility."

The results were impressive. All the best parts of earlier efforts, none of the clumsy—the wonky eyes, the not quite right smiles, the inelegant and generic—all stripped away, and new nearly cubist images had emerged, more resonant. The collage technique became a favorite for Jimmy, and the five or so dozen canvases he moved to Albany represented a couple hundred paintings layered one on top of the other hidden two, three, even four deep, layer upon layer. Some details peeked through, the good bits—particularly expressive eyes now disembodied, a poppy, a door made secret by the removal of its surround. The texture of the built-up paint added a sculptural dimension.

Near the end of the last class before he moved to San Francisco, Mrs. Stacey had introduced the concept of fantasy and surrealism, along the lines of Maxfield Parrish, or Dali.

"We don't have to paint only what we see—we can paint purely from an interior view. For this week's assignment, I want you to imagine a place where you feel completely at home— your best self. This could be your house, a spaceship, an outdoor place, whatever you like."

Jimmy had thought of his parents' house on Campo Drive, the same as every other fifth stucco model lining the broad streets of their subdivision—same beige, same lawn, same palm trees and domestic cars in the driveway. Theirs was the only home he had ever known, but was that his best self, the self that lived there, with them? Please no.

Wondering how his childhood bedroom might feel cut free of its moorings, he had imagined it as a wedge of cake, sliced away and set adrift on an acid green ocean beneath a star-filled magenta sky—a room peeled open—with his bed, chair, trunk, desk, dresser, a miniature version of his landscape *Bungalow with Poppies* hung on a lavender-blue wall (not the actual color, his father had refused to paint his room something, anything, besides white). Jimmy stayed up late every night that week to work on it. Even his mother provided some scant praise.

Mrs. Stacey used his picture for the poster announcing the year-end student exhibition in the gallery space outside the auditorium. *A Room of Our Own: Fresno CC Student Work* was reviewed favorably in the *Central Valley Arts* newspaper insert, Jimmy and his obscurely titled painting *SS Vincent* mentioned by name. By the time the exhibit was cleared out at the end of the summer session, he was already installed as Bob's boy in San Francisco and working at the hip art supply store, ArtHaus.

On his first quick trip back to visit his mother later that fall, he stopped by the school to retrieve his painting one evening after classes ended. The old dear yelped with delight. He guessed she was younger than Marlys, but more mom-ish—never jeans, always blouses, a little mannish with her short, graying hair. Jimmy had come out to her during their first student-teacher conference—when he finally told Marlys the next semester, she rolled her eyes.

"Big surprise."

Mrs. Stacey made tea and they sat for a nice chat as the parking lot outside her classroom windows emptied. The shadows of the Italian cypresses she loved for the students to sketch stretched then melted in the dusk as they talked. Mrs. Stacey had always refused to turn on the fluorescent lighting in her classroom—in the annex wing of the arts building, she was lucky to have a huge wall of windows facing north, and a skylight. As the evening deepened, she flipped on a lamp, the ceramic orange monster with a burlap shade on her desk. Like so many evenings after class, they sat on the cement bench outside with the door propped open for a cigarette and a second cup of tea. Jimmy worried he was keeping her too late and she shushed him.

They discussed art schools he might attend in the Bay Area, though financial aid usually meant exorbitant student loans for those private schemes. She looked through pictures of recent work on his phone, reading glasses perched at the end of her nose. Jimmy stuttered with embarrassment as he described his efforts, thin pickings he realized. He had been following too routinely the Parrish-fantasy theme, only the month before painting yet another miniature castle floating in the clouds, complete with pennants, tiny gargoyles, and turrets. More of an exercise to keep his brush moving, though also an experiment in size. These were some of his largest paintings, playing with negative space but still the same old crazy-color skies and dawn-stained clouds, cozy rooms morphed into mansions.

Despite her attempts to sugarcoat it, Mrs. Stacey pursed her lips and fretted.

"They're technically well executed, dear, you could be an illustrator, if that's the direction you want to go in." He admitted it was not. "Parrish started out as an illustrator, remember." Maybe it was the splash of cold water he needed to move past those half dozen rote studies. She encouraged him to see with new eyes: inspiration lurked in plain sight.

When he returned to San Francisco, he began to notice reflections. In puddles, slices of buildings and skylines upside down. Houses reflected in windows, superimposed over a City visible through the glass. Up the hill behind the Castro, Bob's apartment had spectacular views from Twin Peaks to downtown, all of the Mission, Potrero, and Bernal Heights. Jimmy snapped a picture through a window cranked open halfway—at just the right angle, a reflection of Sutro Tower photobombed the Bay Bridge behind, a jumble of landmarks crowded together. He needed a new technique to render it accurately, not simply one image painted over the other—he must manipulate the paint of the reflected TV tower as a shift in color and texture, sometimes carving into the first layer with a knife. He realized soon enough he did not need an actual reflection to create the effect.

In the last few months before he left the craziness of Bob's, Jimmy took hundreds of pictures of the San Francisco skyline with the digital camera his father bought and never used before he died—purchased for Marlys's sixtieth birthday then abandoned because James Sr. liked to hold pictures in his hand, godammit, not stare at them on a computer like some kind of moron. Marlys detested nearly every picture ever taken of her, and made Jimmy delete all record of that hateful occasion.

He began his *Ghosts* series in earnest after he broke up with Bob and moved down to Vern's, his new housemate in the Mission. He liked his painting *Bay Bridge and Sutro I* so much, he made several versions. Then he posed Coit Tower next to the Golden Gate Bridge, and Treasure Island with a monumental Alcatraz plopped dead center, looking more medieval monastery than prison. To save money, he painted over some of the old castles, keeping details of those fantasy palaces nestled among real landmarks of the City. Jimmy framed eight of the best ones and had hung them with some others at Coffee Lab.

He started a few portraits, and Dee asked him to do a caricature—"Wild! Colorful! Mad!"—for an e-flyer on the Stallion website, actually paid him a hundred bucks out of the advertising budget from the bar, courtesy of Dan. He painted a small but sober portrait of Dee as a present for Ricardo on their five-year anniversary for free but asked if he could hang it at the cafe as an example of his portraiture. And he did the one of himself, the one that Paul had noticed, spending a full three weeks perfecting it. There had been some interest in all of these, but though two or three people had emailed about commissions, none came through. About this time, he began sketching more, suspecting illustration might be his best option after all, just as ArtHaus announced it was closing its Market Street location and Vern decided to move home to deal with his crystal meth problem.

Ten a.m., right on time, Paul bellowed through Jimmy's intercom. "Kindercamp!" He wasted no time grabbing hold of Jimmy the second the door was closed—full frontal kiss and groping hands, no please-may-I. Jimmy was swept up in that crazy New Yorker charisma all over again and left breathless.

"Can I get you a drink—water, or...?"

"I don't mind a Bloody Mary for breakfast."

Jimmy laughed and flapped his hand around the kitchen, still packed. "You caught me with my pants down. Vodka martini?"

"I like your style, boy."

Jimmy directed him up the stairs to the loft. Paul was so fair, with that strawberry blond hair and those invisible lashes and eyebrows. Jimmy already fretted over how to render his skin tones in a flattering way in paint. Tall and lanky was no problem in a portrait—ruddy pallor was.

"Nice space you got here!" Paul called down. "It's got a real New York vibe..." He was going through the canvases propped against the wall when Jimmy came up with the shaker and glasses.

"Here's that one I liked." Paul held up *Bungalow and Oak*. "This screams California to me, ya know? Minus the palm trees." They sipped their drinks as he sifted through the *Ghosts* series. "These are nice too—shimmery, like reflections in water." He made no comment about the rooms or castles, but when he came to a figure painting of Vern, his old roommate, he paused to look closer.

"This is different. I don't remember seeing this at the cafe."

"They didn't want me to hang it—too edgy for the tourist and theater crowd down there."

Paul nodded. "Friend of yours?"

"My old roommate."

Paul considered, then put it aside with the bungalow and spent another ten minutes flipping through the rest.

"Should we get our business out of the way?" He asked how much for the little painting of the bungalow. Jimmy gave him the price he'd listed at the cafe, maybe this was a gauge of his honesty, no need to get greedy. "Sold." Paul downed the rest of his second martini and pulled a checkbook out of his coat pocket. "Any chance I can get another?" Jimmy trotted downstairs for a fresh batch.

Back in a flash, he found Paul with his jacket off, and a fat check—not just a deposit but the full amount of the portrait commission he had quoted and the bungalow painting, the most money Jimmy had ever made from his art, combined. *Say nothing!* a voice screamed in his head. He was so pleased, so busy swooning over two-plus months of rent that when Paul moved in and started kissing him again he was half-melted already and happy to seal the deal in any way required.

Another round of martinis later, Jimmy was braced face down in a pillow wearing nothing but his Kindercamp t-shirt. Once Paul finished, he rolled off with a grunt, no reciprocation. They spooned for a few minutes while Paul caught his breath, then checked his Bulgari watch and was quickly back to business.

"Can I get a shower maybe?" Of course, of course. Jimmy wondered out loud if he had packed the clean towels in the trunk by the bed.

"I got it." Paul opened the trunk, pulled out a towel, and a handful of Happy Meal toys, mint in wrapper. "What the hell are these?" He laughed. "And this!" He held up Jimmy's father's rifle. "Oh wow, I had one just like this when I was a kid, my grandfather took me hunting." He checked the chamber, caressed the wood of the stock, looked down the sight. "This is in good shape, might be worth something. I'm thinking nineteen-fifties, but it looks new."

"I don't think my dad used it much."

"You interested in selling it?"

"Oh! Probably not, I was just telling my mom it's one of the only mementoes I have from my father." Paul set it back in the trunk and went to the bathroom for a quick rinse, emerging again in barely two minutes to towel dry.

"I gotta get going—first race starts in half an hour. Can I take some pictures of your work? Show them to a friend of mine?"

"Yes!" And Jimmy needed pictures for the portrait, too. They took turns, Paul with his iPhone, canvasses against the wall, and then Jimmy with his camera. They agreed he would start working on the portrait right away, but since Paul was flying home the next day and not back for a couple months, he would leave the bungalow picture for now and make arrangements for both when the portrait was done.

Not long after starting classes in Fresno, Jimmy had driven out of town to sketch some of the scenery, attempting watercolors (disastrous) and pastels (better) on the spot. He headed toward the hills at the end of March to take pictures and sketch for a landscape assignment.

Coming around a bend in the road, an expanse of hills sprang up in front of him drenched in California poppies with such a bright, intense orange, they looked aflame. The brilliant carpet glazed the tops of the hillsides, sent a thrill through him like someone had snuck up behind and screamed. He pulled over so abruptly the car almost skidded off the gravel shoulder into a ditch. On the flattened top of the nearest low hill, a desolate adobe bungalow and the skeleton of a half-dead oak tree stood surrounded by the pool of liquid orange. The radiant hills soaked into his brain and dazzled his eyes, but more than seeing almost a flavor too, like eating a mandarin so sweet his cheeks hurt.

He perched on the old ice chest from the trunk of his dad's Oldsmobile and spent a good hour sketching different versions of the poppies and the house, tried pastels, took lots of pictures too, and then sat in the front seat with the windows rolled down eating his PB&J. For the first time he imagined this was a future he might wish for—a whole life could be built on such moments as these—room to breathe, quiet to think, immersed in a pure, thoughtless beauty.

With the pastel drawing as a study, Jimmy painted his most successful oil landscape from those college days, even won first prize in the *Freshman Art Show*. When he went back to the same spot late in the summer, the poppies were gone, the hills dead brown, and the little bungalow sat fossilized in the August sun. The only living thing left on the ridge was a great clump of mistletoe hanging in the shriveled oak.

Jimmy: ***Aw yeah thx I'm good,***
tell you about it later
You at the store tomorrow?

Vic: ***totally, see you!***

[Interview transcripts edited for clarity.]

So you really never heard of Paul Allenson, or at least his wife, when you met him?
True. But I couldn't tell you the name of a single writer in the Chronicle even now—I've never been much of a reader.

Of course. I mean, if you lived in New York, you might have heard of him. He had many protégés, not just you and me. I knew who he was when I met him, knew of his wife too—I cultivated the relationship as much as I let him cultivate me.
Paul knew helping people was a good bet, and if it was a cute boy, even better. He did set my career in motion so at least at first it was a win-win. I've made the most of it, so did Paul, and Dexter.

Dexter Bash, the dealer representing you for your first official show.
Yes. And we're still on good terms, Dexter and me, though I'm with Suzie Coupar Gallery now. Paul too, right up until the end—I was only sort of a footnote in his troubles, legally speaking. We still had dinner now and then when I was in town, or when he came out to SF. I spoke to him not that long before he died. Anyway—what else about Paul? Let's get it out now.

Here's a rumor that's been swirling for a while: Did Paul steal those three Ghosts series paintings from you?
No. I abandoned those paintings at his apartment and forgot all about them. The plaintiffs tried to claim that because they felt cheated they weren't what he represented, tried to say

that he had acquired them dishonestly in the first place to bolster their case. Not true.

Have you ever thought about the #MeToo angle in all of this? I mean, I loved Paul, but he really pushed the limits of ethical behavior—he rarely offered help without expecting some sugar in return.
Not really, I mean, I get what you're saying, but he wasn't vindictive if someone said no—he never held grudges, if anything he was incredibly generous even later. He introduced me to Suzie, too, right before things went really sour for him. No, it was all mutual. As my roommate Vern used to say, 'All gay men are whores, it's just that the service and the payment happen to be the same commodity.'

Fair enough. So Suzie. Now this is your second show with her—total departure from both the previous ones. Your current show, "Phantoms," features, among many others, the early self-portrait, the one you mentioned caught Paul's attention. But that was the only one from before—
Yes, it was a nod to my work before my first show *Broken Spirits*—a name I did not choose, by the way, but Suzie suggested that since my latest work is such a departure in style and subject, we might tease out a thread in the name for continuity.

A show featuring many self-portraits. Everyone mentioned Frida Kahlo, of course.
Of course. But she was never an influence—no symbolism, no landscape of imagery—just me, groundless, and for the

first time considering myself as a subject, and the mark of that transition in my life. People who experience a significant trauma are changed. They may go through the full grieving or recovery process, but it changes their trajectory forever.

SIX

When Jimmy arrived for the interview at the Albany apartment three weeks earlier, Kitty Castro toured him round the garden before even letting him in the front door. With its funny French roof and faux half-timbers, the "Regency Suites"—so named on the cursive bronze sign above the "557" of Ulysses Avenue—held itself apart from the flat-roofed 1960s low-rises and Eichleresque houses terracing the neighborhood. The apartments stood back from the sidewalk some twenty feet, and the garden was, yes, enchanting—the landlady's pomp and pride.

"That wisteria was planted when it was first built," she whispered, still awestruck after all these years at the curling wonder, emerging from the deeps of the earth and lashing its writhing stalks up three stories like some amorous sea beast. "Wait until it blooms next spring! It's a wonder!"

Rowdy beds of daylilies and dahlias encircled a Japanese cherry tree. "You missed the cherry blossoms! I made pie!"

"From the actual cherries?" Jimmy asked, suitably impressed.

"No, no—in homage—it's ornamental." Pea gravel crunched deliciously under their feet, the path neatly edged with mossy bricks.

And then the roses. On this subject alone Kitty was speechless, could but wave her hands with a sigh in front of the twenty-odd shrubs—*enough said* without a word—and demonstrate as though to a simpleton how to smell a lavish red bloom. ("Now you," she urged with her eyes.) For an old lady, Jimmy found her quite hip in her kerchief and mad glasses. Like some latter-day Rosie the Riveter, Kitty Castro wore t-shirt sleeves rolled up to show off two identical cartoon cats tattooed on her left bicep, a touch of blue in their eyes. ("Siamese, if you please—you like? My seventieth birthday present to myself.") Jimmy realized straight away he was dealing with a would-be Queen of Hearts, and this garden, her realm.

The summer before starting junior high, Jimmy's mother took him to the Filoli estate in Woodside during a rare family trip to San Francisco. Maybe it was the other way around, really: Marlys wanted to go to Filoli, and she convinced her husband San Francisco would be a pleasant base camp for a day trip down to the "Dynasty" house—its abrupt cancellation never forgiven, nor forgotten thanks to reruns—and other points of interest.

"What other points of interest?" James Sr. asked.

"The Golden Gate Bridge."

"Hmmm."

"Chinatown."

"Are you kidding me?"

"There are several museums, and cable cars, Golden Gate Park. There's Berkeley, and Beach Blanket Babylon. North Beach. Fisherman's Wharf." She rattled off her prepared campaign notes.

Truth was, Marlys feared bridges, and despised Italians, cabarets, hippies, and fish. She just wanted to see the "Dynasty" house—tour its grand gardens, stroll along bricked pathways—and sure, peek inside the mansion if it was included in the admission, why not? ("But you know they only shot the exteriors there, the inside was a set in West Hollywood.")

"We could visit Alcatraz." Now she was talking. Perhaps she should have led with that, knowing what an Eastwood fan her husband was, or perhaps she knew his mind all too well and saved the best for last. In the end, she soldiered through a musty prison, Chinese Food, and a hair-raising walk across a windy bridge all for the opportunity to follow in the footsteps of Crystal and Alexis (but mostly Alexis).

James Sr. excused for the day to watch a game, Marlys and Jimmy's drive down the Peninsula was unremarkable except for the resemblance of the San Mateo hills to all the other gold and brown hills up and down California, which was also the source of the sudden fit of disorientation that possessed Marlys, her driving glasses forgotten at the hotel.

"What'd that sign say?" she cried, startling Jimmy from a groggy doze.

"What? What sign?"

"Were you asleep? You're supposed to help me navigate. Where are we? We're lost! How the hell did we get here?" A sign loomed beside the road: Filoli Estate—Next Exit. "Oh. Never mind."

The tour included the interior, as disappointing as expected. ("The show was better," Marlys sniffed.) Meanwhile, a perpetually awestruck woman named Gabby, all too true to her name, constantly interrupted as Marlys recounted with mounting frustration how she'd swaddled a newly adopted baby Jimmy to watch "Dynasty: The Reunion" with her on the first night in his forever home. Gabby glommed onto Marlys as they waited for the house tour to start, sensing a fellow "Dynamo."

"I hadn't heard that term," Marlys said cautiously, glancing at Jimmy.

Gabby was thrilled to spread the good word. "That's what me and the boys upstairs used to call ourselves."

"Boys?"

"Well—Rod and Sid—they're a couple. Maybe it's a San Francisco thing."

Marlys would try to extricate herself from this precarious person for the remainder of the tour, but Gabby was an expert glommer. When the group momentarily paused in the grand hall, she beamed at Jimmy and asked him what grade he was in.

"Seventh," he announced pertly. He would not turn twelve until late September, technically outside the age cut off. Marlys was forever debating her early push to get him into kindergarten and whether she should have held him back a year considering what a late bloomer he was turning out to be. In the end, he was more glad than she to be out of her hair.

Unfortunately, Gabby was a titch deaf in that ear.

"Oh! You're seven? What a big boy you are! What is that, third grade?"

Chuckles erupted from the other milling visitors.

The rest of the estate exceeded all expectations. Coming upon the lily pond, Marlys was beside herself. It wasn't the actual one from the famous catfight, but close enough and who would know anyway except a fellow—

"Dynamo. Oh lord, listen to me—where's that Gabby? Thank god she didn't hear me, we'd never be rid of her. Take a picture of me in front of it. No. No. Not there, stand there—the sun is in my eyes—further. Further! Perfect. How do I look? Wait! Let me put on some lipstick."

Fifteen minutes on, and mere moments after Marlys stepped away from the tour to find a ladies' room, Jimmy got lost. Wandering Filoli, trapped somehow behind a hedge, he turned a corner around the backside of a rustic shed where tourists never went. Geraniums hanging in terracotta pots mingled their spicy perfume with a riot of jasmine nodding over a bower. Relieved to be free of his mother's vitriol and Gabby's gaffe-strewn patter for a quiet moment, he stepped through the shady gateway. He would have welcomed a white rabbit, or for that matter, a cozy rabbit hole.

Instead, there were two gardeners, brown and handsome in the chaparral sun, tools abandoned for more urgent work. They might have been uncle and nephew, cousins, brothers even, very alike but from different decades of the same family. Jimmy froze, rapt, as though chancing upon bare-chested satyrs in some Arcadian grotto. The one with the wonderfully round belly, burly arms, and curling brown locks shot with gold sat enthroned against a stone wall. The other, leaner and younger, knelt before his senior and ran his lips up and down a fat, uncut cock, teasing and admiring as much as sucking.

Jimmy froze, transfixed, suddenly jelly-kneed—the path beneath his feet tilted sharply astern. He stopped breathing, and when finally he did take a breath, it was to gasp. With a start, the seated man turned, saw the boy, alone. He relaxed. The younger was too engaged to notice. After a few moments, seeing him watching them, the beefy bull winked and reached out his puckish hand.

Agog, Jimmy raised his sneakered foot—to flee. But like a toy boat slipping inexorably toward a vortex, he could not escape, could only stare at that thick brown hand beckoning.

"James?" At that moment came her vaguely worried call.

The spell was broken. He turned and raced toward her voice, fighting tears.

Over the years, Jimmy's fantasies would often turn back to that moment.

What if he had taken that rough hand? Did he sometimes wish, on the edge of ecstasy and despair, it had all ended there? Spirited away. Annihilated. As though everything since was an endless rehearsal for a terrible opportunity that would never come again?

He was left with an ache all afternoon, a solemn dissociation for the remainder of their tour in the verdant gardens and the drive back through the tumbling hills to San Francisco. He was so unusually quiet his mother thought he must be coming down with something. She suggested, when they returned to the hotel and located his father in the bar, that they cut the visit short and return home—the main event was accomplished now anyway.

"Have you ever been to Filoli?" Jimmy asked Kitty as her own garden tour concluded.

"Have I? Do Muslims pray toward Mecca?"

Jimmy had no idea, which Kitty thought a real knee-slapper. Also—as though reading his mind when he squinted at the front door to decide if it was painted lavender or—"French gray."

She showed him around the front hall, the "foi-yay" she called it (same as his mother—"the French way, the correct way") noting for his benefit the original oak woodwork ("Never painted, thank goodness!") and the inglenook with handmade art tiles where she set up a Christmas tree each year for the tenants. "You'll see," she said, coming off more ominous than generous.

No elevator to the third floor "Studio Apartment For Rent" unfortunately.

"I'm going to let you climb up to the loft by yourself when you're ready, hon," Kitty said, still puffing from the stairs. It was really more than a studio, less than a one bedroom owing to the lack of walls. She pointed out the first-level kitchen made recently industrial with metal counters and open shelves from a restaurant supply outlet on the advice of her nephew, who said it might attract an artist-type. "And here you are!" Jimmy had to agree it was nice and warehousey with its stainless steel everything and old divided-pane wall of windows running up the two stories. Sitting on the shoulder of lonely Albany Hill, the east-facing windows had an expansive view across North Berkeley even to the Campanile on the UC campus, and the Claremont Hotel.

A zigzagging metal staircase with ringing, perforated treads led up to the bedroom and the loft. "Wow! More windows!" Upstairs, a step down and a change in ceiling height separated the bedroom from the living space, all by itself bigger than the room Jimmy had rented from Vern in the Mission. Here, though, he might hang a curtain to create a separation between the two. Fancy. On the wall opposite the stairs, dormers along the front roofline faced the Bay. There might have been another magnificent view if not for the enormous redwood tree in front of the building opposite, and the hill's collar of eucalyptus running right down into the neighborhood by the hill's park entrance. He peeked into narrow closets either side of the bedroom area dormer—inside one, a built-in chest of drawers with curling, daisied shelving paper.

The run of old factory windows continued from the kitchen space across the top of a low bench seat to a small bathroom with a claw-foot tub crammed behind the door, a pedestal sink, more of those windows. Everything was dusty, bathtub and sink rust-stained, floors scarred and well worn.

Metal windows from the twenties, metal staircase from the eighties, metal kitchen brand-new: the old studio reminded Jimmy of a recently refreshed aunt, upgraded piecemeal with bionic parts—new knees, new hips, new boobs—ta-da. And there she stood, down in the kitchen sniffing the drain and yikesing as though discovering her own breath not quite fresh, an exhalation of Kitty Castro's own body. She turned on the faucet and swished some water around in the sink.

Jimmy rested against the railing and cleared his throat gently so as not to startle her. "It's like a set from an old movie. When's the last time it was painted?"

Kitty gave a reassuring cluck. "We saved the choice of color just for you, honey. Don't worry about the painting—I have a live-in handyman. Ramon'll take care of anything you need."

So. "It's a little rough," he probed gently, "no elevator, and no parking." (Not that he had a car.) "Would you knock $50 off the rent?" He deployed his most beguiling smile.

"Oh alright," she said without a moment's hesitation, "you're cute as buttons—it's a deal. But maybe I should tell you why it's been sitting empty for a while..."

"Oh?"

"The last guy who lived here might have hung himself from the railing, right where you're standing." Oh! Jimmy fought the urge to snatch his hands away from where he leaned. Were those rope marks rubbed into the scuffed paint? The poor guy must have been determined—you could stand on the stairs and reach the railing easily. More of a choking than a proper hanging.

"He had AIDS," Kitty continued. "This was back in the day—1991, I think—they didn't have the drugs you kids have now, back then." She eyed him meaningfully, as though he might wish to volunteer some pertinent information, but he was still so flustered by her announcement, "That was the year I was born" was all he could blurt out. She waved him down from the loft to join her in the kitchen.

"Of course not everybody handles that sort of information very well—I've had a devil of a time with this place. How do you feel about it?" Jimmy supposed it had happened so long ago. "Exactly," Kitty said, "over twenty years." And then, to change the subject: "I don't suppose you'd like to join me in a glass of chardonnay downstairs? It's almost lunchtime."

Jimmy laughed. "Oh my! I couldn't possibly." Kitty pouted. "I don't suppose you know how to make a greyhound? I missed breakfast." Kitty brightened.

"Have you ever had one with fresh-squeezed grapefruit juice?"

"I have not!"

"Oh, honey." Kitty looped her arm in his. "You are in for a treat."

Confounding expectations, Kitty Castro's apartment contained no cats. She did have an actual bar, though—"My husband built it himself!"—upholstered on the front and sides in the same carpeting as the floor, an olive-green, low-pile shag. An abalone shell lamp hung in the corner like three globular jellyfish, white and translucent. On the coffee table, a giant chartreuse brandy snifter—"My dad had one in yellow," Jimmy said—filled with a jumbled collection of casino chips.

A baker's rack full of blooming orchids sunned themselves in front of a window. "How about these, huh?" Kitty enthused. "Some of them are from the estate of Eva Gabor. They're probably older than you!"

"My mom has some of her wigs."

A pack of Virginia Slims Menthol Superslims and an ashtray on every surface meant Kitty never need go very far to indulge. There were dogs playing poker on black velvet on the wall. There were framed posters of corvettes, a random beach on Maui, and a night scene of the Las Vegas Strip. The walls were white, the furniture, Danish modern. Kitty's lair smelled of equal parts elbow grease and lemon Pledge.

On the bar she had collected every implement of cocktail making Jimmy could imagine, and many he could not. Liquor bottles lined sparkling mirrored shelves on the wall. The vodkas, gins, and rums were in various stages of emptiness, replacements at the ready behind, but the rest—the bourbons and scotches, the tequilas, the brandy and cognacs and liqueurs, the vermouth, Kahlua, Bailey's—all untouched but stocked, just in case.

"Gosh," Jimmy said, "I love your eyeglasses." Kitty wore pink rhinestone cat glasses, rose-tinted. She preened as she poured grapefruit juice from an extra-large glass juicer over very healthy measures of vodka.

"Smirnoff OK? But you know my real name is Margaret. After my husband died, and I started taking the casino bus up to Reno, I got these glasses—not these exact ones, just some I found down at Rite-Aid I think, or maybe it was Walgreens. Anyway, the girls who fetch the drinks always made such a fuss about them and they started calling me Kitty Cat, and then just Kitty, and before you know it all my bus friends were calling me that too, so here we are. A late bloomer, I guess you'd call me." She raised her glass and Jimmy realized the deal was sealed and they were buddies all at once.

"Hair of the hound, honey." Kitty downed half of her cocktail in a gulp. "Aaah! Say, you don't have wild parties all night?" Jimmy agreed he did not. "Too bad—the tenants are all so boring, but not nearly so cute!"

"I might entertain a gentleman friend now and then," he offered.

Kitty finished her glass. "Good for you!" She filled him in on all the personal details of the other tenants as she fixed two more drinks. "Got any family, hon?"

"Yeah, my mom's down in Fresno—but my dad passed away—" Kitty knit her brow over the top of her highball.

"No kidding—Bakersfield!" she said, raising her hand, guilty. "Brothers? Sisters?"

"No, I was adopted, kinda late actually." Jimmy was trying to read the contract she'd set on the bar for him, but a good bit of it was now wet. Already half smashed, he finally gave up and scrawled his signature while he still could. "My folks didn't get married until my dad was over fifty. I don't think he really wanted kids, but my mom did, only she couldn't so ... just me then."

Kitty wobbled sympathetically. "Me, I had two brothers—bit of a tomboy, I was—I know, right?" They both laughed, for different reasons. "But family—so important!" she slurred, deep into her third greyhound. Jimmy sipped quicker, vaguely afraid for how he was getting back to the City.

"Speaking of which," he ventured, momentarily emboldened. "Who do I gotta fuck to get free WiFi in my new studio?"

SEVEN

After Paul left for the track, Jimmy lazed on the window seat, his new favorite spot since he had no sofa. No point in unpacking—he would ask Kitty about the handyman and painting next week before he started at Albany Art. Still fuzzy from the morning's exertions, he shuffled down to the freezer to retrieve the vodka. Less than half full—fair enough, it was barely lunchtime.

Back upstairs, he sipped straight from the frosty bottle, the glass bitingly cold.

Google: "Paul Allenson." Oh! *Vanity Fair. The New York Times. Wikipedia*? Not his own page but: *Claire Hopper, American writer and socialite—Spouse Paul Allenson (m. 1980) Children 2,* etc. What the...? *Died 2005.* Ah. Still, Mr. Paul Allenson was doing an amazing impression of an extremely gay man, but there you go, black and white for all to see on the internet.

Google: *James Christopher Traywick.* Ugh. Obituary for his father, obviously. Well that was enough of that shit.

When in doubt, sketch.

Which box? He took another slug. "S" for sketchbooks? No, that was school stuff. Was he drinking when he packed? "ART" for art supplies for sure. But where was his sketchbook? No matter, he cracked open a new one, always kept a spare. Charcoal? No, Conté would be better for Paul's ruddy complexion.

Another good belt from the bottle to get him going as he flipped through the pictures he took earlier. Looking up, looking down, to the side, smiling, no smile, over the shoulder, making a funny face, and the real, natural laugh that came after, that was the one. Jimmy decided he had a good heart, Paul did, to laugh so disarmingly. He played with thumbnail sketches across the page.

He dug out a photocopy kept from Mrs. Stacey's class, a classical master's drawing of a Roman statue. That was a good model to ground his sketch. He thought of the shadowy, darker background as the marble removed, and what was left—white paper—the marble that remained. Like Michelangelo said. Good start, very flattering.

He fixed himself a good stiff drink. "To you, Maestro." He paused and thought and sipped.

The unfortunate former tenant must have climbed over the railing right where Jimmy was sitting. He would have had to make the length of the rope short, looped on the top rail, or his feet would be touching the stairs. Good and tight around the neck, and once he passed out his dead weight would have dangled, tightening more, cutting off blood to his brain. He could have put a plastic bag over his head to be double sure, Jimmy saw that on a TV show. Once he was unconscious, no need to fight the urge to reach and pull himself back up. That must be how they did it with sheets in prison.

Maybe he would finish off the dregs of the bottle and lie down for a nap. He barely slept the night before on Dee's sofa.

Thing was, he never even really liked Matt that much.

Jimmy shut his eyes to shimmering streaks, like sticks of striped candy—sometimes a good buzz produced these delicious spectacles. He was spinning a little, not too much, not enough to worry. In the satin twilight behind his closed eyelids, the streamers arranged themselves in bright rows of saffron, maroon, jade—as though someone had dipped their fingers into pots of paint and brushed them on the air. These traveled forward and back, up and down, like an LED sign transmitting some plaid language, a code—he was meant to understand, ought to know, but had forgotten. He need only remember the patterns of color and sequence, and later, when he recalled the key, he could unlock the message to reveal a great truth. But there were so many symbols, so many colors, and all moving so fast. He let go, accepted he'd never discover their secret, the equation forever unsolved.

Dusk had fallen outside—all the blinds still wide open—when a dim light washed the studio from below. A jingle of metal disturbed Jimmy enough to crack open an eye. He had stripped away the sheets in the warm afternoon and lay naked and sweating.

"Hello?" No answer.

After a moment, a door shut, and the studio plunged back into darkness.

Jimmy peeked over the stairs. No one. A ghost then.

Spreading out through the eastern windows, the wide expanse of hills and East Bay suburbs—El Cerrito, Albany, Berkeley, and Oakland, spun off from San Francisco a hundred years earlier—had just begun their evening sparkle. A BART train slipped by along the Greenway, its howling whir faint but clear even through the closed windows. His eye fell on the drawing of Paul gazing up from the window seat, and then he realized his hand rested on the hanging rail. This time, he did snatch his hand away. He shivered again, spooked, and crawled back in bed.

Moonlight streamed through the kitchen window, full evening now, getting on toward ten. Jimmy opened a fresh bottle and fixed himself a real cocktail, no reason to be uncivilized. No lights in the house except a single sconce over the kitchen sink, and another over the mirror in the bathroom—no ceiling fixtures, the place was that old.

In the mostly dark, charcoal would be easier to see as he worked. He loved the squeak and rasp of its dryness on paper. First, he sketched the windows looking east. The moon hung just past full above the hills, and through each pane of glass a similar but altered tiny world, like TV screens all on different episodes of the same late-night mystery. On a new page, he turned his attention back toward the empty studio.

Jimmy imagined the whole apartment stacked askew on the floor like his boxes, his whole life packed and ready for departure, trunks and suitcases belted and tagged. Then—affixed in an enormous tree as if by birds building a nest—a very big tree it would have to be, bigger than the redwood across the road, much. It was the tallest tree to ever grow on Earth, and old, to reach such heights. An ancient tree, old as the continents. Older. Like those Swiss Robinsons, his bird family settled their gabled house in a low notch that slowly rose over generations to a high perch shot through with branches, sunbeams, and the calls of sons and daughters.

"I'm not going to the store just for tonic," he said aloud.

He drew his rooms on a steep outcropping of the hillside, surrounded but dwarfed by eucalyptus—back to normal size, the trees—the bright moon rising behind, a pristine hole in the smeared charcoal. Now it was an elf's house in a shadowy dell, shrunk, even smaller, small as a mushroom, and he saw himself the size of a ladybug, candy shelled.

Jimmy stretched and ate spoonfuls of peanut butter in the kitchen. Behind the building, an alley ran the length of the block. Single-family neighbors kept their garbage cans back there with the apartment building's dumpster parked against the back of someone's garage, just the front edge peeking out from deep shade cast by a streetlight. As he peered, the glow of a cigarette flared. Someone in the shadows, puffing, low to the ground, on a stool or milk crate maybe. Then there was another glow, longer this time, and a second cherry lit, the first snuffed out in a pop of sparks against the dumpster. Thick bare legs stretched stiffly from the shadows. A man, chain smoking in the alley.

He got up to pee, took his bottle downstairs to stash back in the freezer, missed the last step, crashed into the wall. Bottle was safe and sound though, more than half full. He took a last swallow, half thought the apartment needed no lamps with those big windows, crawled back upstairs. The lights dusting the flats and the hills, the lampposts outside—these would be his nightlight. He stood by the window seat, still naked, looking down at the alley. Another new cigarette smoldered to life, the old one flicked across the pavement.

Jimmy supposed he was plainly visible down there. Whassup, fucker?

After a minute and no sign from the apparition in the alley, no come hither or wave, he gave up and fell into bed.

In the Mission, this old queen in the window across the way used to watch him whenever he felt like showing off with the blinds open. This went on for about a year, furtively at first, the man peeking as Jimmy painted half-dressed, or he would wake up out of a blackout, naked, all the lights on and find the old perv masturbating furiously at him. Jimmy felt admired, and OK, sometimes he reciprocated. But one night, there was a buzz on the intercom, and there the guy was through the glass of the downstairs door, smiling and brandishing a bottle of Absolut.

Jimmy recoiled and retreated, and the door shivered with a single, frustrated blow. The next time the guy stood naked in the window waving what looked like a dollar bill, Jimmy closed the blinds and left them closed from then on.

HOOKR CHAT

Fballer26:
Hi

tWinkS:
Hey stud what's up?

Fballer26:
Can't sleep your close 50 feet?

tWinkS:
The chat is coming from inside the house!

Fballer26:
??

tWinkS:
JK you live in the suites?

Fballer26:
Yes! Are you the new tenant?

tWinkS:
Yep, you?

Fballer26:
Lived here awhile yer fucking hot!

tWinkS:
You too big guy grrrrr sexxxy

Fballer26:
Thx

tWinkS:
What are you into?

Fballer26:
Football mostly

tWinkS:
For real? Top or bottom?

Fballer26:
Oh! Top I guess

tWinkS:
You guess?

Fballer26:
Def with you

tWinkS:
You want to cum up? ;)

Fballer26:
Well Ramon's asleep, he'll freak if I'm not here when he wakes up

tWinkS:
Ramon? Boyfriend?

Fballer26:
Sorta

tWinkS:
You sneaking around on him?
I can be discrete

Fballer26:
No nothing like that he just doesn't like it if I sneak off without asking

tWinkS:
Wow OK strict Daddy

Fballer26:
What does your profile mean?

tWinkS:
tWinkS W+S = watersports

Fballer26:
??

tWinkS:
Piss play

Fballer26:
Oh shit

tWinkS:
No scat

Fballer26:
OMG piss gross

tWinkS:
No dude, warm from a cock it's champagne of man juices

Fballer26:
I'll piss on you

tWinkS:
What's your name?

Fballer26:
Oscar

tWinkS:
I'm Jimmy – maybe you and Ramon both come up, two for one special

Fballer26:

You don't even know what he looks like

tWinkS:

I'm very democratic

Fballer26:

Maybe another time, Kitty wants us up early tomorrow morning to work in the garden

tWinkS:

Oh shit, are you the handyman?

Fballer26:

Yes! Ramon is, I help

tWinkS:

Can we talk about painting my apartment?
Kitty said you could help me out

Fballer26:

No problem, I can come by tomorrow

tWinkS:

Cool thx I'll be around

[Interview transcripts edited for clarity.]

Tell me about your first few years in San Francisco—you moved there not knowing anyone?
Actually, no—Dee had already moved to SF. We used to come up for the weekend and stay with his friend in North Beach, she moved up after they graduated two years before me. He was still drinking back in those days, and anything else he could get his hands on, but then he met Ricardo and fell head over platforms, as he says. Ricardo broke up with him at one point because he was getting trashed all the time, so he got sober and traded partying for wigs. Up till then Dusty Davenport was just a messy Halloween kinda gal.
Anyway, Dee didn't officially move in with Ricardo in the Marina until he was twenty-two. I stuck it out in Fresno for two years after high school, art classes at community college, but of course I was up there almost every weekend. I'd been working at an art store since I was sixteen, and I had seniority over the other kids who worked there, so I only had to work during the week. I pretty much drove up to the City Friday night after work, and didn't come home until Monday morning, sometimes straight to work without even stopping home first.

You were—twenty? When you moved to San Francisco.
Right—I was up in the City, hanging out with Dee. Hookr was relatively new, and I was meeting more guys on the Grid than at bars or clubs—

The Grid?
Hook-up apps, on your phone—Hookr, RRuff, Watrboyz. I had a fake ID, but Dee quit drinking and partying, and he wasn't the

famous Dusty Davenport quite yet. He didn't mind me partying and running around as long as I didn't bring anyone back to his place, so I was mostly on my own and hooking up with guys right and left. And then along came Bob—no last name.

We can keep it off the record...

No, it's better we just leave it because he was—is— a bigwig in the District Attorney's Office and he knew a lot of cops and city officials and I just don't want to get into any of that. I met him on Hookr—like on a Friday night, I logged in to sniff around and he was front and center, "Hey boy—you're hot" blah blah blah and we're off and running. He made me show him my ID when I arrived at his apartment. I mean I was over eighteen, but under twenty-one, so he made me show him both my real and my fake ID and he looked at them real close. Of course once he was sure I wasn't underage, he was wetting himself about the little blond twink he caught. Or wetting me, anyway.

Watersports. People talk.

Ha, yeah, by people you mean Paul. Yes—I mean, we don't have to get into any of that if you're uncomfortable with it.

I'm a journalist—I'm comfortable talking about anything—don't be shy—even if it doesn't make it into my article, it gives insight into you as a person. Feel free to talk about absolutely anything.

Alright, we'll see. Anyway—Bob. Bob loved to party, and Bob loved young guys, the younger the better, and at the time I still looked maybe sixteen—I got carded buying cigarettes into my twenties, so Bob was over the moon. I went over there on a Friday night, and I didn't see Dee again that weekend—I think I came up for air a month later, and Dee was like "Uh, you need to come by before you go over to Bob's this weekend so I can be sure you're still alive and not pickled in someone's basement." It went fast with Bob.

You fell in love.

I thought so. He was really good looking—mid-forties, great shape—he worked out with some of the cops he hung out with—salt and pepper hair, super handsome. He loved to drink, and fuck, and party with friends. He never tweaked, actually—some of his friends did, and that became an issue later—I'll get to that. But in the beginning, I mean, it was wine and dine, and presents—not a lot, but he took me shopping one time in the Castro to buy some sexy underwear and stuff, and he bought me a really nice gold necklace—not that expensive, but nice enough that a kid from Fresno thought it was pretty special to have a Daddy buying him things.

You called him Daddy?

I did—he asked me to, and I did, and eventually I wore his collar too, even though if I'm being honest it never really felt right. I mean, some of his friends had boys who called them "Daddy"—I don't know—I gave it a try, once in a while I'd forget and call him Bob instead of Daddy, and he'd act all disappointed.

So when you first moved to San Francisco, you moved in with this Bob.

Yes. Maybe three months in? I'd spent every weekend with him, was texting him constantly when I was home in Fresno.

And then, out of the blue, he said he got me an interview at an art store and it should be a cinch for me to get a job and move up to the City with him—and, big plus, since he knew the manager there he made sure I didn't have to work on the weekend. I'd have to help him with the rent, but I could have my own room to do my painting. Of course what I didn't know then was that his rent was next to nothing—he had been living there for over twenty years under rent control, and the amount I was paying him was more than half—I paid about a thousand a month, not nothing for an art store clerk, but still incredibly cheap for the city. I'm sure his landlords hated him.

So you were paying more than your fair share.

Plus half the utilities—and I came to find out later I wasn't the first boyfriend he had sort of groomed to be a paying roommate and fuck toy. He was always monetizing things—he kept a strict spreadsheet of expenses, groceries and so forth, but I didn't much mind because I wasn't looking for a sugar daddy in the first place, and also he pretty much paid for all the alcohol. He said I shouldn't have to pay for his friends to come over and drink and party, and he drank a lot, so he would make his own special run to the liquor store by himself and didn't ask me to pony up for it.

Another thing he did, which I suppose I should be grateful for, was to get me on Truvada as soon as I came up—he had a doctor friend write out a prescription, and got it filled under his own health insurance for the first couple of months before my new insurance kicked in. So that felt big—like he was looking out for me. I mean, it was all about liability, in the end—always talking about liability—he wanted to be sure I couldn't come back at him later and say that he was responsible for me getting HIV, and he only fucked bareback.

Was he HIV positive?
No—not as far as I know, I assume not—he was one hundred percent top, and I never saw him take any medications, but it wasn't his status that he was concerned about.

Whose?
His friends. I mean—of course it started out all fun and games, with the parties. Friday night would roll around, he'd make his liquor run, a few friends would come over, smoke some weed, cocktails, hanging out. And then one of his friends brought a boy over—cute kid, maybe twenty-two—older than me, but he seemed like he'd been playing this game for a while. I don't think he was serious with the guy he came with, he just liked partying. That was the first time they pulled out the meth pipe, and pretty soon it was the boy bent over an armchair in front of the big screen TV with porn on, and the guys were taking turns fucking him. Bob hung back with me, just watching, carrying on like it was no big deal, making sure I wasn't freaking out or anything—which I wasn't, I mean, he knew I'd been partying down in Fresno as early as high school, so it was just a tester, I think.

I want to circle back to that—but go on.
Right. So pretty soon, I was the boy bent over in front of the big screen, and it was non-stop from Friday night until Monday morning. I wasn't tweaking, just drinking. I mean, there were moments of more or less clarity, but at some point I was always going to black out, and get moved from

the living room to the bedroom, and I'd wake up to find some old man huffing on top of me, and my ass in various states of sloppiness.

Forgive me but that seems pretty rough. How did you feel about it at the time?
I guess I was in such a daze—so much drinking, and this gradual disappointment that this guy I thought I loved turned into such a callous pimp. It all went downhill fast, I think for most of the year I was living with him I was just trying not to think about how messed up it was—I mean, I was having fun too, so. But then there was this big wake-up call, literally. I woke up out of a blackout one night, and I was alone in the bedroom with a guy who had just injected me with meth. I mean, that shit will wake you up out of a dead sleep, so I was instantly awake, and he was shooting himself up right in front of me after pulling the needle out of my arm. I pretty much freaked. I yelled—Bob came in, but he was more concerned about making sure I kept my voice down and didn't make a scene than about the slammer. Anyway—that was it—I found a new apartment and moved out within a week.

That's awful.
Yeah—it was—I had plenty of experience with drinking, but almost none with meth, and I hate needles. I hadn't ever seen anyone slamming at Bob's parties, but of course, shit-faced and face-down in the bedroom, who knows what was going on, I probably missed a lot. So that was that. It was the middle of the month, and I had pulled out some cash as the deposit to give to my new roommate Vern, four

hundred bucks, and I just packed the last of my bags and left Bob's. No goodbyes—I don't know if he was ashamed, or irritated, or what. But when I got to Vern's I realized the cash in my wallet was missing. I assume he took it—I guess he figured I owed him for the half month I was living there before I moved out.

Wow. So that explains Dee's joke that you left him the four hundred dollars in your will. But what about getting shot in the ass—is there a story behind that too?
Yes—another time, before the slamming incident, I woke up out of a blackout feeling something strange in my ass, like cold and jagged or rough. I woke up and there was a guy in his cop uniform—it was real—like, he was a real cop, in his real uniform, but he had his dick out and he was jacking himself at the same time as he was fucking me with his gun. Honestly—he was hot, and the whole thing seemed kinda weird and hot, so I let him finish.

Afterward, he's wiping off his gun and he makes a big point of showing me that the gun had been loaded the whole time. Anyway, I told Bob about it, and he just laughed it off and said, "The dude's a cop, he knows what he's doing—don't worry about it." I think that was just a few weeks before the end—if you can imagine, even that didn't freak me out as much as waking up with a needle in my arm. I hate needles.

EIGHT

His first ever proper commission! Paul's would be the same size as Jimmy's own self-portrait, but oil, not acrylic, and he would prime the canvas with several coats—primer and gesso—as professional as possible. Also underpainting. Paul was so fair he would need some deeper tones underneath, less blood bag, more bronze—nothing wrong with embellishing, the guy was already good looking. One picture Jimmy snapped had turned out especially handsome, his best angle. If Paul was pleased, maybe he would talk up his talents to people out on the East Coast. This must be his greatest work. To the art store!

Out in the front garden, though, a fraught scene unfolded. Two men stood gawking, shovel and shears in hand, one linebacker size, the other smaller and older—less football, more couch coach. Ah, Oscar and Ramon. On the sidewalk, Kitty wore gardening gloves, hands on hips, laughing at an unfortunate man in a car towing a powerboat, wedged in the street trying to turn around.

"I knew he was headed the wrong way the second I saw him! Should have made that hard left down the hill, oh well!" She said to the two guys, "¿Vas a ayudar?" They shrugged their shoulders as Jimmy approached.

"Hi Kitty—oh, hey, Oscar?" They all turned.

"Hey, bro! Jimmy! How's it going?" said the big one—Oscar.

"Oh good, you've met," Kitty said, throwing up her hands at the spectacle in the street. "I'm going back in then. Don't forget to put the tools away." She added something else in Spanish to the older man, but he either didn't hear, or didn't bother to acknowledge her comment anyway, just kept smiling at Jimmy. Both of them extended calloused paws at the same time. Curiously, the older extended his left so that Jimmy shook both their hands at the same time. Awkward.

"Good to meet you," Oscar said, "this is Ramon."

A magnetic charge ran through Jimmy—Ramon was his wet dream come to life. He had dazzling amber-green eyes, a thick beard and buzzed hair, meaty arms and shoulders. Jimmy wished the handsome Daddy had reached out on Hookr first. Oscar was huge, easily three hundred pounds, messy hair about six months too long, a patchy scruff on his full, round face—yes, cute, but, Oh, Papi! Sizzling hot Latin Daddy AND his big brown boy? ¡Ay, caramba!

"I was going to run out, but maybe you got a second to talk about the painting?"

"Sure thing!" Oscar spoke a few words of Spanish to Ramon. Interesting. Daddy didn't speak English. They headed up the stairs, Jimmy in front to make sure they got a good look at his ass.

They would handle everything, Oscar said in the kitchen, he only needed to pick colors. Jimmy supposed a neutral white so any reflection off the walls onto his paintings would keep the color true. Daddy Ramon followed the conversation only for a moment, then continued up to the bathroom.

"There was a leak from the toilet, he was supposed to double-check before you moved in," Oscar explained. They went up and found Ramon in the studio, absorbed in Jimmy's paintings leaning against the wall.

"Good!" he declared. He inspected several of the canvases, sweating through his tattered t-shirt. Oh, that steamy working man's stink—and a waft of beer, before noon! Jimmy stood closer. Ramon collared him playfully around the neck, and that's when he realized why the guy shook with his left hand: he had no right hand, just a smooth, tanned stump, seamed with a scar and resembling an oddly tapered cock. He jerked slightly at the realization, the truncated limb bobbing near his face, and Ramon chuckled and squeezed him a little tighter.

Somewhere, sometime, Jimmy heard if someone does a favor for you, they will like you better, you must be worth the effort so the mind fills in any gap. A fantasy swept over him, himself crushed between the one-handed Daddy and his big boy, naked and afraid. He melted into Ramon, who pinched his side teasingly, testing for love handles or ticklishness maybe. Clearly, Oscar had shared his pictures and their online flirtation with his Daddy—maybe they'd decided to share him, too.

"We got you covered, Jimmy, anything you need," Oscar was saying, standing right behind, close enough for Jimmy to smell the beer on his breath, too. "We could start tomorrow if you want, or next weekend—I start a new job Monday." Cool, doing what? "Helping with deliveries—my cousin's got a liquor distributorship."

"Wow, thanks—tomorrow would be great, but maybe just a little tester swatch on the wall, so I can be sure of the color?" Another favor. "The wrong color shift could throw off the light on my paintings—it's important for my work."

Oscar nodded and clapped him on the shoulder. "You got it, bro, I'll stop by later with some options." Now he rested his hand on Jimmy's shoulder too—look here, look there, he pointed. "We could maybe do a different color in the bedroom, yeah? A pale, sandy color—like your hair—stop there at the step, and your neutral white in here." Ramon still pressed against him, fast friends. "How's that sound?"

It sounded perfect. "You know what? Don't bother with the swatches—I trust you."

Oscar shook his head, protesting. "No, no, no problem at all, we want you to be happy." They took their leave, Ramon giving him a rough, final squeeze and Oscar a fist bump. "Welcome to the building, bro."

Welcome indeed. On the walk up San Pablo to Albany Art, Jimmy reeled at the thought of playtime with those two.

Before meeting in person Friday night, he and Dee's friend Vic had spoken on the phone only once after a couple of emails about the job. Jimmy was grateful for their help and pleasantly surprised by their friendly reception when he stepped into the store. He wondered what he might have said at the Stallion.

"Hey, Jimmy!" Vic cried, going in for a big hug. "So what happened the other night?"

"Ugh, yeah sorry! I know, I—stepped out with a friend."

Vic was unfazed. "You wanna go get some lunch? I was just about to clock out." Jimmy's stomach was off, but he could hardly say no.

Nathan, the manager who interviewed and hired him, was in his office upstairs and rarely wanted to be disturbed. Christine, a chubby coworker trying to hide bad skin with bangs, kept up a friendly patter as he browsed and waited for Vic.

"Vic said they saw you at The Stallion—I've been there, with one of my other gay friends—I wonder if we've seen each other before? Although I think I'd remember you," she flirted.

("Don't be stingy with the hags, they're harmless and just want attention," Dee was always saying. "They're worth their weight in baked goods on lonely Saturday nights.")

"I'm not really a regular," Jimmy offered, not entirely lying—in total he had spent far more time in the Trough than in the bar itself.

"I can't wait to work with you!" She was unable to stop herself from hugging him, too, as he and Vic headed out across the plaza.

"We only get half an hour, I was just going to grab a crappy sandwich at Starbucks and some chips," Vic said.

"Perfect—but really I need coffee more than food."

"Hey, maybe grab this table here outside, it gets busy. What do you want? My treat."

"Oh my god, I should be treating you," Jimmy said, "and more than just a Starbucks, you really helped me out."

Vic beamed. "Dude, I'm totally happy to help—just a latte?"

Jimmy scanned the parking lot as he sat, feeling as though he had been whisked away from the Bay Area and plopped back down in a strip mall in Fresno—from Oz back to Kansas—a sea of cars shimmering among big box stores.

What if Kansas had never been home, though? He was half hoping Paul would be the connection he needed to make a move, to New York, to any place big enough to really lose himself, whole oceans of artists, men, fellow minnows. San Francisco had a bigger name than it deserved. But maybe bigger was the problem? Among the kids at ArtHaus he had felt like a pod, buying his plain old paint and brushes, going home to cocktails and canvas while they experimented with spray paint, tattoos, Burning Man, and acid. Maybe he would feel more grounded in the East Bay. The weather was nicer anyway, and here came Vic, his new best friend, with a venti latte. "So yeah, I looked for you after Dee's show—I figured you hooked up with your boyfriend, Dee said he was meeting you?"

"Oh shit, we broke up—you must have missed that part."

Vic gave a passable impression of sympathy. "Sorry to hear it. Were you dating long?"

Not long, turned out not as serious as Jimmy thought. "It's cool, things were going to get complicated with me moving over here, you know, no car, new job and all that."

"Oh yeah, I forget you City people don't have cars—over here they're almost a requirement, especially living up in the hills at my mom's, but where's your new place?" Jimmy told them. "I know exactly where that is, we used to pass it on the way up Albany Hill. I used to know a guy who lives over there somewhere, Junior—wow, I haven't seen him since high school. You're pretty close to BART anyway, and walking distance to work, that's nice. But if you ever need a ride anywhere, text me—really, you got my number. Anytime."

Jimmy's heart skipped a beat when he arrived back upstairs with his supplies to find his front door open and Kitty milling in the kitchen by a ladder, smoke alarm screeching.

"What's happening?"

Kitty shook her head and pointed up to Oscar as he pulled the alarm off the wall. The screech died. "Whew! That gave us a start," she said, "can't be cooking the tenants the first week they arrive!"

"Probably a short, I just changed the battery but the unit's pretty old." Oscar descended and lumbered out the door. "I think we got a couple new ones, I'll go check."

"Thanks, Ramon honey," Kitty said. "All under control—what would we do without our big strong boy, huh?" She followed Oscar out, a little wobbly Jimmy thought. She got Oscar's name wrong, and he assumed she had already had a couple.

Come to think of it, he was on vacation! He could stand a belt before lunch. He dumped his bag on the counter and grabbed the vodka from the freezer. He was taking a good deep slug straight from the bottle right as Oscar walked back through the open door. Caught!

"Forgot the keys!" He whisked the jingling janitor's ring off the counter and headed back out.

Jimmy swallowed another gulp and stashed the bottle back, then headed up to the bathroom to piss, that big latte already running right through him. He came out to find Oscar back up the ladder changing out the alarm. So hard to tell with Latinos how old they were. Close to his age? Maybe a little older? God, he was a big boy, though—a whole lot of bear to have humping on top of you. Delicious.

"Thanks, man—big plans tonight?"

Oscar hemmed. "Nothing special—game on TV—you gonna watch?" Jimmy had no idea what game, or even which sport.

"Nah, I gotta get started on this," he said, pulling canvas and supplies out of his bag.

"Cool, bro—I'm heading out to the paint store now."

"Cool, thanks, see you later."

Jimmy opened the freezer for another belt as soon as the door shut.

Dee called to see if he wanted to get some late lunch, Ricardo would be home from Sacramento around five. "He says it's better when I stay home because his sister loves me more than him, and when we go up to Sac together she gives me all the love and he ends up babysitting. See you in a bit!"

Not a half hour later, the buzzer rang. "Avon calling." Dee was still carrying on about the walk up as he surveyed the new studio. "Perfectly perfect! You can paint, you can turn tricks, you can leave your douche hose up in the shower and nobody will care—not that Vern did, or Bob, I'm sure. Panda?"

Until Dee started doing drag, Jimmy had always thought he was passably cute in an Uncle Fester sort of way. Balding early, he clipped his hair short and was one of the very few men in the entire world who looked better clean shaven. After his "dragening"—his drag awakening—Jimmy realized Dee's face and skin tone were the human equivalent of a blank canvas, pre-primed and ready to receive Dusty Davenport's Zone of Beauty, or Zona Bonita as Ricardo called it.

As they headed out the door, Ramon was in the garden finishing up. He nodded as they smiled their way past.

"Holy shit!" Dee climbed into his Miata. "He's got a stump! I love a good stump—Ricardo's missing a toe, you know."

"Yes, freak."

"Now you know I can't take a fist—god knows I've tried—but a stump is a whole different ball game."

"Please stop."

"That would be—what? Phantom fisting? Hot."

Dee's old silver Miata, Mildred, was well into her ninth life, and impossibly small to accommodate his wigs and costumes. Ricardo was a wizard with Gorilla Tape, but the old black cloth top was so faded the patches looked better than the original fabric. Then there was the blood-red splash down the dash and glove box from his first show, when he had painted his nails and left the top loose on the bottle in his haste. ("Drag is war! Never forget it!") And on the passenger seat, a frayed hole from one time when they both still smoked—Dee thought he flicked his cigarette out the window, and no one realized it had landed between Jimmy's legs until he started screaming. Now the stereo was on the fritz.

"Bluetooth is out—just radio." Jimmy fiddled with it, and Dee slapped his hand away to turn to a country western station. "Ah! Remember the good old days in the Banana Boat—what did that thing even have, an 8-track? Christ! How did we survive high school?"

"It had a cassette, but we only had CDs, so we listened to my mom's. Kenny Rogers!"

Dee screamed. "And Don McLean, destined for obscurity if not for old whatsherpuss. Bye, bye, shut your American piehole, hag."

"And my dad's Jim Croce, fuck sake."

"Settle down," Dee said. "Leroy Brown is one of my standards. Gotta love a big-dicked pimp."

"It doesn't say anything about his dick, or pimping."

"A girl can dream. Aw! Panda! Loves me some Beijing Beef, baby."

By tradition, they got their food to go and kept Mildred company in the parking lot, top down, radio on. They discussed the ins and outs of Daddy/boy relationships as they ate.

"I don't see a collar on Oscar," Jimmy said, "but I don't think Ramon even speaks any English—I get the feeling they're not really plugged into the scene, you know—I mean, Albany for god's sake."

"Seriously. But you've got a great new space, new job—and maybe some in-house dick—let's pretend this is the fresh start you needed. You're not going to finish that?" Jimmy had started to put the lid back on his half-eaten bowl of orange chicken—he might be wanting a few more shots in the afternoon and didn't want to fill up. He handed it over, then pulled out his phone to show the picture Oscar sent last night. Dee grabbed the phone. "Oh! Big boy—talk about Country Bear Jamboree, huh? South of the Border edition. Yum."

Jimmy snatched his phone back before Dee could swipe for other illicit pics. "That's so racist."

"Impossible, I'm Mexican by marriage. Well, the boy's cute, but that Daddy's gorgeous, right? Jimmy sandwich anyone?"

Jimmy doubted they were into kink. "And threesomes are not everyone's cup of tea—especially Daddys and boys—the power dynamics can shift when you add a third person in the mix."

"At least it sounds like they might be open, or the boy is allowed to play with other boys if he gets permission. But yeah, he might not want you fucking his Daddy. He's damn big, he could eat you for breakfast."

"Yeah, just my luck—I got fat boys up the wazoo, but a hot older top—"

"HAD fat boys!" Dee smacked his lips, orange chicken decimated. "You OK with Matt and all that?"

Jimmy sighed. "Yeah, it's fine—you were right, he was just a boy after all, masquerading as a bear. Topping from the bottom doesn't count—my fist got more action than my wazoo with him. And he was definitely not into piss play."

"So, not a love connection," Dee observed, finishing off Jimmy's Coke too. "This is diet, right? I'm watching my figure."

While he was out, the guys had been in to paint some swatches of neutral whites on the walls in the kitchen, and upstairs, a patchwork from a bright ivory to pale straw picked out in a grid. On the kitchen counter, he found a diagram in pencil with numbers, and paint chips stapled to the back. Two of the colors had stars next to them, the ones he would have picked. Oscar got him, alright.

Jimmy turned on his radio and tried to find the same country station Dee had tuned in. The old boombox had belonged to his father, the one he listened to puttering around the garage workshop, his escape from "the wife and her egg" Jimmy once overheard him say to a neighbor as he sat quietly forgotten by the kitchen door. The signal had been clear in Dee's car, but scratchier now.

Over the rest of the afternoon, he set up his easel and unpacked a few things from the ART box. He primed the canvas for the portrait. Waiting for the first coat to dry, he knew already he was going to run out of vodka and popped out to the corner store.

In between coats of gesso, he took stock of his tubes of oil paint and rummaged to find new brushes he remembered packing. He worked his way steadily through the rest of the open vodka bottle.

"The Night the Lights Went Out in Georgia" came on the radio—that took him back. It had been a favorite of his father's. He'd sung along in a rich baritone that thrilled Jimmy as a kid, though the part about the puddle of blood always scared him. He would sit in his corner of the garage on his yellow Playskool stool, out of sight, never invited to tinker, in fact warned never to even look at the pristine tools. Years later, Dee would laugh about his humorless father loving a song made popular by Vicki Lawrence. "Mama! From *Mama's Family*! And Carol Burnett! Imagine!"

The workshop remained untouched after his father's death, though Jimmy plainly saw tools he could have used for art projects. As they were packing up Ricardo's Volvo to move Jimmy up to Bob's, Dee had stolen the boombox and hid it in the trunk while Marlys was distracted. It might have been older than Jimmy, but the radio still worked. He felt a certain kinship to its AM/FM vibe on a swiftly digitizing planet.

He had done as much as he could do with the portrait for one evening. Jimmy fixed himself an extra-strong vodka tonic and settled into bed for a wank and an early blackout.

HOOKR CHAT

Fballer26:
Hey Jimmy you still up?

Want some beers?

Horny bro?

K have a good night

NINE

Was it the morning light or the knocking at the door making the gigantic noise? Jimmy pulled on some briefs to shuffle downstairs, hair everywhere.

Oscar peeked through the crack. "Oh, shit—you were up late too?"

"What's happening?" Jimmy croaked.

"Ready to paint?"

To be polite—or maybe to be bold—he opened the door all the way. "Is it Sunday already?"

Oscar's eyes went wide. "Whoa. We can start on the kitchen if you want to go back to bed, bro."

Jimmy crawled back under the covers, pillow over his head and marching band in his stomach. The guys started taping in the kitchen, quietly, and worked their way up the high walls, not much to tape really, just the outside edges of the windows. The steel counters were freestanding and pulled away from the walls in a jiffy, the open shelves popped right off. Ramon hopped up the ladder to sand while Oscar continued taping up the stairs and on through the studio.

Jimmy drowsed waiting for his stomach to settle down but never fell back to sleep. By the time he sat up in bed, Oscar had worked his way halfway around, down the long wall Jimmy was calling the gallery and back to the dormer windows. Ramon worked in the bathroom with the door closed.

"Better?" Oscar asked. "Had a few last night?"

"Maybe more than a few." He felt ridiculous sitting up in bed with Oscar sneaking looks, and some fresh air would wake him up. He pulled on some shorts and a tank top, grabbed his keys and wallet.

"Tell you what, I'm gonna run down to Dunkin' and get us some coffee and donuts, yeah?" Oscar nodded with a thumbs up, and he headed out.

Good morning, Albany!

Dee had a theory about Daddys and boys.

"A true boy is not a guy who finds older men attractive, but one who eroticizes an image of himself as a powerless object in order to cope with feelings of shame over his attraction to an indifferent and/or dominating father. I've given this a lot of thought—on your behalf, I might add, I should send you an invoice," Dee said the day before. "Most so-called 'boys' are just narcissists who love the attention and like to run the show with their asses—but real boys want to lose themselves in the sex and will do anything Daddy tells them. You're somewhere in between."

"Do tell."

"You're not a narcissist, but you're not a true boy either—far too sassy, in my opinion—you find older men attractive, but you have art to work through your feelings. You're like me—I've got drag, you've got painting."

"But I thought you were a narcissist," Jimmy said.

"As I was saying—I've got drag, and you've got art and alcoholism. You're welcome. Five cents, please."

Maybe Dee was right. More power to Oscar—he had a sizzling hot Daddy, and if he was open to sharing, Jimmy would present no real competition as a boy. His experiment with Bob had shown him he actually did have some limits. Losing himself in sex, even freaky sex with weed and liquor and poppers, got him out of his head, but if anything, power plays and trust games drove him deeper in and left him instantly sober—definitely the wrong direction. For another nickel, Dee had said he could formally diagnose some sort of attachment spectrum disorder, treatable with enemas.

When Jimmy got back with a dozen donuts, three coffees, and a handful of baby creamers, the taping in the studio was done, and Oscar was working on the bedroom. Ramon was missing. "He's out smoking." Jimmy glanced out the window and saw him by the dumpster in the alley.

"Help yourself—I didn't know what you liked, so I got extra of everything I like."

Oscar ate three donuts in three minutes, powdered sugar dusting his lips and wispy goatee. He had that rosey-brown Latino smoothness, like maybe he only needed to shave every month or so. Jimmy imagined he was smooth all over—a brown, hairless hulk. He picked at a devil's food and sipped his coffee black while Oscar doctored his with four sugars and half the creamers.

Should he ask Oscar about their relationship? Most guys loved to share the dirty secrets of their gay liberation. Oscar seemed different though—like most boys, probably a bottom, but maybe curious about topping someone younger and smaller? Jimmy had played with one throuple—a boy, a Daddy, and a GrandDaddy. G-Daddy had the biggest, thickest dick on a white man he had ever seen, and liked to blow cigar smoke up his boys' holes. But some boys were not too eager to share—MY Daddy—and that was as often true of the Daddys loaning out their boys. The fact that Oscar had mentioned asking permission meant such permission could be given— encouraging, but he could also be making shit up and sneaking around.

Ramon returned, trailing a sweet, earthy odor. Why did smokers always smell different? His mother tried to cover her smoking with Tic Tacs, and she smelled spicy, like black pepper and mint. Kitty smelled of furniture polish and a cold fireplace. Ramon's musk wafted up the stairs like the inside of a cedar chest full of whiskey. Ignoring the open box of donuts and the cup of coffee, he extracted a can of beer from a paper bag he brought up, and popped it open as Oscar continued to tape in the studio. He listened from the window seat as the boys chatted.

"Technically the best light is north facing," Jimmy was saying, noticing when Oscar realized he was the only one doing any work and stopped for a moment to glare at an oblivious Ramon. "You don't want direct light, you want lots of indirect, but I never work too early so my next favorite is east facing like the big window in the kitchen—the sun will be up and out of direct line by the time I ever get going." Ramon was nodding, evidently able to at least follow a conversation even if he was hesitant to speak English.

"You got the blackout in the kitchen if you need it," Oscar said.

"Blackout?"

"Oh, you don't know. Behind the soffit—there's a blackout shade. Kitty had us install it awhile back, trying to get this place fixed up to rent—she said some people were turned off because there was no shade on the big window, so she had one custom made." Oscar spoke to Ramon in Spanish, who retorted gruffly and made no sign of moving.

"I guess I'll show you how it works, then" Oscar said, tossing the roll of painter's tape at Ramon as he headed toward the stairs—it bounced off his chest, and he chuckled as he opened another beer and watched it roll across the floor.

Jimmy leaned over the counter to try to see up the window wall. Without a word, Oscar lifted him up under the arms and set his feet on the kitchen counter as easily as if he were a child. He could see now past the deep lip of ceiling ending six inches shy of the windows and a hidden shade running the length. Behind the shelves and a stack of boxes on the counter, he had missed the cord that operated it. These last five days he had been waking at sunrise and flipping a pillow over his head to block out the light.

"Fantastic—do you think she might spring for some more along the window seat?"

Oscar fiddled with the cord to show him. "Probably—she likes you, but maybe you want something different in there? This sucker's just big and plain, she was thinking maybe curtains."

"Yeah, maybe."

"So what about the paint colors?"

"I like the ones you chose," Jimmy said, and Oscar smiled, pleased. "Roman Forum in the studio, Dunegrass everywhere else." Oscar yelled up to Ramon, who came reluctantly, his heavy work boots clumping on the stairs. Daddy and boy left for the paint store.

Jimmy decided scrubbing out the rust stains in the bathtub and sink would make him feel a little less upstairs-downstairs while they painted. No scrubbers, sponges or cleaning supplies though, so he needed to head to the store. But first, since Ramon was drinking, why not?

While he worked his way through a couple of vodka tonics and moved around some boxes, Jimmy wondered about the logistics of a hot Daddy with such a massive boy. Definitely he had met Daddys who were bottoms, boys who were tops, tiny men with huge dicks, and butch queens with voracious holes, but he was holding out hope he might get two tops for the price of one. He could see himself on the bottom of that dogpile, close to five hundred pounds of Latin love grinding him into a paste. With a healthy measure of liquid self-help, for that hour or two—fingers crossed—he might erase the tangled mess of his brain and feel useful to his fellow men. He giggled to himself as he downed his drink and floated down the stairs.

For no particular reason he took a different street down to San Pablo, and lookie there, a BevMo not five minutes away, hallelujah ClubBev. The corner store had no rust cleaner though. Kitty had mentioned a Safeway halfway up Solano, so he decided to walk and see how long it took for normal people groceries.

No denying Albany had its own charm if you wanted a nice sleepy place to raise a family or retire. It amused him to know this vanilla village dabbled its feet in the same Bay as Dore Alley Street Fair and Fist City. Wandering lazily up the avenue, he peeped in at shops full of this, that, and wicker, nothing too compelling. He had spent so many years living in Old Navy shorts and t-shirts to afford art supplies and rent—and maybe the odd bottle of vodka or two, who's counting?—that he had lost the taste for things like fashion, or Dee's favorite, pet accessories. Trixie B. Davis, Bulldog Princess—"the long lost love child of Alice the maid and Sam the butcher"—enjoyed a gilded life.

"You should get a puppy," Dee would say, "then Trix would have someone to play with, and I would be relieved of the crushing burden of being your best and only friend." But the infamous episode of the one stray sock down Trixie's gullet and the thousand-dollar vet bill later had proved daunting. Dogs were not a struggling artist's best friend.

He passed under the raised BART tracks he could see from his studio. A real shame there was no stop at Solano, a ten-minute walk to the train would seem somehow less than half the solid twenty minutes to El Cerrito Plaza. Safeway was also a bit of a hike, and for what? Fresh limes? He did not want to believe his mother and Vic had been right about needing a car in the East Bay. The corner store had his mainstays: peanut butter, jelly, Wonder Bread, and mac-n-cheese. Tonic was always optional, and he could make ice at home. At least now he knew where the store was. He spent a good half hour exploring BevMo on his way home.

The studio was silent when he returned, smelling of wet paint, and Jimmy guessed the guys were out for lunch. He helped himself to another vodka tonic. Small as it was, the kitchen was half painted already, top down. The new color was clean as a white sand beach. Perfect choice. He swept and dicked around for a while, expecting them to come back any minute, but then he saw Ramon in the alley smoking again. He hated to be pushy, but he started to wonder if they had knocked off for the day and was also curious about the laundry—he had not been down to see it yet.

The basement was two stories below the foyer, the stairwell illuminated only with a green exit sign. He passed a humming utility door at the first landing, ceiling snaked with pipes and ducts like a descent into a submarine. Fluorescent lights flicked on from a motion detector in the laundry room as he popped in his head. One washing machine on spin was making an insane racket, a hurricane echoing off the concrete walls and halfway up the stairs—it knocked up against the next machine, drum off-kilter maybe, or one of the legs out of level.

Past the laundry, another glowing exit sign over a door into the alley propped open with a cinder block. Never one to miss clandestine spots for fooling around, he noted the drain outside the door, the unpainted concrete, no security light. If he ever needed a quiet spot to lure a trick for some indecent exposure, this might be a good candidate. He mounted the steps to the back gate, a piece of cardboard keeping it from latching.

Ramon waved from his seat on a crate by the dumpster, lighting a new smoke from the cherry of the last one. The alley bisecting the block was just wide enough for a garbage truck to get by, and nearly every building up and down the lane warned "NO PARKING – VIOLATORS WILL BE TOWED."

"Hey, dude," Jimmy said, "smoke break?"

"Yeah, yeah—back soon." What did bros do to break the ice? He squatted against the wall next to Ramon, close but not touching. "Smoke?" Ramon asked, holding his cigarette between his lips and fumbling for his pack of Lucky Strikes.

"No more—I quit." He wanted to say yes, to anything Ramon offered.

"Weed?" From the pack, Ramon pulled out a joint, well rolled, not too tight, and now Jimmy did say, "Yes please." He made sure to touch Ramon's hands as he cupped his own around the lighter flame. As always, he pulled deeper than he should and coughed. Ramon laughed and slapped him on the back a few times, left his hand there, puffing on the cigarette stuck between his lips. "Good, eh?"

The problem with weed, he remembered after taking a few more smaller puffs, was how his mind scattered into so many interesting directions. Like Ramon's stump, resting on the inside of his thigh. He wore frayed and ragged khaki shorts, his legs dark caramel brown, thick, hairless and smooth. The end of his handless wrist looked like a huge cock lolling against his leg. Jimmy fought the urge to reach out and touch it. Of course it was his arm, not his cock—that would be weird.

To distract himself, he faked another cough and handed the joint back. Ramon set the stub of his cigarette on the lip of the dumpster, but a gust threatened to roll it off, and now Jimmy did reach over, leaned languidly on Ramon's thigh to rescue it, smoked a couple puffs after all. Now the cigarette smoke and the weed smoothed out the noonday sun, framed the moment as though a scene in a movie, cameras slow-rolling on Jimmy and his handsome costar.

Now they were enjoying the sun together, beside the prop dumpster, feeling chummy and warm, a mood shot, no dialogue—you only have eyes for each other, this is the moment you realize your longing—Action! But in his muddle he could not remember what the script called for next. Was he supposed to lean in for a kiss? Squat down on the pavement in front of this "Ramon" character, pull up his shirt and kiss that adorably round belly? Was it as smooth, brown, and thick as his legs? Or perhaps fumble at his fly, release the manly musk into his nostrils, and—

Line?

Jimmy stood up to adjust the growing tumescence in his briefs and shake off the trembling, uncertain energy of their dumpster moment.

"Should we go in?"

Ramon nodded, pinched out the roach, and stashed it back in his pack.

"Where's Oscar?" Jimmy asked.

"Back soon."

But already upstairs when Jimmy and Ramon returned to the loft together, Oscar was finishing his first burrito. "I got you one," he said, "chicken—I wasn't sure?"

Jimmy was enjoying his high. "Thanks, maybe later."

Oscar washed it all down with two beers, while Ramon took a few bites, and then handed the rest of his over to Oscar to finish too. Jimmy got to work on the rust stains in the bathroom.

He was in the tub on his hands and knees with a scrub brush when Ramon walked right in, unzipped, and pulled out his cock, balls too—the whole meaty package flopped free—and started pissing. Their eyes locked. Ramon's flow was good and strong, and lasted a long time. Jimmy almost spoke, almost invited him to hose him down then and there in the tub instead of wasting it in the toilet, but could not find his voice and only managed to motion him to approach as Ramon finished. Jimmy leaned forward and slurped the last golden drops off his cock. Nice to finally meet you, Sir. Ramon stepped back and tucked himself back into his shorts.

"What do you think about the railing?" Oscar had finished in the kitchen, all the way up the stairs and halfway through the bedroom by the time Jimmy emerged from the bathroom. "I think latex would make a mess—could use oil, but I kinda like it this way, all rough and industrial and shit—like the windows and the kitchen." Jimmy agreed, he was so amped he would have agreed to anything. Ramon nodded, back on the window seat, seemingly done working and well into the second six pack in his paper bag.

Maybe some painting of his own would steady him. "You don't mind if I start working on my stuff while you guys paint, yeah?" He tried to sense any strangeness coming off Oscar, if he was upset that Jimmy had been tasting his Daddy's dick, but found none. They seemed to enjoy just hanging out, Oscar working, Ramon belching and drinking his beer watching the two of them. Jimmy got his stool, his cart, his palette and brushes set up and flipped his laptop to the one super handsome picture of Paul.

"Wow, you got the real setup here." Jimmy could tell Oscar was distracted by the process as the figure took shape, underpainted shadows slowly built up, defining the head and face. Oscar kept stopping and coming back over to watch.

"This is just a study for now, I'm just playing with the composition."

Oscar finished in the bedroom and moved into the studio. The cutting in on the walls took no time at all—it was all one color, ceiling and walls, and they had already taped the floor. Oscar was so tall he had no need to climb on a ladder, and he was rolling on the walls within an hour. The gallery wall was already done by the time Ramon drained the last beer and mumbled in Spanish to Oscar on his way out.

"You want some beer?" Oscar asked, and Jimmy nodded. He yelled down to Ramon on his way out.

Now it was Jimmy's turn to be distracted as Oscar worked in the studio. His shirt was too short and kept hiking up whenever he reached overhead, revealing the bottom of his belly, and in back, the top of his ass crack, glistening with sweat. Jimmy had a fondness for plumber's crack, and Oscar had that gold standard of bellies: big and round, swollen but firm. He began to imagine what it would be like to be squished between the bellies of Daddy and boy both.

He had realized around puberty, poking around on the internet for naked men after school with Dee, that a belly resembled the head of an enormous cock. A belly button looked like a pisshole. The image mesmerized him. Once he started seeing it, he saw it everywhere—at the pool, in gym class, walking down the street in Fresno—he would see Latin men, rednecks, older guys with big guts, and imagine a gigantic cock straining through their shirts. He loved touching bellies, rubbing his face all over fat guts, nuzzling and sucking and slobbering over them—especially as he got older and discovered the vastly under-acknowledged hallucinatory powers of poppers. It was like he was shrunk down to miniature, helpless insignificance, in awe of a monumental manhood. He loved the big, careless strength of blue-collar working men, construction workers, the city workers of Fresno, gardeners his mother and neighbors employed. He ached to worship their raw masculinity and power, himself a powerless captive, prey, a thing, used.

When Ramon returned with two twelve packs, they cracked open a couple for a quick break, and then Oscar got back to work. In an hour and a half more, the bedroom and studio were done, and he came to watch as Jimmy worked, standing close behind him. He downed another beer and let out a huge belch, then an adorable giggle. He examined the photo of Paul, standing so close behind Jimmy his belly was pressed against his back.

"Good looking man." Yes, he was.

"Not as sexy as you, bro."

Now Jimmy leaned back into his big belly. Oscar reached around and started playing with his nipples.

Ramon sat on the window seat, watching them as he fooled with his crotch.

TEN

"New Yorker," Jimmy explained to Marlys on the phone. "Journalist. I think he's pretty well known." He told her the name.

"Never heard of him."

"He really liked the self-portrait I did—I'll send you a picture of it, it's pretty new, I don't think you've seen it."

"That's OK, James, I'm sure it's very nice—you know how I hate fussing with computers."

He made the mistake of telling her how much money Paul had given him for the commission. "Oh! That's good, then you can start making payments back to me for the money you borrowed. A check is fine."

Fuck. He sighed audibly and she seized on it.

"Now you listen to me, young man—it was a loan, I made that very clear."

"I know—I'm not complaining, I just don't know how long I'm going to have to wait before I get my first paycheck—or how much it's going to be after taxes and everything. Can we wait a month and see?"

"No—you can certainly afford to send two hundred immediately—I assume your rent is already paid for the month, and you shouldn't have to wait more than two weeks for your first paycheck, I'm sure there is some law. No, this is part of being a responsible adult, James Christopher—you may start repaying me immediately."

"OK."

"Your father didn't exactly leave me in perfect financial shape, you know—there was no life insurance after he retired. I told him he should get some term insurance to make sure I was taken care of, but he never got around to it before his heart troubles, and then after ... well, by then it was too late, nobody would insure him, what with his age, and his health."

Jimmy knew all this, he was there, and she had given him a refresher when he borrowed the money in the first place. Never mind his seventy-two-year-old father had also never bothered to make any provisions for his only son, but he knew, having helped Marlys get everything transferred over to her name, that between Social Security and pensions she made far more money than him each month, and the house had been paid off for years.

"You're OK though, right?" Calling her bluff—just a little poke.

"That's not the point," she snapped. "The point is I loaned you money, and you agreed to pay it back when you got a new job—this little art job counts."

"That's not what I meant, mother—I just want to be sure you are taken care of."

"I'm not a child—I can take care of myself." Abrupt silence.

"OK then, good—I'll send a check as soon as this one clears."

"That will be fine."

"Anything else? Any word about Maryann?"

"I spoke to her husband the other day—he was rather rude, but then he always was—well, I should say, he wasn't at first, but then he became rude after that one time."

This was new. “One time?”

“Oh, have I never told you this?” she began, the familiar prelude to many a long-smoldering grievance. “Actually, Maryann became somewhat cool after that, too, but her husband was downright rude—came over and talked to your father about it, but it really wasn’t any of his business, now was it?”

“Mother, what are you talking about? You never said anything—did Maryann and dad have a fight?” Marlys let out a long, throaty chuckle, and he heard the crisp snap of her lighter—she was settling in for a good dish.

“No, no—well, James, I suppose I never told you because I didn’t want to tarnish him in your eyes—a son should look up to his father—but he was not perfect, good heavens, not even close.”

“I never thought he was, trust me,” he said.

“I won’t have you talking ill of him either—I’m his wife, but you should be respectful.”

“Jesus, mother—just tell me what happened.”

Deep inhale. “Fine. I guess you could say the reason I’m practically living hand to mouth in Fresno instead of the south of France is that your father had a gambling problem.”

“What?”

“Yep. I mean, we kept it from you of course because we didn’t want you to know how precarious things were at times, but yes—your father had a problem, a big one—he lost several fortunes over the years, which is why I live on a fixed income.”

“Wow, I had no idea—I mean, he liked his poker night, and he went to the track now and then.”

“He calmed down quite a bit after the loan sharks came knocking and scared the living daylights out of me and Maryann.”

"What?"

"That's why Maryann's husband came over—Maryann was here having coffee one day, middle of the afternoon—I don't know where your father was, probably at the golf course—and these two goons show up at the front door. Dressed in suits, if you can imagine—good marketing, I suppose, I mean I looked through the peephole and I thought, 'Oh, these could be police detectives, good lord what if something happened to your father?' Anyway. They walked straight into the foyer and shut the door behind them, and I thought, 'Uh oh.' Maryann peeked her head around from the dining room, too—it was so strange."

"What'd they say?"

"You must have been at school, I guess, so it was just me and Maryann in the house by ourselves and these two big men—I mean, they were white, so I was a little nervous but not actually scared even when they barged right in. They knew my name, for heaven's sake. They said, 'Mrs. Traywick, is your husband home?' and I said no, he was out, could I help them? That's when they pushed their way in, and they said, 'Mrs. Traywick, we're here to tell you that your husband owes us some money, and it is now overdue. We know where you live, and we know where your son goes to school. We'll be back tomorrow at the same time, and you will need to give us ten thousand dollars or there will be consequences.'"

"Oh my god."

"And then they left—and sure enough, they came back the next day, but your father was home, of course I gave him holy hell, and he handed over ten thousand dollars to them—which I went to the bank myself to withdraw that morning, because honestly I didn't entirely trust him not to hightail it out of the country with all our money and I wasn't going to be left alone in the house waiting for his friends to come back. I was nervous as hell thinking the bank wouldn't be able to give me that much in cash, and then having to walk around and drive home with all that money in my purse. What if I'd been mugged? What if it was over the daily limit?"

"Jesus Christ."

"Anyway. That's why Maryann's husband came over to talk to your father—of course he was worried because she'd been here, and she never did come back over for coffee—I went over to their house now and then, but I always got such a chilly reception from Steve. Anyway, like I say—fair weather friends—who needs 'em."

"So that's why you had to hear she died from the gardener."

"Yes—you know, despite their social standing, at least those people have a strong sense of family and friendship—they have to, poor people can't afford to discard friends over a little trouble, they might need to borrow money when the going gets tough. Oh. Well, family is different, of course."

Tuesday. Wednesday. Thursday. Friday. Saturday. Paul's portrait was coming along. How to make his cheeks flushed, fuller, less pale—he had great bone structure, and good hair. (He had done a sketch of his father once and added hair where there was none. "It looks like he's wearing a toupee," Marlys said. "Never show this to him.") The underpainting had been a good call. With a bit of restraint, a slightly sepia approach, the color blooming through conveyed a healthy tone, the way black-and-white photography flatters pale people. The angle of the picture was perfect. He was no photographer, but somehow, carelessly, that one shot struck exactly the right note—good light, Paul's most handsome side, fifteen years erased.

Marlys, also freckle fair, was always up in arms over how she looked in photos.

"I look like a ghoul!"

"I'm the least photogenic person in the world!"

"Can't you adjust the exposure or whatever so I don't look like a corpse?"

People often mistook her for Jimmy's real mother because of the blond hair, the set of their blue eyes, and a general similarity of features. But while she could not tan despite hours in the sun, prayers, and special lotions from European laboratories, Jimmy took on a deep bronze in summer like those Swedes with their ski tans. A few afternoons in the backyard, smelling of baby oil and blushing brown, he would come in through the kitchen door and find her glowering.

"I hate you," she would say, and he would laugh and pull down his Speedo a little for her to see his tan line. "Go away!" she would shout, slamming the dishwasher shut.

Spring vacation, second grade maybe?

"Come here, sweetheart, let me put some lotion on you—you're getting a little pink!" said the nice lady by the pool of the Palm Springs Marriott, beckoning as Jimmy walked past the line of them, all the mothers of the cavorting kids, bare legs like hotdogs lined up on a grill. "Thank god for golf," another wife was saying. The cement was toasty hot in the desert sun.

He presented himself and let her sit him down between her legs where she straddled the chaise, pink toenails splayed, freshly painted. She perched her Jackie-O-big sunglasses on top of her blonde updo.

"Aren't you cute. Marlys! Your boy is so adorable!" she cooed and another mother in the next chaise rolled over on her side to regard him with a serene smile. This was nice. He crossed his legs facing the pretty lady, smelled her frosty pink lipstick, wished he might stay and let her fuss over him for a while. She squeezed out blobs of sunscreen—another delicious summer smell—and dabbed his nose and cheeks, his neck and shoulders too.

Out of the corner of his eye, he saw his mother sitting two chairs down. She had not turned to look, only stared straight ahead for a moment before reaching for her pack of Parliaments on the table.

"There you go sweetie, we don't want you getting burned." The sweet mama lady friend rubbed the lotion into his skin so softly and delicately he thought he might melt right into the neon pinkness of her bathing suit. "Where'd you get this beautiful tan, sweetie? Marlys! Where'd he get this beautiful tan skin from?" she called, not realizing the peril of her question.

"He was adopted."

The smile froze on the woman's mouth for a moment, her eyebrows raised slightly. She winked and booped him on the nose.

"There you go, sweetie, brown as a berry." He loved that she said it.

"By the way, Jimmy," his mother said, examining her cigarette and manicure as she spoke in her calm, sharky way. "Mr. Mitchell told me you did poorly on your last English test. If you don't buckle down before the end of the year, he said he might have to think about holding you back a grade."

He looked at her and saw the familiar set of her jaw, the lopsided way she pursed her lips as though she had a toothpick jammed in the corner.

"Might be for the best—you're so much smaller than your classmates, it would give you a chance to catch up."

"Thank you," he said to the pink lady. He stood up and walked toward the pool, but instead of jumping in, he passed it and, gathering speed, ran out the gate and up the stairs through the lobby to the elevator in bare feet and damp bathing suit. Realizing he had no key when he reached the room, he sat on the swirling paisley carpet. Deep in his chest where his weeping emerged, he felt with a bitter sureness something he had suspected before but now knew, and which he confessed tearfully to Marlys when she arrived minutes later, as though rushing after him to clean up a spill.

"You don't love me."

The portrait must be perfect, and the sooner Paul saw and loved it, the sooner he might recommend him to other clients. Even if he was able to up his price to three thousand each, he figured, that was at least twelve portraits a year just to make ends meet, and how realistic was that? Twelve New Yorkers, all wanting to have their pictures painted by an unknown artist in California? Jimmy doubted even Paul could coax that much interest. And time spent on portraits, however well done, was time away from his real work. He had started no new paintings since he was laid off. But maybe portraits led to dealers led to galleries. If Paul was his foot in the door, at least it was a New York door.

Despite his hopes to spend most of the day working on the portrait, Ramon and Oscar arrived unannounced to finish the touch-ups on the walls. While they were brushing out missed spots, Jimmy's phone rang. He wandered down to the kitchen as Paul jabbered.

"Kindercamp! How you doing, boy? All good? How's the portrait coming?"

Good, good—he would text a pic of his progress when they hung up.

"Great! Hey, so I had lunch with my friend, you know, the gallery owner—Dexter—and he had some good feedback."

"OK..."

"I won't get into all of it, I mean, it was a quick conversation, but I showed him your work, and one in particular he really liked—you know the one with the guy in leather?"

"Vern?"

"Was that his name? Your old roommate I think you said? Yeah, he liked that one, if I'm being honest he said—I'll cut to the chase—he said you should forget the landscapes, and the buildings and the views of Twin Peaks and all that crap, excuse me, I mean, he said there wasn't anything new or exciting about those, but he was interested in that particular one, and if you wanted to focus your work in that direction, that's the one he would want to see more of—more like that... What'd he say? 'Like the stain on the sheets after Mapplethorpe raped the shit out of H.R. Giger.' Anyway—I think you've got a shot, he actually put on his glasses to take a look at that one—I've got his ear, so if you can scrape together some new work more along those lines, I'll try again in a couple months, we get together pretty often. It's all about who you know, right? OK, gotta go! Talk soon—send me that text!"

Jimmy slammed his phone on the counter. He grabbed his bottle of vodka out of the freezer and took a deep slug.

Ramon and Oscar popped their heads over the railing.

"Everything alright?" Oscar asked. "We drinking?"

How the hell was he going to start a whole new series of paintings based on just one image he painted—when he was high!—of an old roommate lost to rehab in Oregon?

"Might as well—let's get fucked up," he said.

"Yeah!" Ramon growled, pulling his shirt off.

Jimmy grabbed some shot glasses. "I'll come up."

Oscar was closing up the paint cans and wrapping brushes in plastic, but Ramon was already sprawled on the bed, hand down his shorts. Feeling the first hot flush of liquor, Jimmy had an idea as he nuzzled his face into Ramon's belly.

"How do you guys feel about modeling for some paintings?"

Later, restless, Jimmy was sorting through canvases he might paint over for new work. Oscar lazed on the bed, but Ramon stood naked holding one painting he had been admiring, and he murmured to Oscar.

"He says this is the best one."

But now Jimmy was disgusted by the whole bunch of pretty castles floating in the clouds.

The Christmas after his father died, his mother and he had put up a tree and decorated it with all of the mercury glass ornaments they loved—Santa heads and teddy bears and a gingerbread house—big, gorgeous ornaments Marlys had collected over the years. She never let him hang them. It had to be done just right or they would fall off the more spindly boughs and break. But she did let him put up the tree, and he raised it on a big heavy box so the ornaments on the lower branches would dangle freely, not scrape the floor. He wrapped the sparkly red blanket around the bottom, and they turned out all the lights, and put on the TV yule log to listen to the carols by the twinkling lights of the tree until late. They had even shared a bottle of champagne—granted, he only had one glass and she finished the rest and cracked open a second. He smoked a cigarette in front of her for the first time, actually felt that though his childhood had been a wash, perhaps they could be friends now that he was an adult. Marlys finally went to bed with her bottle, but Jimmy fell asleep on the sofa.

It must have been the weight of all those heavy ornaments, probably, that crushed or shifted the box under the tree. Just after midnight the whole thing came crashing down. Jimmy startled wide awake to the spectacle of the tree flopped over like a drunk, the lights still blinking, and his mother's precious mercury glass smashed to bits, so many elves and reindeer in jagged shards on the floor—a Christmas catastrophe! Marlys came rushing out of her bedroom and stared at him as he gaped in horror from the sofa, shock hardening into grim reproach on her face. She turned and went back to her room without a word. He cleaned up the whole mess, saving the few that had not broken but most of them he junked.

In the morning, she was not mad. He showed her the few he had saved and she shrugged her shoulders. They exchanged gifts and had a quiet dinner in front of the TV, and she went to bed early Christmas night. Jimmy drank half a bottle of rum from the liquor cabinet, and when he woke up late the next morning, she had put the surviving decorations away, pulled down the tree and dumped it at the curb.

Next December, Marlys set out Gramma's white porcelain tabletop tree studded with red icicles next to the cards received from cousins they never visited, and that was it. They never had another real tree. Christmas was dead to her, deader than if she had only just learned there was no Santa Claus, and Jimmy was the one who told her.

"Why don't you keep that one," Jimmy said to Ramon. "For everything you've done, yeah? Oscar, pick another one of those paintings if you want—I want you guys to have them. It would mean a lot to me."

"Wow, really? Hey! Thanks, bro, thanks a lot," Oscar said. He translated for Ramon, who was visibly moved.

"Jimmy," Ramon said, pulling him into a warm embrace. "Love you."

"Aw, you're sweet."

[Interview transcripts edited for clarity.]

After Bob, you moved in with a new roommate. And you painted him—that painting was in the show at Bash Gallery…

Yes. THAT painting. One of the few times I tried meth. Vern was a complete pig and got off on being naked while other men were fully clothed, especially in any kind of uniform. Anyway, one night we were hanging out, and he said, "You should paint me in my sling!" and I was like "Yes!"

That painting has been noted as a turning point in your work.

You know, something clicked in me after I did the painting of Vern—I lost my shame about what people would think, the fear of revealing the depravity of my life in my art—thanks to Vern and his meth pipe. It was the real life I was living rather than the pretty fantasy world I had been trying to paint. It must have resonated with Dexter, too—that was the one painting that caught his eye out of all the pictures Paul showed him. At the time I thought, if that's what he wants, I'll give him more—which is why I started painting Ramon and Oscar.

But that painting Vern reminds me of an incident in high school.

Tell me.

So I went to hang out with this guy, Hector—he had already graduated, but he still had a couple cousins at my school. Anyway, I ran into him at a gas station, we were both getting gas—I had my mom's Banana Boat and he was like, "Hey,

I remember you, crazy car, dude." I mean I recognized him right away—sexy as hell, little bit cholo but not in a gang or anything, and he was all, "We should hang out," and I was like, "When?"

I went over to his house on a Saturday night, and one of his cousins and another guy were there, white dude, couple girls, too, just a normal house party—parents out of town, whatever. I got pretty wasted, of course, Hector's pouring tequila shots, there's beer, and pretty soon he invites me up to his room to smoke some weed—says he doesn't have much and doesn't want to share it with everybody, just me. Anyway, we get up to his room, smoke, things are getting pretty blurry. Next thing I know his dick is out and I'm sucking him off, and then he's fucking me. And then there's another guy in his room, and they take turns.

Long story short—I have class on Monday with his cousin and his friend and they start trash talking me in the back of the room. "What's that whistling, Jimmy, is that your ass?" and "What's that smell? Smells like sperm." Stuff like that. Just loud enough for everyone around to hear, loud enough for the teacher to tell people to settle down.

That must have been difficult.

Yeah, nothing new. Anyway, me and Hector started having parties out at some of the construction sites at night—no one was around, no streetlights or anything because these tract home developments weren't hooked up to the city yet, no roads. Him and one or two buddies, they'd bring a boombox, and beer, and at some point I'd get stripped naked and down on my knees sucking their dicks, and then bent over the hood or tailgate of one of their cars—Hector had an old El Camino. I mean, most of them I didn't recognize—I assume they were friends or cousins, some of them didn't speak English. I think it was funny to them that some fifteen-year-old white boy was taking all this brown dick and loving it. But then, of course, a few months later, I was out at a construction site partying and who shows up? Hector's cousin from school, and his friend.

Wow. OK.

And they take their turns on me too, and you know, bent over that tailgate with these two assholes gooning on me—I owned it. If I felt bad because of what they said, imagine how much more twisted they were, trying to humiliate me, and then later, fucking me. It was a kind of power I had over them. I started to like it when guys called me faggot, or cocksucker, like I knew what they were really thinking when they said that stuff. I really started partying the last half of my junior year, and senior year, meeting guys at night in parks, construction sites, online.

Exciting but scary at the same time?

Scary? That was part of the excitement—getting blitzed and not knowing or caring what or who was going to happen next, not seeing faces, not having to talk or be interesting or figure out what people wanted to hear to make them like me. I knew what they wanted—I just had to open my mouth, or bend over—it was easy, and it felt good. No, I wouldn't say mixed feelings—I loved it. Even when I got gonorrhea and had to go to a free clinic to get a shot, and got lectured by this very straight doctor asking me a lot of questions about how a kid my age gets gonorrhea in his ass—I didn't care.

And then my dad died and I went into a tailspin.

What happened?

Yeah—that's when I first started blacking out. One morning I woke up naked in a cold puddle of piss in this random house being built and two construction workers poking me with their boots. I blacked out during a party the night before, and I guess they left me. So basically I was instantly sober, jumped into my clothes and booked it out of there. That wasn't even the end of the construction site parties, if you can believe it.

I understand—small price for a good time.

Right. Anyway—it all sort of came together with that painting of Vern—it was wild, and dark, almost grotesque, reds and black—we were high as kites, and I wasn't trying to put a pretty spin on things anymore, didn't care if people were shocked or grossed out. Anyway, that's how it felt. *Broken Spirits*.

Whatever happened to Vern?

It was my fault he ended up moving back to Oregon and I had to move across the Bay—I'm the one who called his mom. I came home from work one day to find a mess of paint cans in the hall, and Vern's bedroom painted black, walls, ceiling, tinfoil on the windows. He said people were peeking in at him.

His mom—you know, I never did get her name, she made me call her Mom from the first time I answered the phone at the apartment. Anyway, she was like, "Vern, it's time for you to come home," and she made him go to rehab. But I wasn't on the lease, so once Vern left, I had to move out. I met Matt thanks to Vern. I bumped into him in the hall on the way to the bathroom, and he was like, "I'm pretty sure I'm never gonna get my turn in the sling." His arm was all greased up with Crisco and he was wearing an assless singlet. I was like, "You are not the first random guy to say that to me." Vern didn't even know we hooked up that night—some other guy was already there as I was slipping into Matt, elbow-deep on my first try—now that's a weird sensation—you can feel bone, vertebrae. It's freaky. Anyways. Then I got laid off from ArtHaus. They wanted to develop the land it sat on, this whole new retail/residential complex. Some of the employees moved to the other location in the Sunset, but I was still a relative newbie so I missed the cut. Vic helped me get the job at Albany Art, and my severance paid for the deposit and last month's rent on the new studio, but that was it. I was back to square one—no gallery, no boyfriend, no money. Thank god for Vic—new job, new apartment, new town. But moving out of the City felt like a huge step backwards.

And did Vern get sober?

No idea. I called his mom to check on him once and she's like, "Don't ever call here again," and hung up.

ELEVEN

Jimmy's new manager, Nathan, was a total hottie, and an unabashed asshole. The guy wore a tie by choice, for fuck sake.

"Here's the deal at Albany Art—with seniority, you can hope to have Sundays off, but until one of the old timers leaves, you're stuck working with a hangover, no excuses. For now, just focus on getting through your first three months."

"Three months?"

"Your probationary period."

"I'm a company man," he went on to say as they reviewed procedures in the office. "I don't mind coming in to train you, but you'll need to get up to speed quick—I don't work Sundays. But you've had plenty of experience." He peeked at Jimmy's resume as though it were a secret dossier. "And you've got all week to figure things out. It would please me if this were the last Sunday I have to come in to train you."

Vic had warned him. "He's like the bitchiest nun from Catholic school trapped in Tom Cruise's body. But not cute dancing around in his underwear Tom—crazy jumping on the sofa screaming 'I'm heterosexual' Tom."

There was some debate about whether Nathan was even gay, apparently—he was tight-lipped about his personal life. Christine and Vic hoped Jimmy would tease out some evidence one way or the other.

"Let him be on my team," Christine begged, "you guys get all the good ones."

Albany Art stocked few novelty items but an excellent selection of staple products, including a framing service.

"That's where the real money is," Nathan said, "not many other options this side of Berkeley—sell lots of framing and we'll get along great. Vic is an assistant manager, so they'll be doing some of your training." They would be working together, Jimmy and Vic, and Christine, just the three of them on Sundays. If anyone was sick, Nathan said he would not be overjoyed to arrange a replacement, or come in himself. "So don't get sick."

"It's nothing earth-shattering," Jimmy told Marlys at the end of his first week. "Basically the same job as I had at ArtHaus, with an extra dollar an hour and basic health coverage—my copay for PrEP is a lot less through Kaiser."

"Well an extra buck is better than a sharp stick in the eye—nothing wrong with a steady job. I worked nineteen years for minimum wage at the college cafeteria before I met your father." He had heard this one ad nauseum: the respectable food service salesman trying to make inroads in the Central Valley market, and the pretty cashier he always talked to when he stopped by for a meeting. "The only new contract he got out of that was at the altar, ha!"

"You never know," Jimmy continued, "my supervisor is cute..."

Loud sigh. "I'm sure I've told you before, James: Don't shit where you eat. Pardon my French, but you just started this job—you have higher rent, and debts to pay, remember—at least you're finally living on your own."

"Alright, mother, Jesus!"

"Don't take that tone with me, young man—it was one thing when I did it—I was already forty, my trailer was paid off, and your father wasn't working for the college after all, he was trying to do business with them. I could have lived very happily on my retirement pension if push came to shove—I got lucky, I guess—your father was a good provider even if he did have his troubles. And now at least I have his Social Security, it's more than twice what mine would have been, and his pension too—we both squeaked in before they started shutting all those down."

"Yeah, I've got to look at starting an IRA—this place doesn't have a 401K either."

"That's what I'm saying, James—the world is different now. I was a single gal back then, I turned down proposals from two other men before your father because the one I just knew was a slob and I'd spend my life picking up after him, and the other one was jealous—spied on me! Actually spied on me," she interrupted herself to light a cigarette, "I came home from work one day, and he called me and he said, 'I know you're home, who are you with?' So I knew he must have followed me, or waited outside and watched, never mind the gentleman who had given me a lift home because my car battery died and he came in for a cup of coffee, but he was just a cook at the cafeteria after all, I mean nice manners, but I could never marry a Mexican, good heavens—no one had jumper cables in the parking lot, and I certainly couldn't afford AAA back then, but can you imagine? Spying on me! What a creep. But you—I don't even want to think about what's going to happen when you get older, you hear so many sad stories of bachelors, no one to take care of them, and then you know there's still no cure for..." Uncomfortable pause.

"That's what PrEP is for, mother."

"Don't get smart—I will not have you throwing that in my face, James—I won't have it. And you can't survive on a Trupep pill or whatever it's called—it's about food and rent, and security, and what about enjoying your golden years? It's not all about ... AIDS!"

"I know. I'm trying! I didn't expect to lose my job—I'm just glad I found something so quick, even if I did have to move across the Bay."

"Out of harm's way maybe—it sounds like a break from your wild ways will do you some good."

The big bottle of turpentine, or the small? Jimmy considered the price of the two and put back the big bottle. He had spent more than he anticipated on bedding for his new queen mattress, but the twin-sized comforter in Southwestern pastels his mother bought when he started high school had more cum than threads holding it together at this point. His guests would now be entertained on a fashion-forward ombre stripe in cream and charcoal, shams included, an entire bed-in-a-bag on sale for $59.99. Luxury!

He also had splurged on a distressed birch nightstand with drawers for toys, lube, cum rags—the essentials. But his checking account balance was hemorrhaging the money Paul had paid, and he was waiting for the first check to his mother to clear any minute. So. Small bottle of turpentine. He also picked up a few new brushes, and tubes of cadmium red and yellow ochre.

As he was contemplating anything else he might need, Nathan rounded the corner of the shelf.

"What are you doing?" he asked coolly.

"Just grabbing a few things for myself," Jimmy said, holding up the basket for him to see.

"Are you on the clock?"

Jimmy's breath caught, but he wasn't doing anything wrong. "I'm on my lunch break."

Nathan sniffed. "Can you come up to my office please?"

"Um, yeah—I was going to grab something to eat. Do you want anything? We could eat and chat."

"No. Come up when you get back."

As he walked to Subway through the parking lot, he tried to guess what Nathan wanted. He already hated him. Who else did he remind him of besides crazy Tom? Of course, his father—they had the same unnerving bluntness. He got a small sandwich and barely choked down half.

The cement bench on the plaza was cold, the sky dull gray, a typical Bay Area summer—drab and drabber. The sleeves of his shirt were frayed, not as crisp white as he liked, but he hated to think how much new work clothes cost. The rest of his sandwich looked like a good option for dinner. He must start economizing, invest some money promoting his own art. If this dealer Paul mentioned took a pass after all, he would need to ramp up his other efforts again. What about a website? Vic had done really good work for Dee, but he could never ask them to work for free. What about a new gallery in the East Bay? He would have to start doing some research. Etsy? Bah.

He stamped his timecard five minutes early back from lunch, oh well, and checked the "NEW INFO" board on the wall running up the stairs to Nathan's office with all the requisite employment notices, minimum wage and workers comp, official State of California stuff for anyone who was interested.

(Nathan: "Check the "NEW INFO" board regularly—it's not my job to remind you.")

Feet on the desk, Nathan did not rush to end his phone call, glancing up but not acknowledging him. Jimmy hovered near the door for a moment, then drew back into the corridor and read all about his right to a workplace free of sexual harassment and discrimination based on his gay white male atheism. Sensing the end of Nathan's call, he paused outside the office door and stared through the windows looking down over the store. ("So I can keep an eye on you," Nathan had said during the interview, as if in jest.)

"Come in, sit down." Nathan finished typing a note for a solid minute while Jimmy waited. "So," he finally said, with a few last violent strikes at the keyboard, "how's your second week going, do you think?"

Jimmy nodded his head, fakely earnest. "Yeah, good—everyone's great, excellent selection, wonderful customers—smooth."

"Smooth," Nathan repeated back with a cock of his head. "Good, could always be smoother, I guess."

"Yeah, always—finding my feet, but I'll be up to speed in no time, not so different from ArtHaus—the product is more streamlined, so that should make things simpler."

"Yeah, I guess they do have a lot of novelty crap over there—we're a little more serious." Jimmy nodded sincerely as Nathan handed some papers across the desk. "Anyway, here's some additional paperwork to look at, employee rights I'm obligated to show you, employee handbook, your responsibilities to us, and the notice about your probationary period—take a look at those, initial, sign, put them in my box by the end of the day."

"Got it."

"And to be clear, because your first three months are probationary, no vacation, no time off. We're required to offer sick time, of course, but it would be better if you didn't need to take any, especially on the weekend."

"No problem."

"And. About leaving the register unattended—you know you're not supposed to do that."

The day before, Jimmy had a momentary lapse when a customer asked him about pencil sharpeners. Of course, they were right across from the register, but he had gone off in the wrong direction at the wrong moment and Nathan had hassled him in front of the kindly lady who tried to smooth things over to no avail.

"Oh, yeah, I'm sorry—I got flustered, I needed a quick price and no one was around—I thought I knew where the sharpeners were, but they were right in front of my—"

"You're going to need a cool head working here, you know, this isn't the 'boutique' atmosphere you're used to."

He tried to keep his face as placid as possible while his stomach twisted. He took a couple of deep breaths while Nathan continued to impress the need for professionalism.

"Of course," Jimmy said. "It won't happen again."

"Better not."

Oh. My. God.

"OK," Jimmy said, "I think I'm on the register now, actually—Christine needs to go to lunch."

"Fine, you can go—bring me your timecard and I'll adjust your clock-in from lunch."

"I clocked in before I came up." He was already halfway out the door, but Nathan brought him up short.

"You clocked in early from lunch? Why'd you do that?"

"I thought it was better to clock in a few minutes early than have to adjust it later. I—"

"Overtime has to be authorized by me—you can't just take it on your own. Bring me your timecard," he said, shaking his head, "I'll fix it. This time."

Jimmy was struck by how often art stores failed to show any imagination. ArtHaus, the "boutique" store in the City, had attempted to entice its customers with more color and design than most, slick displays and an edgy vibe complete with punked out employees. Not so Albany Art. The shelves were parallel; the lighting, fluorescent; walls, white. They had a uniform: white button-down shirts and khaki pants; black or brown belt and shoes—more of a blanding than a branding. Only some small amount of thought had been given to the framing department, but even that was just a touch of gray with some nice signage in the back corner of the store.

Vic was supposed to show him the ropes of mats, frames, miter saw, and glass. Luckily, Jimmy had experience with all of these from his Fresno days. ArtHaus never did framing. "You'd think they'd get wise—freaks don't make money, product and service make money," Nathan had said.

Three things made for a good frame job.

Mat or no mat, the color, the frame itself—none of these details mattered too much. The customer was always right, or could usually be steered in a more tasteful direction. No, the quality of the workmanship was most important, and that took practice.

First, the glass must be cut cleanly, an art in itself. It was all in the touch, feeling when the cutter scored the glass just right, how to hold and tap perfectly to get that clean cut. If you did it wrong, of course, the glass could chip along the edge, or crack instead of snap, but he had worked out those kinks years before. He practiced on a few pieces of broken discards before he worked on the first frame. He barely needed the file to smooth the edges after a couple trial cuts—you wanted to hear a whisper as you ran it along, no crunching on invisible jags. Also, keep the glass super clean, especially on the inside.

Next, the frame stock and miter saw. The trick to these, he knew, was measuring perfectly, and the right blade—it must be sharp and clean so no particles of sawdust could catch and cause the wood to splinter. Jimmy noticed right off they were using the wrong blade and changed it out for the correct one he found in a drawer. Again, with a few practice cuts, he was producing perfect, clean cuts, measured exactly. He even made a couple of teeny tiny frames out of discarded pieces for practice.

Lastly, the mats. These must be cut precisely, and like the glass and wood, had their own peculiarity of touch. A person could waste a lot of money messing up mats with uneven cuts. Card stock could fray at the inside corners, or you might overcut and have tiny unsightly splits, or your angles might be off square. Sharp blades changed frequently were key.

These were all ingredients, but what saved him was the experience of cutting thousands of mats in his four years in Fresno. Vic was supposed to be teaching him but quickly stood aside and leaned against the counter to watch as he worked.

"You could teach me a thing or two."

Nathan exclaimed later over the quick work he made of a custom order. "Wow! Finally someone who knows what he's doing." Vic rolled their eyes.

Jimmy had left two of the three backs open so Nathan could examine them, the last finished in the standard heavy brown paper with the finishing tape and a special little fold on the edges and corners for a fancy touch. Nathan defrosted as he looked it all over, including the scraps of glass, frame stock, and mats set to one side, in good shape and salvageable for odd jobs. "Damn, boy, this looks amazing! You really know your shit—I'm impressed." He almost seemed elated.

Jimmy showed him the tiny practice frames. "Suitable for framing a glory hole," he said in a mad attempt at humor. Nathan giggled and held one down in front of Vic's crotch with a smirk, like a taunt. Vic knocked Nathan's hand away and floated off, shaking their head. At least Nathan knew what a glory hole was, so there was that question answered.

"Random question," Nathan said as he continued checking the joints of the frames. "Do you like scary movies?"

Jimmy and Vic chatted during the week and Sundays, of course, but had not hung out after work yet. In the course of slow afternoons slumped at the counter, Jimmy unpacked Paul, his artwork, Daddy handyman and his boy, Fresno, Bob, "tWinkS" and Matt. Vic was an attentive listener, as Jimmy had always supposed himself to be, too, but he'd seldom met someone just happier to let him talk.

"Oh, you know," Vic would say. "What's to tell? I grew up here in Albany, my mom's a nurse practitioner—I lived in the City, that's when I met Dee, but I moved back home after a minute. SF wasn't really my speed and I needed to save up some money."

"Significant someones?"

"Nothing too serious. You know."

Jimmy supposed he did. While he bonded with his shy admirer, he was taking loads from Daddy and boy at all hours of the day and night, finishing his portrait of Paul, and working on his new series of paintings.

"So remember that art show I told you about?" Vic asked him another Sunday. "I finished the flyer, look!"

"Very nice."

"It's not for a couple weeks, but do you think you can make it?" They settled the day's receipts at the accountant's desk in the back office, the last two out of the store.

Vic did not look at Jimmy as they asked, "So what are you up to tonight?" Jimmy wondered if this might be the Big Move. Vic's interest was obvious, if their actual intentions were still not entirely clear. Jimmy would never make the first move on anyone but wondered if they'd ever screw up the courage to proposition him. And what would he even say?

After work, Vic drove them over to Jimmy's, but finding a parking space took longer than the trip. "Nice place—it's like some Parisian courtyard," Vic said as they passed through the front garden.

"I know, right? They do a good job—oh, here's Daddy," Jimmy said.

Ramon was fussing with a stepladder and lightbulbs by the inglenook.

"Hey Ramon! Meet my amigo, Vic." Vic put out their hand to shake, but Ramon had his hand full and rather than extend his stump, he just nodded with the barest of gruff acknowledgements and stared.

Vic made a fist and bumped the air instead. "Hola."

They continued up to the studio. One flight up, a great crash below, followed by Spanish curses. Jimmy shrugged and went on as though he had heard nothing.

"Oof," Vic whispered, "you do like 'em rough."

"Rough likes me."

Vic popped in long enough to look around and admire the studio before remembering an errand they had to do for mom and scurrying off. Squirrely, Jimmy thought. Endearing.

TWELVE

Back and forth and back to work again, Jimmy grew familiar with the side streets on the way to El Cerrito Plaza, the homes snapped together on Monopoly-neat lots. Here was a clapboard bungalow with arched window and Juliet railing, trimmed in lavender. Next door, a stucco sister in cream, pointed window with petunias, steps painted brick red. Before McMansions and freeways to the burbs ever existed, these were the original tract houses, lined up and down one-way lanes with lava rock lawns and grizzled roses—there was a drought. There was always a drought in California.

He had visited the insides of similar houses when Bob, swept up in a house hunting spree, had imagined an economical retirement in the East Bay. Besides the frontiers of Vacaville, Vallejo, Benicia, even Stockton, they had spent a few Sundays touring El Cerrito, Albany, the Berkeley flats. Snug two bedroom-one baths with Barbie-sized pedestal sinks seemed just right for placid widows and thin cotton dresses loosely hung in twenty-inch-wide closets. Said the real estate agent, "One or two linen suits were all they needed—these were the summer cottages of the well-to-do from San Francisco back in the day."

Bathrooms could be remodeled, but views into neighbors' spare bedrooms gave Bob pause. Jimmy pictured Marlys trying to pull the Banana Boat into any of the narrow driveways or Model

T-sized garages and understood the good sense of hardscapes instead of lawns—like a fixed income, there was zero room for error.

He would never grow fond of summer gray mornings, a problem in the East Bay as much as the City. As far as he knew, there were no parks like Dolores Beach in his new neighborhood. For that matter, the nearest gay bar was in Berkeley. Steamers the sex club was nearby but they had no outdoor area for tanning, and no bar. Also, he knew three guys who all got syphilis there, and the one time he had visited, the hot tub was closed because someone sharted. He foresaw himself growing pale and weakened in his khakis and windbreaker as he trudged to and fro on his new daily grind, the cougars of Albany stalking him through lace curtains.

Strange to say, he missed the sunny-and-nineties summers of Fresno—no school, lots of yard work, his mother cursing her fair skin's premature aging. She had spent a good deal of time researching cosmetics and procedures to variously tighten, firm, or soft focus her complexion over the years, but James Sr. would never allow a surgery for fear she would end up looking like "one of those goddamn lady jokers at the club." She freely admitted to Jimmy she had chosen a husband twenty years older than herself in part to avoid the inevitable discarding.

"I AM the trophy wife," she declared one boozy afternoon in the shade while Jimmy mowed the lawn shirtless, turning an enviable Coppertone. "Guess how many of my girlfriends who married young are still married! Guess! None! Well, two, but they're miserable!"

The summer morning his father went to the hospital to die, Jimmy was awakened from a sound sleep by a commotion down the hall. Loud enough that he guessed there must be some kind of emergency, he stumbled out of his room to an unearthly green light suffusing the carpet and wood paneling outside his parents' door. What the hell? There came a crash and a plate breaking. Alien abduction crossed his mind.

When he reached their bedroom, he recoiled. It was just after dawn, the July sun already ablaze and casting the room in the murky shade of the thin green drapes. His father had messed the bed. His father was naked, shit covering his ass and the backs of his thighs. His mother was already dressed, face on, probably two cups of Folgers in her, and struggling to keep James Sr. upright. Jimmy froze, gaping.

Though his father accepted her help, leaning heavily with an arm around her neck, he lurched like a wild man, yelling obscenities, and attempting with his other hand to strike at Marlys. The bedside lamp lay broken on the floor, and she kicked shards out of the way under the bed. Now her white pants were smeared with shit too where he leaned against her. She managed to half carry her disintegrating husband from the bed toward the bathroom and fend off his weak attack.

"You fucking bitch!" his father moaned, slapping at her. "You ruined my life! Aw, god! Aw, god! Goddamn bitch! Jesus!" he raved hoarsely. Jimmy saw his face and lips blue from lack of oxygen, his fingernails almost purple where he gripped her shoulder.

Her face grim, she noticed Jimmy frozen, one hand extended toward the door handle.

"Close it," she said.

The windowless hallway plunged back into morning darkness, and the cursing faded to a muffled drone. Once she managed to clean James Sr. up and get him dressed, Marlys sat him in his easy chair, called the ambulance, threw the bedsheets and her clothes in the trash before the paramedics arrived.

Alone in the house for two days, Jimmy wandered into his father's rarely used study. In his childhood he had sometimes snuck into that formal room abandoned for the comforts of the La-Z-Boy and ESPN, but still off-limits to Jimmy and his mother. He felt like a detective mooning around the executive suite of furniture—matching mahogany desk, credenza, bookshelf—the old hunting rifle mounted on the wall, black and white photographs of sports teams, aircraft carriers, generals, and baseball heroes. The Case of the Man of Few Words.

His father owned precisely five books—*The Old Man and the Sea, The Grapes of Wrath, All Quiet on the Western Front, Moby-Dick,* and *A Tree Grows in Brooklyn*—all paperbacks of the same size as though a series, so browned and crackling they might fall to pieces. They sat on the highest shelf surrounded by bookends of old-timey globes larger than the mass-market books they propped up—spheres printed with sepia-toned continents and cartoon sea monsters.

He had climbed on to the credenza and examined the books and other altar pieces. A signed baseball so faded there was no telling who. A bronze sculpture of a matador and bull, death spears and all. A gigantic glass brandy snifter the color of pee, filled to the brim with matchbooks from sports bars and holes-in-the-wall up and down the West Coast, his father's sales territory.

On a lower shelf two other bookends, no books in between, tiny sailing half-ships, fore and aft, mounted on polished driftwood, rigged and pennoned with real string for rope and curling, shellacked flags immobilized as though snapping in a gale. These vessels drunkenly listed and reared in opposite directions—one up and forward, one down and back—as if sister ships capsized in a squall, or one ship snapped in half by a real-life leviathan. Jimmy stood immobilized for many minutes examining these vessels in distress, nearly as intricate as a ship in a bottle. He wondered again if his very own father had assembled these, that man of short patience and shorter temper. Though Marlys would forever profess how out-of-the-blue her husband's death had come, Jimmy knew already when he stepped into that velvet-roped sanctum he would never see James Sr. again.

The memorial service proved a prickly affair at the house. Marlys sat stone-faced on the sofa accepting well-wishes from golf buddies, former colleagues, and wives she had never met and hoped never to meet again. Her friend, Maryann, did most of the legwork with the sandwiches and the flowers, while Jimmy and Dee snuck rum into their glasses of Diet Coke and made a game of saying the same three phrases in order to each person who expressed condolences: "How kind of you to come." "He will be deeply missed." "Please sign the 'Memory' book by the front door, if you haven't already." Once it became clear the changeling son would not have the good sense to offer any words, an exasperated associate from The Elks thrust a bookmarked Bible into Dee's mortified hands and, pointing at the text, made him read "Isaiah 40:28—there, now!"

"I'm sorry for your loss," the Elk said sternly to Marlys on his way out, "I have a homosexual son, too."

In the after days, Jimmy would remember the glare of the morning sun whenever he walked down the dark hall. Had he never seen his parents' room that early in the morning? How could they bear to have that claxon light burning them awake first thing every day?

He was struck again by the submarine glow through those thin green drapes a few weeks later. They both had been having trouble sleeping, and his mother took to comforting herself with an epic housecleaning. Ragged from a fitful night of flushing toilets and vacuuming, Jimmy wandered down the hall through the green gloaming of dawn toward her bedroom door, imagining they lived now at the bottom of the sea, looking up at their life before, with him.

He found Marlys abstracted, sorting through his father's dresser drawers, and he wordlessly set to holding the Hefty bags open. She lifted each article individually, not stacks at a time, sometimes refolding and laying them in fresh piles on the bed, cardigans all together, snow white undershirts separate from boxer shorts separate from the madras shorts she always bought for him to wear in warm weather. These stacks she placed in turn neatly at the bottoms of the bags Jimmy held, then folded the plastic over like wrapping paper, and cut pieces of clear packing tape to seal the corners shut. They may be going to Goodwill, but they were not being thrown away, they were being delivered.

"But I was a good wife," she said to herself blankly as she finished one drawer. Then to him, "Wasn't I a good wife?"

Jimmy sat woodenly on the bed. He guessed the reason for the rage directed at her in the last hallucinatory days of his father's failing heart.

She had been barren. And Jimmy was the result.

Dee also had Wednesdays off, and invited himself over to see the new paint job and help turn the long studio wall into a gallery.

"Salon style, a nice jumbly grouping," Jimmy said.

"I love jumbly."

First, though, Paul's finished portrait. Jimmy spent longer on it than any other painting he had ever done, even scrapping the first attempt when he realized the skin tone needed to be a little less bronzed god, a little more marble and pearl to be a true likeness.

Dee took a good long look as Jimmy fixed him a double Tazo Passion tea in his special mug, and for himself, a celebratory martini. They clinked cup and glass.

"Amazing," Dee admitted. "First question: Is he married?"

"No, but you are."

"Details, details. Seriously, your best work, portrait or otherwise. Have you flattered the shit out of him? Of course. But it's the same person, just run through a wow filter." Dee sipped his tea again then swirled his cup as he looked inside. "What the fuck?" He fished in and pulled out something glittery. "Your dad's ring! Are you giving it to me? Is this a proposal?"

Jimmy had a habit of hiding things when he was drinking, valuables and whatnot. One of only two keepsakes he had received after the funeral, his dad had bought the diamond and sapphire pinky ring to wear for poker parties at the house. Marlys had played hostess in a French maid's apron she'd bedazzled with *Diamond Jim's*, and had strict instructions to freshen the players' drinks promptly and make sure they got a good look at her ass, two decades firmer than any of their wives.

Even with the homefield advantage and Marlys as a distraction, his father lost heavily and eventually suspended poker night. The ring became a symbol of shame to Marlys and easily sent away with Jimmy when he moved to San Francisco. Dee had come to covet it, feeling it should rightfully have been left to him to go with the bedazzled apron he finagled from Marlys. Blacked out and feeling clever, Jimmy had hidden it in the one place he felt sure he would remember it: Dee's cup.

"No, sister wife, I'm not proposing, and I'm not giving it to you, but you can wear it when you come over—that's why I put it in there."

Dee slid the ring on and held it up to the light. "Thank you, Precioussss."

"How's your Russian neighbor? Did he get his tooth fixed?"

"Feo? I have no idea, I haven't seen him. You're so judgmental!"

"It's not that!" Jimmy protested. "I get all self-conscious when people have shit like that going on."

"You're self-conscious? What about how he feels?"

"No, it's just—I don't know where to look, and then I feel weird, and then I feel like they're staring at me and they know I'm trying not to look, it's like they can read my mind and I panic and..."

Dee waved the explanation away, distracted by the ring as his hand moved and held it up again to admire. "Ask your doctor today if electro-shock therapy might be right for you."

They set to work on the gallery wall, and Jimmy caught him up on Ramon and Oscar.

"So they're Daddy and boy." Dee held up a painting against the wall while Jimmy stood back and decided about placement. "And you're having three ways. Do you think they want you to be a throuple? Would you consider that sort of arrangement?"

"I don't know, maybe? It's hard because I feel a real connection with the boy, but I'm way more attracted to the Daddy, but he barely speaks English, so I don't know. He told me he loved me when I gave them those paintings. Like, I don't think he meant in love, but..."

"Oh shit! What'd you say?"

"Not I love you back, that's for sure. I mean, I like them, but … they're fun—they were tag-teaming me most of the week I was off."

"That's the hottest thing I've ever heard, can I jerk off on your ass?"

"For a thousand dollars."

"A prostitute and a gentleman…"

Jimmy sighed. "Daddy shows up with a bottle of vodka any time he's horny so now I'm not just a cheap floozy but an actual Kirkland vodka whore."

"I wonder if they'll get married now? By the way, are you coming to the party at the Stallion on Saturday?"

"Party?"

"Hello? Gay marriage? Supreme Court? Pride?"

"Oh, that. I have to work on Sunday, so I'll probably just celebrate with a couple of burritos up my butt."

"Bean queen. Do you call him Daddy? Or, what—Papi?"

"No, neither does Oscar. I'm not a thousand percent sure they would even call themselves Daddy and boy, and I don't really care as long as they keep making deposits in the Bank of Jimmy." He also told Dee about his sexy new boss, Nathan, and what his mother said about shitting and eating.

"She's got a point. But enough about you. How is Marlys Momroe? You know she made me promise to stay your friend after I got sober."

"What???" Dee was always dropping delicious little bombs to watch the explosion.

"Yes or no?" Dee said, nodding at a painting.

"Yes." They pounded in another hook and moved to the next one.

Dee went on. "I was down at my parents—it was after I got sober, you remember, Ricardo said he would break up with me if I didn't quit, and so I did—surprised even myself. Anyway, don't you remember, I didn't see you for almost six months—you were ass up at Bob's by then, I don't think you even missed me. Yes or no?"

"No."

"No you didn't miss me, or no painting?"

"Yes. Try the other one."

Dee switched one painting for another. "Better?"

"Go on then," Jimmy said, knocking in another hook.

"So I stopped by your mom's to say 'Hi'—also I was plotting Dusty Davenport's official debut and I thought she might have some freaky old dresses she might want to part with—and she did! You know that day-glo number I wore for my eighties round-up, 'Madonna Who?' I had to let it out in the bosom and with side panels, of course, I mean your mom's no waif, but I had this acid-green lycra left over from Halloween, you remember, Ricardo was Kermit and I was Miss Piggy ... I looked fabulous." Dee lost himself in the memory.

Jimmy swore and pushed him out of the way, started knocking in hooks by eye. "Oh my god, get to the point, lady."

"Oh, she was just asking how you were, how you looked, because of course you talk all the time, but she could tell you were drinking a lot—Ha! If she only knew! Anyway she wanted eyes on you, but I was seriously thinking about cutting you off—you know, newly sober, it was hard with you and your vodka and your bloody martinis and backrooms and golden showers and whoregies. Who the hell drinks martinis anymore, ferfucksake?"

"Wealthy clients from New York are drinking martinis anymore, thank you. Yeah, you were almost as big a drunk as me."

"How dare you—I was a much bigger drunk than you! Anyway, when I told her I wasn't sure if I could handle you and your partying she got super serious."

"Really."

"Yes, really, and she pretty much begged me not to abandon you. I mean, I might have agreed under duress, I pretty much ransacked her closet. She was three sheets to the wind herself, guzzling her rosé in that princess chair in her bedroom, you know the one, your dad definitely popped Viagras and nailed her on that, no question—in case you were wondering, you get your drinking from your mother. No not that one," Dee said about the painting Jimmy was hanging. "That other one. Yes, that's nice. We're the same shoe size, by the way. I have remarkably dainty feet, everybody says so."

"Fascinating," Jimmy said. "I wonder who I get my party ass from...?"

"Also your mother: while I was rummaging, I found her shoebox full of vibrators."

"I'm going to slap you til you're dead."

"You're mom's smarter than she seems—scrappy—you should pay better attention, considering..."

"Considering what?"

"There's two kinds of people in this world..." Dee began. Jimmy was familiar with this line, but the ending always changed. "Owners and renters."

"Excuse me?"

"There's people who own the world, right? Sinatra, for example. Your dad, for another. Me."

"You?"

"All drag queens own, they have to; if they don't, they melt at the first splash of cold water. But your mom, and you—you just rent, or in your case, are rented. You're at the mercy of forces greater than yourself—luck, chemistry, passing fancies. People choose you, you don't get to choose. Your mom gets it, that's why she wouldn't sleep with your dad until he married her, and why she asked me to adopt you. I'm your Bay Mom. Lucky."

"She told you that? I could have gone to my grave without that information, thanks. But my BM sounds about right. As usual, Dr. Strangelove, equal parts sensible and psychotic."

Dee scoffed. "That's my line! You don't even know who Peter Sellers is."

"Well who is he then?"

"Being There? Inspector Clouseau? Pink Panther?"

"Being where? Steve Martin?"

"Have you cleaned your ears out lately? Peter Sellers! Peter SELLERS! PETER SELLERS!"

"Never heard of him. So you agreed to keep an eye on me. Is that what this is, keeping an eye on me?" Jimmy set down the hammer and downed the rest of the martini he was working on.

"It doesn't bother me anymore, you know—coming up on four years sober now—but don't thank me. You're alive, that's thanks enough. You're the youngest old lush I ever adopted."

"I'll drink to that," Jimmy said, pouring the rest of the martini shaker directly into his mouth.

"Also, your mom thinks you were born with a wee touch of fetal alcohol syndrome. Can I get some more tea, please?"

After Dee left, the guys came up with beer and vodka so Jimmy could take some pictures and make a start on his new painting series. Maybe they'd had a fight before they arrived. Maybe the weirdness between them was Jimmy's fault, insisting they do the photo session before they got too hammered, fearing nothing would be accomplished. Ramon and Oscar were testy with each other, exchanging barbs in Spanish. When Oscar pointed toward the foot of the bed where Jimmy wanted them to sit back-to-back, Ramon slapped his hand away.

"C'mon guys," Jimmy beseeched. "Give me a little lust, if not love."

They managed to hold the pose for a few moments, but finally, Ramon simply wandered over to the liquor, cracked open the vodka and took a big belt before returning to the bed with a beer—the rest of the pictures included the can.

Trouble? Maybe he was seeing just the two of them together for the first time, naked, no Jimmy at the bottom of the dogpile. Come to think of it, lately, they mostly visited him separately. Gay wedding bells? Maybe not. Lovers' spat, none of his business—he had to get the pictures done. Some ad hoc photos of them separately from other evenings had worked well so far, but he wanted a few specific poses with the two of them together for the new series, part Vern in a sling, part mystical creatures—extra eyes, arms and legs, suggestions of wings and tails. In the first painting he completed, he had portrayed Ramon's stump as a penis, complete with peehole.

Jimmy positioned him now on his belly with one leg cocked and the other outstretched, Oscar on top, spooning. Jimmy liked the look of a smaller man smothered by the bulk of a much larger. But Ramon fidgeted and huffed, and finally growled and pushed Oscar off him. Jimmy snapped pics as the two squirmed around, fighting over position. This was good too, like the dynamics of movement in an old book of wrestlers he had also been using to compose layouts.

"OK, one more—how about Oscar on your back, head toward me—legs spread—Ramon, get between his legs like you're fucking him." At this they both seemed more comfortable—Ramon practically leaped into position. Now they were mirrored at the hips, Oscar down, Ramon up, like an inkblot. He could always invert the picture on his laptop to get Oscar on top.

"OK, that's good for now, I guess," Jimmy said, scrolling on the camera's viewscreen. Ramon smiled, pulling back from Oscar and stroking his boner. Oscar rolled out of the way and started playing with his phone. Jimmy glanced up at Ramon and took his position bent over the bed.

THIRTEEN

Balloons, drag queens, a busker dressed like a Native American playing folk techno on a fiddle—all these spilled across the sidewalk in front of the LGBTQ+ Center for Vic's event in Berkeley. Jimmy was glad to see the turnout as Vic burst from the crowd like they'd been waiting for him to arrive.

"Hey! I'm so glad you made it!" They seemed a bit edgy, maybe just "on" for the event. *PACKING MEAT* read the headline on the poster hung in the case out front, Vic's flyer blown up large. They plunged through the front door into the cavernous main hall, art lining the exposed brick walls up to the steel rafters.

"Great crowd," Jimmy observed. "Is there a bar?"

"Where do you think I'm taking you?"

Heads turned as they made their way through display spaces and knots of people, Vic greeting many by name with fist bumps and hugs. Nearer to the bar, they grabbed Jimmy's hand and pulled him through a group of drag queens determined to continue gossiping. All eyes appraised Jimmy as Vic pushed straight through the middle of the clutch.

"Puta!" The bartender was already pouring two vodka cranberries for them with a breathy wink. Like some bastard child of Jack Sparrow, he had a smoky eye, big glam eighties hair, flawless skin and perfectly arched eyebrows paired with a five o'clock shadow, a drawn-on beauty mark, and maybe a hint of cherry lipstick. Jimmy had never seen such a pretty man.

"Wow, he's beautiful," Jimmy said.

"I know, baby," Vic said. "Fucking gorgeous. Arturo, friend of mine. Trans man."

"Woof." Jimmy couldn't take his eyes off Arturo, but also took note of the "baby."

As Vic was paying and exchanging a few words with their friend, Jimmy stepped back with his drink. Behind him, a mass pressed—more of a warmth and a breath on his neck than a touch—with a throaty, rumbling whisper.

"Hey, blondie."

He turned and, bottom to top, tracked the biker boots, the jeans, the massive appliance in their crotch, the keychain and belt, the white t-shirt and leather vest, and a penciled beard and pompadour hair—the Elvis impersonator who swallowed Marlon Brando whole.

"You're the hottest piece of ass in here. Call me Butch," they said, and Jimmy found himself strangely compelled.

"Nice to meet you, Butch," he whispered, mesmerized.

"I want to pound your pussy so hard you puke," Butch said, wrapping one tentacle behind Jimmy's back and sniffing him. "You ever been fisted in both holes at the same time?"

"I'm a man!" Jimmy squeaked. "I'm a man!" This took Butch by surprise, and they drew back and Jimmy up and down with more scrutiny before Vic interceded and hustled him away.

"He's with me, Butch."

"What was that?" Jimmy asked, unable to escape Butch's glowering eyes as Vic put some distance between them.

"Your worst nightmare, little boy."

Jimmy gulped most of his drink while they approached a wall of photographs, mainly figures—drag queens and kings—also close-ups of costumes, feathers, sequins. A cute Latin boy was standing to one side talking and laughing in a small group. Vic slid in and kissed him on the cheek. While he waited to be introduced, Jimmy polished off his cocktail and wondered if he could sneak over and get another. Butch was still shooting glances his way, so he figured he better stay put. Then he heard the familiar cackle behind him.

"Jimmy Jimmy, lady killer!" Dee yelled, charging through the scattering crowd. "As I live and breathe!"

"What's up? Vic didn't mention you were coming."

"I don't think they knew—I have more than one friend."

"Bitch, I have more than one friend."

"Vodka doesn't count, sweetie. Stick around, I'll be performing a short set long on innuendo. Vic! Introduce us!" He barged into the middle of the group and leaned in for air kisses.

"This is my friend, Jorge."

"Whore, hey! Nice to meet you," Dee purred. "Is all this your work? I love it! You should photograph me! In fact, why haven't you connected us before, Vic? Naughty!"

Jorge seemed unfazed by the towering theatrics and proceeded to steer Dee through the display. Jimmy laughed to see the diminutive Jorge next to the psychedelic bulk of Dee, like a plucky tugboat dragging The Love Boat behind. Hardly a moment passed, though, before Dee was blowing kisses at someone else and screaming off. Jorge slung his arm around Vic's shoulder, cute and cuter.

"So! Jimmy! I've heard so much about you!" Vic groaned at this, and Jorge laughed, clearly a little tipsy already.

Across the room, a makeshift stage came to life. Dee and his banjo were handed up onto a platform, and he began twanging out the opening bars of an unfamiliar tune. Jimmy noticed most of the butch dykes in the crowd had that same sort of clone look about them, not unlike himself: short hair, white t-shirt, blue jeans. How many times had he caught himself eyeing a boy from the back only to discover he was a girl in the front?

"I see your friend's cup is empty, Vic, why don't you go get us some more drinks?" Vic glared and abruptly exited for the bar.

Dee cleared his throat into the mic and let out a blood-curdling screech.

"Hee-haw! I'd like to introduce y'all to a little ditty bequeathed to me by my dear old Uncle Bonsai. 'Penis Envy!' Not that any of you gentlemen suffer from such an affliction, har har har!"

Jorge went on. "So how was your talk?" He put a conspiratorial hand on Jimmy's arm. "Vic was so excited yesterday. They really are one of the best people I know..."

"Talk?" Jimmy asked, studying a photograph without actually seeing it.

"Oh well, you know, The Talk, I guess."

Jimmy's eyes focused on the small photo in front of him, right there on the wall, a black and white portrait of Vic. They were sitting on a sofa next to an old lady, American Gothic minus the pitchfork.

"Oh," Jimmy said, "Vic."

In the photo, the two did not smile, but did not seem uncomfortable either. They must know each other, he thought. Vic's grandmother? Or Jorge's maybe.

"Well, it was kinda obvious, wasn't it?" Jorge said, as Jimmy stared at the picture.

The sound of the crowd rose and fell with the twang of Dee's banjo, stretching suddenly into a great reverberating echo around them as Jimmy's eyebrows went up and he turned toward Jorge.

"I'm sorry, what are you talking about?"

"They've been totally crush—" Jorge's mistake dawned on him, and he stifled a horrified laugh. "Oh! Oh shit! You didn't have your talk this morning before you got here?"

"Before who got where?" Vic asked, delivering drinks. Jimmy and Jorge both turned, mouths open.

"What?" Jorge said.

"What?" Vic frowned.

"Were we supposed to have 'The Talk' this morning?" Jimmy asked.

"PUTA MADRE!" Vic yelled.

Jorge stammered, "Oh my god! But he knew—Jimmy, you knew! Didn't you? OH MY GOD!"

Obviously, Vic said, they were aware there might be some stumbling blocks, just assuming Jimmy was a diehard bottom, but not so. They sat at Coq Cafe with a carafe of cabernet, retreating from the art fair to finally approach the question they'd been dancing around.

"Strangely, I'm not horrified by female genitalia—Dee would scream to hear me say that. I used to steal my dad's Penthouses for the men but the women held some slight fascination for me. I love boobs."

Vic laughed. "Can't help you with that one—or two, I guess. I had a breast reduction two years ago, just to tidy up, they weren't much to begin with. But you're a total bottom, aren't you?"

"Let's just say I attract a lot of tops, and I love to get fucked. But I am a little curious."

"I'll take curious. I mean, I can strap one on any size or color you want, right? Pink, brown, black, purple people eater, whatever—ribbed for your pleasure, vibrating, German Shepherd—two-headed dragon dick—they even have ones that squirt. Nice, huh?"

With most of the wine down Jimmy's gullet, he had to admit Vic was awfully cute, and after all, there was nothing so sexy to him as being wanted. And he hated to let anyone down.

They continued their conversation the following Friday night after work. Less and less timid all the time, Vic suggested they make pasta and watch a movie.

"You don't have Netflix?"

"I don't live at home with my mommy."

"¡Pinche cabrón! Give me some sugar, and I'll share my password with you." Vic was laying hands on Jimmy more, a touch on the hand, arm around the waist. Jimmy let them. At one point, they pushed Jimmy against the kitchen counter and started kissing him.

"I'm not sure why it took me so long," Vic said as they ate. "I guess I sort of hoped you might be moved to make a play for me. But then it seemed like maybe you're only into cis men and I didn't think you'd be interested. But you're a bit of a unicorn, aren't you? A big old bottom who's not afraid of a vagina.

"Don't tell Dee. And don't call me a big old anything!"

"Sorry, baby. And, uh, Dee's gonna know soon enough if we're seeing each other." Vic set their empty plates aside on the floor by the bed. "So I've been holding back because, you know, I wasn't sure how you'd react, but you're not freaking out and I felt that little chub you popped down in the kitchen."

They laid against Jimmy and began to explore the inside of his thigh. "You're not freaking out, are you?"

"What's to freak out? I'm guessing you packed a trick bag for a reason."

"I'm not here for my health."

Awkwardly, like teenagers slow dancing for the first time, they settled into a routine: Netflix and dinner and vodka and chill. At least it was better than BARTing into the City and $8 cocktails. They were exploring. Jimmy gave topping a trial run.

"Clean as a whistle, huh?" Vic said after the first time they did it in their pussy. "No fuss, no muss."

Jimmy was agog. "I know, cleaning out a butt is such a production. This is so much easier! I'm surprised everyone isn't doing it."

Vic rolled their eyes. "Best kept secrets, huh?"

And it was nice, like bopping along to catchy music, though he kept Oscar and Ramon in reserve. No one was saying "I love you," anyway. Finally, after they started to get the hang of things, Vic asked, "So are you going to paint me too, or what?"

The summer before Jimmy started tenth grade, Marlys signed him up for swim camp at the high school.

"But I know how to swim," he said.

"I can't have you sitting around the house playing video games all day," she replied. "I'm allowed to have a life too, you know."

The six-week program taught younger kids to swim, but also more than a few junior high and older teens either learning to swim, or like Jimmy, forcibly removed from their sofas and PlayStations by working parents and those who could not bear to entertain their children for two months. They played games and attempted to learn how to butterfly and flip turn, some basic dives, safety lessons, CPR and drills, but spent a good deal of time simply swimming laps freestyle. Because there were more kids than lanes, Jimmy got doubled up with Kyle, a junior.

The first day of swimming laps, Kyle squatted at the edge of the pool above Jimmy in the water, farthest lane from the locker room.

"You start," he was saying down to Jimmy, "and then I'll start when you get to the other side." Kyle had dark hair on his legs and chest, and the deep timbre of a man's voice already. From where he crouched in front of Jimmy, the leg of his swim trunks gaped open so Jimmy had a direct shot at Kyle's balls and dick. There was no lining in his bathing suit—he had pubic hair! Jimmy wondered if the semi-hardness he saw twitching and bouncing was what some of the kids meant by the word "hung."

"What are you waiting for?" Kyle asked him, and Jimmy tore his eyes away.

He set off down the lane. He was a good swimmer, and by the time he reached the other side, the rhythm of his strokes and the splashing of the water helped him focus on the thirty minutes of freestyle at the end of the day. He turned in time to see Kyle's dark head diving. As he returned, and they passed near the center, Kyle's choppy splashing jostled him, and the older boy's toe flicked his leg at the last moment as he receded. Reaching the end, and turning back again, he saw Kyle had started back already—he swam harder. This time, they passed quite close at the center of the lane and grazed legs. A few strokes later, and Jimmy swam through a suspiciously warm spot in the water—Kyle had pissed in the pool. Jimmy barely remembered the remaining laps, he was so overcome.

In the locker room afterwards, the older boy lured him into the handicapped stall and taught him how to give a blowjob. It was a short lesson, just the basics: no teeth, tickle the balls, try not to gag, always swallow. The lessons would get longer and more involved as summer wended on. Walking home that first day, he still tasted Kyle's salty cum in his mouth and was so sure there must be some visible sign, he rushed to his bathroom to check again. And there was! Somehow a drop had got in his hair and dried, just a bit of fluff, an ash from his mom's cigarette it could be, but hardly the horror show he feared.

Yet he could not shake off the feeling, a hesitation—could people tell? For years, Jimmy was surprised when the mirror showed no traces of the monstrous secret he wore like a Halloween mask. If he remained always vigilant, the ghastly truth could remain hidden, his true depravity only revealed at the invitation of other freaks as though luring him to run away with the circus.

Finished for the moment with the Ramon and Oscar paintings, and wanting to start the new "V" series in a few days, Jimmy sat on the window seat and sifted through images he'd taken of Vic on his laptop. You might never know what box they'd been put in at birth, and not wanting to insist on boy or girl, he settled on a duality to match the doubling of Oscar and Roman. He found himself mirroring figures—jaw, hips, shoulders—masculine and feminine, blurred.

In his sketchbook he drew an exaggerated outline of Vic's head, no body, and inside it, as if in the mind's eye, a face split down the middle. One side sharper and darker, the other softer, paler. Not quite man or woman but opposed. He erased, redrew, doubled the eyes. Two mouths now, one open, one sealed. Stupid. Too obvious. For the nose he sketched a blunt vertical slash, added two profiles pressed together. Ridiculous, strange—but a starting point.

Did it matter if parts were bolted together, not belonging, if the whole thing looked strained? Maybe the tension was good. The ugly faces people made when they fucked, the slackness, the gooning and intensity, the "I don't give a care just slam your dick into me hard and deep." ("Stump me, papi!" Thank god he'd never said it out loud.) Ramon and Oscar never looked beautiful in that way either—just animals, greedy.

He added lines to the drawing, seams where the halves met but didn't merge, scars. The head seemed to face forward and backward at once, as if caught mid-turn. Where was he going with this? It was as though he were seeing Vic multiplied—this self and that, neither cancelling the other out, but never allowed to settle. And somehow his images of Vic spoke only to this fusion. The more primal forms he painted with Ramon and Oscar refused him with Vic. It was all too proper. Something was missing, and he couldn't put his finger on it.

In high school, Jimmy had drawn a portrait of his mother from a studio photo taken around the time she and his father had been married, one of the few photographs of herself she kept. The sketch turned out surprisingly well, except for her eyes—they had proven difficult, and he had redone them three times before he was almost satisfied. When he showed her, she recoiled and demanded he destroy it.

She fumed. "I don't know who that is, but it's not me!"

He tried to see it as she might and realized (of course) she had always considered her eyes her prettiest feature, exactly the detail giving him trouble. She had aged prematurely from constant, fruitless sunbathing as a teen, and from untreated hormonal imbalances associated with her hysterectomy.

Her figure tended toward voluptuous—"Fat! Fat! Fat as a pig!" Marlys declared herself regularly—and her hair was never as thick and lustrous as she wished, leading to a lingering flirtation with wigs. If the amount of make-up, time, and money she spent on her eyes was any gauge at all, he should have known never to show her the drawing with that rubbed out, cockeyed mess.

FOURTEEN

"Now," Kitty said, "we have before us five vodkas—even I don't know which is which, I mixed them up and there's a sticker on the bottom. No peeking!" Jimmy was just impressed she had five identical mini carafes sitting around.

She had dressed up for the occasion, worn her chartreuse silk capri pants and a floral top with a popped collar. Her hair was done, and she had on her good cat's-eye glasses—the ones with the pink rhinestones. Almost disappointed when he arrived at her door in shorts and flip-flops, she shooed him to the bar in a cloud of perfume.

"Should we have water chasers to clear our palates?" Jimmy asked.

Kitty lit a cigarette. "Oh ho, you child!" she chortled, and then thought better of it. "I suppose we should—it's a taste test, not a drinking contest." She bustled around to the fridge behind the bar, cigarette pursed in her lips. "Evian OK?"

This all came about because Jimmy arrived the week before to Kitty's happy hour—"Every night, five o'clock, three hundred and sixty-five days a year—unless I'm at the casino!"—with an apology for bringing one of the bottles of Kirkland vodka Ramon was always giving him.

"It's crap! I'm sorry!" he said, but Kitty had clucked.

"Don't you know? Kirkland vodka is really Grey Goose—they

deny it, of course, but those in the know buy their vodka at Costco." Jimmy would not believe it. "It's not like you're drinking top of the line with your Absolut anyway, hon—tell you what, we'll do a taste test. What fun!"

Kirkland, Absolut, Grey Goose, Smirnoff and Stoli.

"Do we sip it?" Jimmy asked.

"What? No! You taste it like you drink it—down the hatch!" She grabbed the first shot and threw it back—Jimmy followed suit. "You know, chocolatiers will tell you: Don't eat a piece of candy like a rabbit, nibbling at it because you don't want to seem like a hog. Hell no! There's a specific balance of ingredients in fine chocolate: the mix with the other flavors inside— caramel, nuts, liqueur, whatever—and you can only taste it properly if you put the whole thing in your mouth. Now you know."

"Now I know. Is there a scorecard?"

Kitty frowned. "I'm sure there should be, but shall we wing it?"

"Let's shall."

They smacked their lips.

"How was that? I'm going to guess that was Absolut, but maybe I shouldn't say. I've tasted better—at lunch, as a matter of fact. What do you think?"

Jimmy considered. "Yes, I think maybe you're right." They filed it away for later.

"Alright—next one—cheers, honey!" Number two went down smoothly, they both agreed better than the first. "That might have been Stoli? I thought we should have a Russian—oops, a second Russian! Now I feel greedy!" They realized after the third shot they had failed to clear their palates with water in between, but agreed two and three were barely distinguishable.

"Maybe two and three were the Kirkland and Grey Goose?" Jimmy offered. "If they're made by the same people, just with different labels."

"Very astute." They took another taste of each, forgetting to clear their palates again.

During a short breather, Kitty squinted at the stereo clicker over her glasses. "Oh! I was going to put out some nibbles," she said, bustling off to the kitchen and leaving a cigarette smoldering on the bar in a green, shamrock-shaped ashtray. *Kiss Me I'm Irish*, it demanded. She called from the other room, "And how is the studio working for you? Ramon says you're all settled in—lots of painting."

Yes, yes, all good, and then he remembered the toilet was constantly running, probably needed a new thingamabob.

"Oh, dear—just knock on their door, sometimes Ramon needs a little tap on the shoulder, you know."

"Oh right, but. Where? Do they live?"

"In the basement, next to the laundry room—it really is a nice one bedroom, the rooms are quite big, you know—not a lot of light, but hey, what do you expect for free? I'm sure Ramon is down there now, working on a six-pack probably, but who are we to talk?" She laughed as she rejoined him and clinked her next shot glass against his. "I guess a love of drink runs in the family."

"Family?"

She nodded as she sipped. "Ramon is my nephew—well, my husband's, our roots are down in Bakersfield—didn't I say? I could hardly leave him out in the cold after his accident—crushed," she whispered, as though anyone might hear, "under a big sewer pipe at his construction site, right on his hand, no way to save it, pulped as I understand—god!" So explained the stump. "He didn't work for a long time, and then his cousin on the other side, the one with the liquor distributorship down in San Leandro said 'Come up'—of course, that didn't last long—but I needed a handyman after my husband died, and that big useless space down in the basement I couldn't rent but seemed like a perfectly clean and dry place for someone down on his luck, living on disability. 'Why not?' I said."

Shot number four evoked a purr from Kitty. "That's my Smirnoff!" Jimmy was disappointed by number four, but he would not risk offending her.

"Very clean," he did manage, trying to sound sophisticated. Kitty nodded her head a little too enthusiastically and almost slipped from her barstool.

"What the hell is going on with the music?" She was beginning to slur, and retrieving the stereo remote, handed it to him. "Do something with that, hon?" She started to pick up number five, blinked, and put it down. "Whoops! That's not water!" They cleared their palates while Simon or Garfunkel crooned, then hit shot number five.

"Aha! On second thought, this one is definitely Smirnoff," Kitty pronounced slowly and clearly. "But that would make the last one..." Genuine befuddlement now. Perhaps another sip of number four.

She paused as she caught her breath and looked at him strangely. "You remind me of him, you know."

"Who?"

"Grady, the boy who lived in your apartment."

He tried to sound more empathetic than drunk but had to shut one eye to focus. "Were you friends?"

"Oh yes, sweet, very sweet—like you—a little serious, but quite a looker, my goodness. Was he even thirty when he died? He lost a lot of friends, and he was just wasting away, lost his job too, on disability—we didn't ask for the rent the last four months of his life, but I think he felt it, you know—the obligation. I'm the one who found him."

Jimmy could barely muster words. "Terrible. I'm sorry."

They never did arrive at a conclusion about the best tasting vodka, though an hour later it was absolutely definitely determined Kirkland was just as good as Grey Goose, if not better, but certainly no second fiddle to Absolut, and why waste good vodka after all? Jimmy had two more bottles sitting unopened in his kitchen from Ramon's last two visits, though he kept the part about screwing her nephew and his lover to himself. And really, of the two Kittys sitting in front of him he had no idea which one to address such a comment to, and none of their business anyway. He decided it was high time to throw himself down the basement stairs and find someone with a penis, though not entirely clear how he got from the bar to hugging Kitty goodbye at her door. Opportunely, Oscar was walking through the foyer.

"Oh! There you are, Ramon—we were looking for you! Be a dear and see our Jimmy upstairs, love," Kitty said.

Oscar carried him upstairs. They did it on the kitchen floor with hand soap for lube and then Oscar put him to bed.

HOOKR CHAT

BigBadBro:
Hey twinks what's up? Love your profile name

tWinkS:
Chilling with cocktails you?

BigBadBro:
Horny
I've seen you before

tWinkS:
When?

BigBadBro:
Waterbuddies 6 months ago

tWinkS:
Haha sounds like me
What was I up to?

BigBadBro:
Naked in a tub hottest thing I've ever seen

tWinkS:
I remember a lot of loads that night
Any of them yours?

BigBadBro:
I wish, there was a line
I've been looking for you ever since never seen you on here before
Are you really 24 you look younger

tWinkS:
Got the fake id to prove it ;)
Just moved to the east bay

BigBadBro:
Lucky East Bay
Can you host?

tWinkS:
I can host
Get that dirty dick over here stud

BigBadBro:
I have to shower

tWinkS:
Don't bother
Here's my address

At least if Jimmy and Vic had to work the first Sunday of September, they would be out for the Solano Stroll street fair instead of stuck in the store. It would not be a high sales event, mainly an opportunity to get the Albany Art name out in the community and sweep new customers into the brick and mortar. They spent the Friday evening before packing up all the cute stuff normal people with kids might like, art kits, origami packs, balsa wood sculptures of dinosaurs and Eiffel Towers, coloring books—fun shit for the whole family. On that perfect sunny Sunday morning Vic stopped by to pick Jimmy up, and they were setting up their folding table next to "Watercolors by Winnie" half an hour before the crowds.

"You've never been to the Stroll? Go!" Vic said, sending Jimmy out to look around a bit and find them some coffee. There were the usual arts and crafts booths with jewelry, wire sculptures of tiny furniture and fantastic creatures, tie-dye, crystals, beads and incense. Nothing stopped him in his tracks. He avoided eye contact with the people in their booths, hating the uncomfortable marketing conversations, the networking, the chit-chat he knew all too well, some variation on: "Please buy my wares, kind sir, I have a bachelor's degree in art history and my rent is due." He had worked a similar booth at the Castro Street Fair once, and it was an entirely different animal—selling stuff to people who came to a store specifically to buy versus trying to sell people your own artwork, a tiny piece of yourself however small—by many orders of desperation.

Back at the table, he found Vic opening a pack of origami paper to teach a family how to make paper cranes. "Now the legend says," they told them, "if you fold one thousand cranes, your wish will be granted—though that didn't help the little girl who was dying of cancer, haha!" The mother gave them a hard stare.

The morning wore on, many cranes were folded and sent on a merry migration up and down Solano Avenue. They sold a few All-in-One art kits and boxes of crayons. Around lunchtime Vic was in the middle of a Spiro-Graph demonstration and Jimmy volunteered to get pad-thai and iced coffees at the food court.

"I don't want the iced tea if they don't have the iced coffee—that shit's sick—just a coke, then," Vic said.

Maybe the cute East Asian guy working the booth was trying to flirt with him because he ended up with complimentary chicken satay as well. As he was heading back, he began to think he had lost their table when he saw Oscar and Kitty through the crowd. Vic was yelling, "Junior!" as Oscar leaned through a gaggle of children to hug him. Junior?

"Hey!" Jimmy said, kissing Kitty on the cheek. As Oscar turned around his face froze. "Hey."

Vic laughed. "You know each other?" Jimmy handed the food across the table.

"Yeah, we live in the same building—" He almost said "this is the boy" but thought better of it in front of Kitty.

"Oh wow," Vic said, "small world! Junior—I mean, Oscar, haha, old habits—who's this with you?"

"Hello dear!" Kitty said, beaming at Vic. "It's OK, I still call him Ramon sometimes—I mean, the family never called him Junior, you know—but I'm Kitty, his aunt—well, great-aunt..."

Oh. Shit.

Oscar—full name Ramon Oscar Castro, Jr.—had been a freshman when Vic was a senior, and they had been passing friends for a year. So Oscar was only seventeen, and a senior in high school. As the light dawned on Jimmy's face, panic froze on Oscar's, and he made a quick excuse to keep moving through the crowd with his aunt. Great-aunt. Fuck!

"He really helped me out," Vic explained, "he stuck up for me with the football players, even when he was just starting—two-fifty in ninth grade, he skipped right over JV straight to varsity—you better believe they didn't mess with me after he told them to shut the hell up." Vic had already changed their pronouns. "I actually enjoyed my senior year once the football team sort of adopted me—all thanks to Junior—shit, Oscar! He doesn't like Junior. Are you OK?"

Jimmy pretended his pad thai was off and got no argument to his suggestion they pack up a little early when the crowd started to thin.

"Want me to come and nurse your tummy?"

But the only nursing Jimmy wanted was a frozen bottle of vodka.

HOOKR CHAT

Fballer26:
Can I come up?

tWinkS:
No that's a bad idea

Fballer26:
I'm sorry can we please talk?

tWinkS:
We're talking now

Fballer26:
You hate me

tWinkS:
I don't hate you I care about you but you lied
and this puts me in a really bad spot
What about Ramon?

Fballer26:
What about him? He's an asshole

tWinkS:
What about your mom?

Fballer26:
Meth head, she left before they cut the cord

tWinkS:
It doesn't have to be this way
I can help you

Fballer26:
Like how?

tWinkS:
I don't know talk to your school
talk to the police
What do you want?

Fballer26:
I want things to stay the way they are
he doesn't both me anymore since you got here and
I like you
Don't you like me?

tWinkS:
Yes but you're 17 and I could get in huge
trouble

Fballer26:
I'll be 18 pretty soon and I can move out or I could
move upstairs with you and he couldn't do anything
about it

tWinkS:
How long has he been doing this to you?

Fballer26:
I don't want to talk about it

tWinkS:
HOW LONG???

Fballer26:
I don't know since we moved up here when I was about 10

tWinkS:
We have to tell someone
What about Kitty?

Fballer26:
NO!!!! She'll kick us out
I just have one more year and then I graduate
Please don't tell her!!!!
Can I come up?
I love you

tWinkS:
Fuck sake
This is really bad

Fballer26:
Please plese
I just want to talk

tWinkS:
Ok

FIFTEEN

For a few weeks, Oscar came upstairs, same as usual—never together with Ramon anymore, things were too tense. If Jimmy started asking questions, Oscar clammed up, but when he suggested they should end things, the truth spilled out in drips.

Oscar's mother dumped him when he was born and disappeared—she and Ramon only had a short fling, but she showed up ten months later at his apartment in Bakersfield, twitchy and asking for money. When Ramon refused, she started yelling and screaming from the street, chucked a baby wearing a dirty diaper on the hot sidewalk in a third-hand car seat, and drove off with some guy in a sketchy van. No question of paternity: the kid looked exactly like Ramon at the same age, so said his older sister. She continued to live with them for some years, babysitting Oscar during the day and cleaning gyms and offices at night. But after Ramon's accident on the construction site, she finally said she had enough with his drinking—only getting worse on disability—and moved back to Mexico. The offer from his uncle's widow had seemed like a fresh start in a new place.

"Better school for me up here," Oscar said, "free rent, and at first, he was making some money under the table delivering for his cousin, but then he got caught stealing liquor, and he was always late, so they cut him off."

"How did—it—start?" What should he call it?

"When did he start fucking me? We only have one bed, and he never hid when he was jerking off, but then he started touching me—showing me how to do it, he said—and by the time I hit puberty and started to realize I liked guys..."

"Jesus."

"Whatever. But everything's different now, with you."

"With me?"

"Now I know how it's supposed to feel, with a man," Oscar said. "And he leaves me alone—all he talks about is you, and how lucky we are you moved in."

"What are you going to do, bitch?" Dee asked, then came a muffled shriek through the phone. "Trixie! Trixie B. Davis! Drop it! You drop mommy's chancleta right now, young lady. I said RIGHT NOW, dammit! Good girl. Sorry. So what the fuck are you going to do?"

"I don't know, I have a bad feeling about this—like, Oscar doesn't want to stop—he says he's in love with me, and I have feelings for him too, honestly, I mean, I wouldn't say forever and ever kind of feelings, just the ordinary you're sweet let's do it kind of feelings."

"I mean, seventeen is legal in a lot of places, so I wouldn't beat myself up too much over the child molestation thing, plus he lied to you from the get-go."

"It's not just that—should I tell someone? Kitty?"

"You can't tell me she's never noticed anything. Has she never been down to their apartment and seen there's only one bed?"

"Oscar says no, she hasn't been inside since they first moved in—he thinks she feels guilty for not giving them a nicer apartment upstairs and doesn't like to be reminded of what a jail cell they're living in."

"Huh. That might be a can of worms. What about his school? They take that shit seriously, if you tipped off the guidance counselor at his high school, maybe? At least then the snitching to the police wouldn't be coming from you but from the school."

"Maybe, but I think no matter who I tell, if I tell, they're going to know it was me—nobody else knows."

"Alright, and then what? The kid is seventeen, even if he was in foster care for a bit, he'll graduate soon—he could live with your landlady maybe, or declare emancipation and just stay where he is with his dad in jail or whatever. Shit! I don't know. Do you have a lawyer?"

"Are you seriously asking me if I have a lawyer? Do you have a lawyer?"

"Yes—Ricardo's sister-in-law is a lawyer. Hmm, maybe I could ask her..."

"Alright—hold off on that for a minute, I need to think. Should I end it, I mean, should I just tell them it's over? They both keep knocking on my door—I've actually started pretending I'm not here, I just can't deal, and I need to get some work done."

"Yeah, how is that going? When's New York supposed to come pick up his portrait?"

"He says in a few weeks he'll be back out and he'll take a look at my new work and put in a good word with his friend at the gallery."

"OK, well, this is your big chance! Try to lay off the bottle and focus!"

Jimmy groaned. "Yeah, and try not to get arrested for child molestation. Jesus Fuck."

"Forget about that. And who are we kidding—don't take this the wrong way, but you would literally be the queen of the cellblock, the bubbas would be shanking each other over who got to make you his bitch."

"That's the sweetest thing anyone's ever said to me."

Jimmy drank two preemptive martinis the Wednesday he showed Vic the new painting series, but they did little to calm his nerves. There were seven, not counting Paul's portrait: four of (shudder) father and son, and the three of Vic he had all but finished. Paul was expected next week.

He had cleared off the pictures on the gallery wall, tidied up the whole studio, just like an art opening. At first he hung them up, then took them back down and turned them facing the wall to unveil them one by one. Seven seemed a good number to gauge the new direction, and Jimmy valued Vic's opinion. Their own graphic work was beautifully done, incorporating a fair number of their own illustrations. He had rarely had the opportunity to present an entire new collection of work to a fellow artist for feedback. They started with the *Ramon and Oscar* series. He really needed a different title.

"You're not saying anything."

They had discussed the whole situation with Ramon and Oscar, with no more certain conclusion than Jimmy had reached with Dee.

Vic said, "Listen, don't beat yourself up—I had a crush on him back in high school, he's a total teddy bear. I mean, what if I had dated him back then and we kept on after I graduated, right? Same diff."

But though they had not made any definite commitments to each other, Jimmy sensed his relationship with Ramon and Oscar had thrown Vic off-balance. They started cautiously enthusiastic about the group of four—figures twisted around each other. Fucking, or fighting? His vintage book of wrestling photos helped with some of the forms.

"I wanted to put their bodies in impossible poses," Jimmy explained, "something that looks more like how sex feels, my kind of sex anyway—sort of a gay Fight Club, in the moment—not like how it looks later, when you see yourself on video and you think, 'Oh, I'm totally gooning out—I look like an idiot.'"

Vic twisted his lips. "Your kind of sex. Huh. You've done that—videoed yourself?"

"Sure—been videoed, anyway. You?"

"No."

The space between them went still, and Jimmy stopped himself from taking a step backward. The dead air went on a beat too long.

"I like them—really, I think they're good—interesting, definitely a new direction for you—fresh, yes—Fight Club, OK, but. I don't know. I guess I'm having a hard time getting past ... you know." Yes, Jimmy knew—he had been living with You Know for weeks, but it was too late now—they were done, and he was out of time to start over or scrub out the incest.

Once he turned the paintings of Vic around, though, they stood in complete silence for an uncomfortably long time.

"Say something."

Vic hemmed, and gritted their teeth, squinted and fidgeted. "Oh... So..."

"So what?"

"Please don't take this the wrong way, but this isn't what I expected, honestly."

"What do you mean?"

"I don't know, I mean, I see where you were going with the others, Oscar and all that—they're sexy, yeah, edgy—but these are just ... weird to me?"

Now Jimmy did take a step back.

"I'm totally not the kind of person who feels this great need to be flattered—like I didn't expect you to paint a pretty picture and make me look hot, or anything. But this? I don't know. I don't know what to say." Now it was Vic's turn to take a step back. "Of all the ways to depict me, my body, I guess I didn't expect this sort of ... not clinical exactly, but I don't know. I thought you were cool with me being non-binary."

Was he not past all that? Jimmy felt as though he were no longer in his body but another dimension—out of body but also instantly, acutely sober.

"No, no, not clinical." He struggled to collect himself and focus on his thought process. "Not clinical—I was trying to show different sides of you, right?" He pointed to the first painting. "Here's you as a boy but with different parts, and here's you as a girl with boy parts. This second one shows some of the conflict within you, some of the pain you must have felt, disconnected from the body in the mirror."

"I've never told you anything about that, not really." Vic crossed their arms. "I mean we've talked a little, but this is a lot of gigantic assumptions. I don't need to be hemmed into a binary, that's not me, that's you working through something. And what's that, a sling?" He pointed to a box enclosing one of the figures.

"No, it's—I'm—having trouble processing this right now..." Jimmy was feeling the martinis again, and not in a good way. His stomach churned.

"It looks like a sling, like that painting of your roommate. Is that what you want, me in a sling?"

"It's not a sling."

"What is it, then?"

"A box."

"A box? You see me in a box?"

"No."

"What do you mean then, what box?"

"What difference does it make, you don't get it, it's fine."

"No, seriously, tell me—I want to know what you think—do you think I'm in a box, an in-the-box kind of person?"

"No. I mean, I think you know who you are, and what you want—so you're inside, right? It's not a box, it's a space—inside."

"You think I'm inside? Like an insider? And that makes you what?"

"Outside, looking in."

"You're killing me right now, white boy."

Jimmy rolled his eyes. "Maybe we do this another day. Or not at all."

"Dude." Vic reached out, but Jimmy shrugged them off.

"No really—you don't get it, it's fine—I was just trying to paint what I feel when I look at you."

"I'm not just a body."

"Fuck, never mind, I shouldn't have showed this to you."

"Come on—seriously? It's just I don't know if you know what you are saying, right?"

Jimmy tried to cover up the nearest painting with a sheet, but his hands were shaking too hard and he ended up turning all of the pictures to face the wall again. "I'm sorry, maybe, can you just go?"

"No," Vic said, only just stopping themself from shouting. "Jeez, can we talk about this? What are we doing here? Can't friends disagree? Can't we be honest?"

"Oh. Friends? Is that what we're doing?"

"What? Isn't it?"

Jimmy shook his head. "I thought this was supposed to be something more."

"I mean, friends first, right? It's a start, isn't it?"

Jimmy leaned in. "Then when are you going to start fucking me up the ass for real, friend? Oh—you can't."

"Whoa."

"Seriously, I mean this has been fun and all, but when do I get what I want out of this, what I need?"

Vic recoiled. "Wow—alright, what do you need, then? I thought we were having fun—I mean, you cum, I cum—we laugh, we sleep together—we enjoy each other's company, at least I thought we did. What more do you want? Please tell me."

Jimmy fought to keep his voice from shaking. "But you don't cum, not really, do you? I mean, nothing comes out of you, you don't give me anything—no cum, no piss—nothing, not for me anyway."

"What, you want me to piss on you?"

Jimmy threw up his hands. Vic flinched. "No! Fuck! I mean—you don't give me what I need! Your dick is fake. You don't give me anything, you leave me feeling ... empty!"

Vic set his jaw. "Can we take a step back for a second? This is getting way out of hand..."

"I don't need this," Jimmy said, casting about for his glass. "I need a drink."

Vic sighed. "Listen—I'm sorry I'm not vibing with your paintings—they took me off guard. Can you lay off the booze for just one minute?"

"Why? You were just leaving..." Jimmy turned and went downstairs. Vic followed.

"Seriously, is this how you want to leave it? Kick me out, get smashed? That working out for you? Other than Dee I don't see a whole lot of people in your life—maybe you would be happier if you laid off the booze and learned how to work with the few people you've got."

Jimmy slammed the freezer door, uncapped the bottle and took a long, vengeful slug straight from the bottle. "Fucking genius—says the dickless wonder..."

"Oh, fuck you," Vic spat.

"You know what, you're right, I am a lonely, unhappy alcoholic—and you're the fool who chased after me."

Vic turned and walked out the door.

[Interview transcripts edited for clarity.]

Your early work, the paintings from the first show, have been described as brutal, disturbing—likened to autopsies, car crashes. Grim stuff.

Yes—like I said, it was pivotal meeting Dexter, getting real New York feedback. Until then I had focused a lot on fantasies, things I felt were lacking in some profound way in my life or childhood—things I wanted. My parents were not cultured people—high-school educated, no museums, I don't think they ever even went to the movies after I was old enough to go by myself or with Dee and his mom. White walls, canned asparagus, registered Republicans. I never ate a bagel until I was twenty-one, after I moved to San Francisco—my mother still thinks there's something "Jew-y" about them. Wonder Bread was the only brand she ever bought.

My whole artistic vision had to change if I wanted to work with Dexter—the first brutally honest assessment of my chances as an artist, emphasis on brutal. I had to dig deeper, look in the shadows.

Are you fascinated by gruesomeness? You strike me as a gentler sort of soul.

That's not the angle I was looking at things. One thing did stick in my head around that time. I hooked up with a guy who was into watching horror movies while he we had sex, kinda freaky but he was hung like a horse and really handsome, so I was like, alright, we can watch your "Saw" and your "Hostels" and "Human Caterpillar," I mean, weird, but whatever gets you off, dude.

Human Centipede.

Oh. Yeah. Centipedes are gross. Anyway, this was some sick shit he liked, torture porn, and it was strange because those sorts of movies used to freak me out, really bad, but while I was laying there getting plowed and watching all these horrible movies, I started to numb out to it. After a while I stopped believing the violence, I guess, and just saw it, maybe like a doctor sees blood and guts. I wasn't afraid of it after that, and I started to look at my figures differently. I started to let the figures in my paintings morph, to become strange to me—like an alien might see us—like food. Consumable.

Anyway, I remember someone telling me that one part of sex is the suppression of disgust—the smells, the weirdness of genitals, morning breath, the occasional blood and other fluids, that kind of stuff—that disgust itself can become highly erotic to some people. Of course, Ramon—the father—he had that stump, and I incorporated it into the figures of him.

You painted it with a hole, to resemble a penis.

I mean, it looked like a penis—he used it like a penis. Anyway, I thought, people get fisted, Robert Mapplethorpe showed it thirty years ago, right? I can't believe we're still talking about this shit, but here we are, clutching our pearls. Getting fucked with a stump isn't even as extreme, sensation-wise, as getting fisted—only in the imagination. So that's the kind of sexuality I was exploring in my own life, and started to capture in my art. That's how it all started.

What about the box you paint in many of your compositions? The Vern painting, you've said it was a sling, but then you used the image again, many times, including some of your recent work. Some people have guessed they represent coffins.

I don't know—I've tried to explain it, but people assume sling. It's a frame, like, a frame within a frame. Put a frame around a thing and it instantly becomes more, accrues context, has more weight. The box is my way of doing that, imagining the subject as a whole—framing it as already complete.

And the other paintings? The *V* series? There were only three or four. They have bothered some people very much, almost as much as the *Ramon and Oscar* series.

Because they depict a non-binary person. There are a lot of people better equipped to discuss enbyphobia than me, but that's what it comes down to. Vic never liked them much, I guess they thought I was like the sorcerer's apprentice, messing around with a subject I didn't really understand, so I never went back to that subject.

SIXTEEN

One night when Jimmy was about four and needing to pee, he had found his father in the dark bathroom and they peed together, a rite of passage. Transfixed, eye-level with his father's penis inches away and the thrum of his stream hitting the water, it seemed the most bulbous, enormous thing Jimmy had ever seen. He goggled at the gigantic head, that eel-like protuberance, monstrous compared to his own little boy weenie. In the dark, a tiny droplet of his father's piss splashed back and landed on his lip. He flicked his tongue to taste it. Salty.

The event would never be repeated, nor did he want it to be, this demonstration, somehow more estranging than bonding.

He would never completely remember the several hours after Vic left, how he got to the City and came to be buck naked in a clawfoot tub at Waterbuddies, the Wednesday night party at Suckers. The attendants were usually all business about check-in, barring intoxicated men, but Jimmy often walked and talked in a blackout as though he were sober.

The dim basement rooms were humid and warm. Past the clothes check, black leather drapes hung from chains dividing areas with freestanding tubs. Shadowy forms leaned on the railings of raised platforms faced with glory holes, dicks at mouth level so cocksuckers could stand rather than kneel, a gallery view of the action by the tubs and drains.

Jimmy never bothered with the cocks in slots—not that he minded a dick in his mouth, but he knew his place: naked in a tub. Sometimes another boy climbed in with him, but he preferred to be by himself at the center of a crush of men working up heads of piss, the fathers of a beer-soaked baptism.

Was anything so gloriously depraved, the spew of a gang of men? The buttery wetness on his face and tongue, the warm drench of maleness from every side—a magic fountain, men on tap. Better than cum, he thought—not sticky but wet and plentiful. The gurgle as a hard stream filled his mouth, spitting it out to drench his chest, or swallowing it like a good boy should. Cum was a booby prize, merely a garnish. Piss was this little piggy's gold standard. He could lean back in a tub for hours.

"There's a good boy," a familiar voice said in his ear, strong arms snaking around his neck from behind. "Popper up for Daddy." A little bottle pressed to one nostril, he inhaled deeply of the caustic fumes. Here we go—his brain slopped and swirled, his face flushed, his body tingled.

Open for business, gentlemen.

Not Jimmy any longer, no, but a thing, squirming, mindless. A fish flailing in a bucket. His lips gaped, his tongue lolled, he reached up to squeeze and fondle each man's streaming cock by turns, coaxing forth their warm liquor. Around the trough, wordless, leaning and swaying together as one, the crew gave succor to their boy, exultant in his submission and abounding gratitude.

Rod, the freaky mohawked popper pig always telling people he was seventy-two, continuously ministered the vapor to Jimmy's nostril. "Come be my boy," he was always saying in the smoking area. "You wouldn't have to work, or pay rent—just service me, twenty-four seven." An alluring offer, maybe, crazy and tattooed and muscled as he was, except for the horrifying detail he never failed to mention: "I've got two trained dogs."

"Open your mouth, faggot." Jimmy did as he was told. Rod hucked a thick wad of spit into the back of his throat and he swallowed.

"Thank you, Sir."

"Hop up in the sling, boy, I got a load of piss to pop up your hole."

"Yes, Sir."

Jimmy stood in the tub but, slipping on the piss-slick enamel, fell half in, half out, and wrenched his wrist with a strangled scream, narrowly missing a cracked skull on the edge. Rod disappeared. The cries from those who helped him up drew the attention of the clothes check boy. Shook up and suddenly sloppy with the pain, Jimmy was escorted to his locker and bum rushed out the door as soon as he was dressed.

"You can rinse off at home."

Somehow he had the presence of mind to call an Uber and direct it to Dee's house. The car was black and smelled new inside, the techno music a little too loud, the driver maybe thirty, maybe Middle Eastern, definitely suspicious of his fare. Jimmy fought not to puke in the backseat, deep breaths, and finally pleaded for the driver to "please stop talking" through gritted teeth.

The guy persisted. "What was that place I picked you up?" he asked, wrinkling his nose as he peered into the rearview. "I pick you guys up all the time, but there's no sign, just an address." No answer. All four of the windows began to roll down at once. The fresh air felt good.

When he arrived at Dee's door, he rang and leaned against a pillar in the portico, breathing through nausea, his wrist throbbing. He rang again as the Uber sped off, not waiting as Jimmy had asked.

What would he have said? "Take me to the Golden Gate Bridge." What was the closest an Uber would go without asking too many questions, end of Lombard maybe? How far was it to the bridge? Could he walk? Once there, it would be just one tiny step into nothingness, not so hard. He knew how that felt, did that almost every day.

Across the street, the onion domes of Volga Restaurant's neon sign flickered out. A figure locked the front door, stopped to take a deep breath and stretch. They saw each other across the street. The Russian.

"Hello, cricket, what are you doing on my doorstep?"

The liquor and the pain of his arm overcame him before he could answer, and Jimmy rushed to the curb to puke after all. He felt steadying hands as he nearly fell forward into the gutter. "OK boy, you're not doing so good, huh? Let's see if DeeDee is home."

"He's not." Guts on the ground, he was at least lucid again. "You have a mint?"

"Upstairs, we go." Jimmy let himself be guided.

The apartment was spacious and clean, almost spartan—lots of chrome and black leather, art photography on the walls, expensively framed. He tried to stand as still as possible in the front hall without touching anything, aware now that he stank. The Russian popped his head out the door of the kitchen. "You coming in...?" The kitchen was well appointed with shining black enamel stove, built-in refrigerator, black marble floor—custom, custom, custom.

"So, I'm sorry—tell me your name again."

A deep rumble of mirth emerged from the towering man. "Feodor Aleksandr Kuznetsov, at your service."

Jimmy took the bottle of water offered to him and gulped. "Thanks. That's a lot of syllables."

"My American friends call me Feo—you call me Feo, yes? Yes."

"I wonder where Dee is," Jimmy said.

"I'm thinking, I'm thinking." Feo combed his beard with his fingers. "I don't know—you don't know? Nobody knows. He was expecting you?"

Jimmy shook his head, stepping out of the way as Feo lumbered around the kitchen, pulling a bottle of Smirnoff out of the freezer.

"No, I ... I wasn't feeling well, I guess, and I needed a place to crash for a bit. Do you have an ibuprofen? My wrist is killing me."

"Ibu-who?"

"Advil."

"Yes, of course," he said, pulling a big bottle from the cupboard and shaking two out into Jimmy's hand. "Vodka?"

"You literally just saw me vomit in the street."

Feo shrugged. "Yes, but you feel better now—vodka?"

"Why the hell not."

"But sip, yes? It's good." He poured out two generous shots. "Sip," he said again, handing one to Jimmy. He excused himself to the bathroom and the patter of the shower drifted out.

Jimmy sipped as instructed and wandered into the living room. On closer examination, he saw the photos on the walls were not posters from a print shop—some of them were signed, mostly black and white. One in color was some strange killer clown, garish, more clown drag than murderous—unsettling either way—against a psychedelic background. Another was a single poppy in salmon-orange.

"You're very neat," he observed when Feo emerged wearing a towel, carrying his drink and the bottle. Across the expanse of his furry belly, a gang-style Old English tattoo said *CADILLAC*.

"I'm a cook—neat is a good habit in the kitchen. And life."

Jimmy nodded. "Cadillac?"

"Always buy American." Feo sat on the sofa, his towel falling open to show thick furry thighs. "You like?" He pointed at the wall of photography.

"Nice collection." Jimmy stopped himself from gulping the rest of his drink. "Do you mind if I use your bathroom?"

"Of course—first door past the kitchen—you're not sick again?"

"No—sorry, I just—I'm pretty sure I stink—is there a washcloth?"

Feo leaned back and smiled. "I noticed—you're marinated again, like last time, eh? Maybe I don't mind so much."

"You took a shower."

"Kitchen grease, not so fun as golden showers." He rubbed the leather next to him. "Easy clean-up—come. Sit." Jimmy did as he was told. "Wednesday night—you were at Waterbuddies?"

"You know about it?"

"I know—never been—I work always and they close doors at midnight. Tell me, it's only one o'clock now. You left early?"

"They kicked me out." Jimmy told him about his fall in the tub and hurting his wrist.

Feo examined Jimmy's arm, leaned down and kissed it. "Not broken, probably sprain. Advil help? OK. You stay here with Feo tonight, huh? I was hoping I would see you again, cricket—I was going to ask DeeDee about you but not seen him too much, maybe he is busy with his cabaret."

Jimmy giggled. "Cabaret, yeah..." He was feeling better, enjoying the moist heat coming off Feo. He threw back his drink. "Oops. Sip." The Russian poured him another small one. "So, you do know my name, right?"

"Yes, Jimmy, yes, how could I forget?"

"So why do you call me cricket?" He remembered to sip this time. He set his drink down and let himself be folded into Feo's flank.

"Because you're very small, and your name is Jimmy—like Pinnochio—you know, the cricket—Jimmy Cricket."

Jimmy chuckled. "That's not his..." He stopped and shook his head. "Perfect."

"Also many times I thought about you. DeeDee called you ladybug, but I thought, not ladybug—sunshine, picnics, games, no, not you I think. I think you are more serious, and—what do they say, chirping in the dark?" Feo knocked back his glass and poured himself another.

"Whistling."

"Aw, OK, whistling—but chirping. Jimmy Cricket. It's what I thought. Maybe I'm wrong."

"You're not wrong."

"You like big strong Daddy bears, little cricket," Feo said, pulling Jimmy into his lap, towel flopping open.

"You're not wrong," Jimmy whispered.

His legs, wrapped around Feo's waist, could not reach all the way. There was no jockeying for a better position, no bracing himself for the best angle, power bottom-style. For the first time in his life, he could only relax and be taken with full force. The man was an avalanche. Pinned and skewered beneath the vast mass of the Russian, he could only sip air. At moments darkling spots exploded in his eyes. One enormous hand cradled and encircled his entire neck, fingers wrapped and squeezing, sometimes softer, sometimes firmer, as Jimmy alternately fell silent, close to fainting, or cried out.

"Crush me!" he groaned, and there came a reply, so soft and low Jimmy could not be sure he did not imagine it.

"I love you."

Tumbled like a snowflake under a thundering mountainside, Jimmy let out an aching wail, at once a moan of relief and sob of anguish.

Feo drew back, supporting his weight on his elbows.

"Cricket?" he whispered, breath heavy. "You alright? That was big noise for such a small person. Should I stop? I'll stop."

Jimmy clutched at him. "You stop and I'll call the police."

"Can I be honest?" Jimmy asked afterward, snuggled in the crook of Feo's legs, head nestled on the soft scruff of his belly like a pillow. Feo was a talker. His voice resonating down through his torso soothed Jimmy, as though submerging his ears below the water of a bath, the world gentle as a heartbeat.

"Honesty always."

"So—when we first met—you were missing a tooth in front, right? It freaked me out, I couldn't stop staring at it."

Feo laughed. His belly shook, and Jimmy's head bounced up and down with it until he was laughing too. "Yes! I fixed—how's it look?" He smiled big and crazy.

"Perfect! But what happened—how'd you lose it in the first place?"

"Oh, not a fight like DeeDee wanted—who would try to fight me? No. I had my baby cousin, Ludmila—my cousin Ludmila's girl—she's on my lap, I play with her footsies, kiss kiss, each one—so strong—sweet little girl—and she squeals, and she laughs, and BAM! Like a steel spring, she kicks me with her heel right in the mouth! Oops! What the fuck? Out comes my tooth. I cussed! And she laughs at that too."

In the morning, Feo wrapped Jimmy's wrist with an Ace bandage, gave him three more Advil with a glass of OJ and a ride home in his (what else?) black Cadillac Escalade. When he arrived to work, Christine said Vic called in sick. He fumbled through the day with his throbbing wrist.

Dee finally answered his messages Thursday evening.

"Where were you?"

"I was home. I saw the whole thing from my window. So Feo, huh? Did he take good care of you? Was he everything and more? I want every ghastly detail, no matter how gigantic."

Jimmy reviewed Feo's ministrations.

"I knew you two would hit it off! You're welcome for not answering my door at one o'clock in the morning." Then Jimmy told him about the argument with Vic.

"You had a tantrum."

"It wasn't a tantrum—it just got out of hand. I was a bit tipsy, and I don't think I was ready for the kind of criticism they gave me."

"You probably shouldn't have shown them at all—I mean, you're right, they're an artist, but also the model. It's like asking the frog how it feels about your dissection technique."

SEVENTEEN

Was it pretentious for him to have painted Vic so clinically? Was it all just an experiment, because Vic had made the moves on him, why not? A test drive in a car neither of them knew how to handle? Jimmy spent Saturday quietly daubing finishing touches on the *V* series paintings, swimming between image and mortifying memory.

"Put this on," a guy had told him once—a leather hood, no eyes, a zipper for a mouth. Erased, he retreated from the world around him, became an object, floating in darkness, rites performed on him. But rather than enjoying the loss of control, he found himself unmoved. The top became frustrated, his efforts random, almost frantic. Jimmy pronounced the safe word (Utah) out of boredom, and they cut the session short.

Had he performed a similarly oafish escape with Vic?

Pretentious? How could it be pretentious? He was trying to understand, not pretending as though he already did. Was that the offense, that he'd faked his way to a grasp of Vic's gender, cobbled together from hints and headlines?

Jimmy staring at the painting on his easel, brush poised but unmoving, when his phone buzzed, a text from Paul. He'd be in town Tuesday night—want to get together? Of course.

Jimmy: ***I'm really, really sorry***
I didn't want to say it in a text but since you haven't been at work I guess I have to – are you OK?

Nathan was surprisingly cool about coming in to work yesterday

Vic: ***thanks i'm ok***

we need to talk

At Vic's suggestion, they walked the half block from Jimmy's up to Albany Hill. They had mentioned it before, that it was peaceful, a slice of woods on the lone hill at the edge of the Bay. They used to go up there with a friend and a six-pack on warm Indian Summer nights just like this. Jimmy guessed the paintings were now radioactive, a toxic distraction if they'd stayed to talk at his place.

Their shoes crunched on the scrabble of asphalt and gravel at the bottom of the hill, and as they plodded under the leafy canopy, the eucalyptus exuded their cat pee odor. A thin but robust woman marching back down might have been staring behind wraparound sunglasses as they passed. Her wispy water dog sniffed them as it jogged after her. Vic let out a whistle at the view when they reached the bench at the top, on the lip of the western slope that fell away to a group of apartment towers wedged between hill and freeway. *If You Lived Here You Would Be Home Already* a billboard taunted from the top of the tallest building. The air was heavy in the ears with the heat, enough to muffle the traffic noise below.

"They trimmed the trees." Vic stood in front of the bench, looking across the water at the slow fade of dusk. The first flush of lights shimmered like a desert horizon, the bay a mirage. "There was hardly any view back when I was in high school, we'd sneak up here and have a little party in the forest. One time we did mushrooms and ran around with squirt guns playing Shroom Warriors." Their voice trailed off as though the memory captivated them, and Jimmy was too hung up on remorse for the things he had said to interrupt the silence.

Vic seemed tired. They slouched, scuffed the sole of their shoe across the dirt. Certain he was about to receive a scalding indictment, Jimmy broke down to grovel.

"I'm so, so, so sorry—"

Vic stopped him impatiently. "Stop. You already said you're sorry, I get it. I'm not going to say it didn't hurt, but I accept your apology. Let it go, I have. I'm a little sorry too that I wasn't more gentle with my feedback. Just a little."

"I guess I didn't know how to say some of the things I was feeling about—stuff."

Vic shushed him, put their hand on his shoulder and looked at Jimmy for a long moment. "Take a deep breath. Sit down."

Jimmy sighed heavily. "I'm OK—but what do we do? What's next?"

"No, I mean, sit down because I'm about to tell you what's next, and it's gonna be scary."

"Oh god." He sat. "What?"

"I'm pregnant."

Vic had been on a low-dose T regime, so their period had lightened slightly, but when it stopped abruptly, they thought, well, that was unexpected. As a nurse, their mom urged them to put the hormones on pause and go see a doctor immediately.

In the meantime, they bought a pregnancy test—double line on the stick.

While Jimmy held his head between his knees taking deep breaths, Vic danced around the decision they were facing.

"So I always knew I wanted to have a kid, but I sorta thought I would have someone in my life, and we would make the decision together, right? But here we are."

"Here we are? Where the hell is here?" Jimmy moaned.

"I know, I know, you remember that first time when you started poking around—I mean you didn't even finish, I made you put a rubber on but ... you do leak a lot."

Jimmy sat up, hoping he wouldn't faint. "Gee, so virile!"

"Yeah, but, so ... abortion is an option, but there is the whole Catholic thing. My mom's not thrilled about that prospect."

Jimmy stifled a groan. "Catholic? Are you serious? For real, does that even figure anywhere in this?"

"It does for her."

"Your mom isn't having this baby, you are—and me! This isn't happening..."

"It is happening! Jimmy, I'm sorry—I mean, I was an accident—my parents weren't married when my mom got pregnant. And you were adopted. You were probably an accident too."

"Alright, but this kind of accident happens to straight people. We worry about HIV, they worry about babies—that's the deal—they have their pill, now we have ours. Fucking hell!" Jimmy put his head back between his knees.

"This is a fine how do you do," Marlys groused. "I ... don't understand. How could this happen?"

"Well..."

"Stop! I don't want to know. She'll have an abortion, of course."

Why correct her about pronouns now?

"Vic's mom is Catholic, apparently."

"What the hell does her mom have to do with it? You certainly didn't consider me when you got yourself into this, why on earth should she have a say in the matter?"

"Consider you? You're right, mother, I didn't consider you when I had sex with my non-binary lover and got them pregnant because I've been barebacking for so long I don't even remember what a condom looks like." There came such a long silence on the line Jimmy thought maybe she had hung up on him. "Hello?"

"Are you finished?"

"Yes."

"You will not speak to me that way again, young man."

"Sorry."

"You better be. You may take me for a fool, James Christopher Traywick, but obviously I know how these things work—poor Bruce Jenner's been all over the news, for god sake, and he's got a slew of kids, and now what? They're supposed to call him mom, not dad? What the hell is the world coming to? Hold on."

Jimmy sighed as quietly as possible, the crack of Marlys's lighter snapping through the line. She must have put down the phone and opened the refrigerator because there came the clink of bottles, the thunk of the door, no cabinet slamming, though—she already had a glass on the table. She was topping it off with rosé.

"But what do you want, James? Obviously you don't care how this affects me, but what about you? You can barely support yourself—a clerk! At an art store! Living in a studio apartment!" The snap of her lighter again, and then a quiet "shit"—she must have lit a second cigarette while the first still burned in the ashtray. "Have you thought about that? Are you going to get married? CAN you get married?"

"Nothing's been decided—I mean, terminating the pregnancy might still be an option, so is putting it up for adoption, I guess—I mean, I was adopted after all."

"Hm."

"Hm, what?"

"Certainly someone somewhere would be grateful to take the child—your father may not have been entirely sold on the idea, but it was crushing to me personally to think I might never be a mother."

"Excuse me—he didn't want to adopt me?"

"Oh! No, it's not like that exactly—no, no, there was something about wanting to pass down his genes, you know—typical man, thinks he's god's gift, thinks only his own blood is good enough—but he came around. Oh, you know he came around, Jimmy! Your father loved you. Still, I wonder what it would have been like to be pregnant—to feel a child growing inside of me, the closeness. But it was not to be..." Long drag on one of her cigarettes, long pause, long exhale. "And what it would have done to my body! Christ! The stretch marks on your aunt's belly—you should have seen them when they were fresh—the horror!"

Around lunchtime on Tuesday, Paul texted to ask where he could get some coke, but his manner turned clipped abruptly when Jimmy said he didn't know, he never really got into the white powders. Paul would be there at eight. Maybe their visit was going to be more business than pleasure? Then he wrote, "Check out my Hookr profile N.Y.C.T.O.P." and what do you know, there was the picture Jimmy had taken, the one he used as the model for the portrait.

When he arrived that evening, Paul was eager to see the finished product, actually blushed with pleasure. If the photo had been flattering, the painting was more so—Jimmy captured him at his most handsome, a triumphant airbrushed version of himself. "Best I've ever looked. Thank you."

He lingered over the paintings of Vic, Ramon, and Oscar, remained silent for a long time too like Vic had, and Jimmy started to get nervous all over again and poured himself another martini.

"I'm impressed," Paul said finally, almost with surprise. "I guess I wasn't sure what you'd come up with. But these are good. Really good."

Jimmy let out an explosive sigh. "Thanks!"

"No really—it's like you took the advice I passed on to you and ran with it—what Dexter said about your leather painting, I didn't even tell you everything he said about the other ones, but this! I think you're onto something."

Jimmy looked at him sideways. "What did he say?"

"Oh god, something like 'Thomas Kincaide, Painter of Light is already trademarked'—I mean, fuck Dexter, right? But he's got a great eye, so I think he planted the seed. Good job, Jimmy! Fantastic!"

"Thanks," Jimmy said again, more modulated.

"Who is this?" Paul asked, referring to the three of Vic. Just a friend. Trans? Non-binary. "Interesting." His eyes darted back and forth between the different studies, and he paused. "You know, here's what I'm thinking—I've got to have the portrait and the bungalow shipped to New York—my suitcase isn't big enough, I should have asked how big they were," he said, gesturing to the weekender he had brought with him. "Why don't I have all of these shipped out together, and you come out and we present these to Dexter in person? I think they're that good—I think you should meet him and let's see what he says. You ever been? No? It's settled—I've got a good feeling about this, kiddo."

The sex was perfunctory. Nothing wrong with dumping a load in a boy, but Jimmy was glad he had only needed a quick rinse out beforehand because it was over and done in ten minutes of grunting. He was wiping up in the bathroom when Paul said he needed a quick shower.

"I put a fresh bath towel on the bar," Jimmy said as he came out of the bathroom. Paul was snapping shut his suitcase. "Oh, I grabbed an old one from your trunk again—I guess you bought some new ones, big spender."

Feo was free the Wednesday after they hooked up, and the following Saturday too, and every Wednesday and Saturday thereafter, though of course he worked most evenings. He bought Jimmy a few things but nothing extravagant—an adorable T-shirt, sexy underwear—just because. "I walked by a store and thought 'Aw! Perfect for cricket!'"

"Don't you get tired of cooking?" Jimmy asked one afternoon before lunch. Feo had already reorganized his kitchen top to bottom, and installed a few new essential items, including a dozen of his most essential spices and an enormous apron. "You cook every day at work. We can go out."

"Is no problem, for you," he said, waving the suggestion away. "This way you don't have to dress."

Feo knew the magic words when Jimmy drank too much and it was time to go to bed: "Pants down, ass up, cricket." He manhandled Jimmy just so, moved him physically this way and that. "On top, no, like this, face away," he might command, lifting Jimmy bodily, turning and slotting him like a Lego. He gently but firmly showed Jimmy all the things he wanted to do: ropes, hoods, collars, gags, floggers, tit clamps—his toy box overflowed with gadgets and contraptions, meticulously organized. All the freaky shit that had left Jimmy cold before took on dizzying new dimensions in the sure hands of the mighty Feo.

And he was delighted by the news of Vic's pregnancy.

"How do you feel about it?" Jimmy asked the night after he and Vic had the decisive talk—the end of their first trimester was fast approaching.

("Are we keeping the baby? I mean if we're saying 'baby' now we're kinda past the wire hanger stage, don't you think?" Jimmy said.

Vic laughed. "I was not thinking about it in just those terms, but yes, I guess so.")

Feo smiled. "I love babies. Babies love me."

Jimmy pushed a little harder. "And toddlers, and kids, and teens? I'm terrified, to be honest—does this worry you at all?"

"What is worry? Is make believe."

As arranged by Paul, a guy arrived one day to assess the shipment going to New York, unfazed by twelve medium-to-large oil on canvas paintings—four of the boys, three of Vic, the portrait and the bungalow, and three of his best *Ghosts* he had overpainted with some new elements on a whim and snuck in at the last minute. When the crew arrived the next day, they had a plywood crate built to size and wrapped each painting tight as a drum. Jimmy only had to sign the manifest with a description of the contents and an insurance form. He thought they might have made a mistake when he saw the insured amount: $60,000.

"Is this right?" he asked the lead, who glanced at the form again and shrugged.

"It's $219.99 for that amount—did you want more?"

Paul had said he would take care of the whole thing, so Jimmy signed and watched them muscle the crate down the stairs and out the door, his copy of the invoice in hand, dice rolled. Two weeks and a flurry of texts later, he had a ticket for an overnight trip to meet Paul's dealer friend in New York.

Which was more exciting: his first trip to New York, or his first time on an airplane?

"Will you miss me?" Jimmy asked the Wednesday before his flight. Feo was heading back to the City for the dinner shift at the restaurant, but they spooned and dozed for a while.

"Miss? No. Is just one night. But I think of you every day."

"Good enough. You know me and Paul have a thing, right?"

"Yes. You said—just a little thing, you said, not big, like us." Jimmy snuggled back against him, the scratch and prickle of Feo's fur slopped with sweat and lube like a gooey bearskin rug.

"No, not big like us," Jimmy said. "So small I wouldn't even mention it, except..."

"Is OK—have fun with your friend—I have friend too, not seen him in a while and I want to tell him about you."

"Oh!"

"No 'oh', no big deal 'oh'—rentboy, nice, but I think he has crush and maybe hoped for boyfriend? But now, no, not possible."

Later, come time to pack for his trip, Jimmy went looking for his toiletries bag. Not in the bathroom, not in the closet or any of his drawers. A few moving boxes still stacked in the kitchen had never made it upstairs, but he checked the old trunk first.

What had he done with the shaving kit?

And for that matter, where the fuck had he stashed his father's gun?

EIGHTEEN

"10:05 p.m. to JFK has a layover in Dallas." Jimmy read from his phone as they crossed the Bay Bridge heading to the airport. "Two hours. That seems like a long time." Feo leaned over to scowl briefly at the flight confirmation.

"Is not such long time, but not so direct to New York, I think. What time you arrive?"

"10:30 in the morning."

As they slipped out of the Treasure Island tunnel onto the western span of the bridge, Jimmy wondered if the view of New York must be the same as the towers and glowing glass of San Francisco. "Have you ever been to New York?"

"Yes, of course, but I have family, I flew to New York when I first arrived, before coming here." Feo paused. "But your friend could not get direct flight? You'll be all night in the air."

Jimmy would not let such pesky details interfere with this milestone event. "It's fine, I can sleep on the flight and be nice and fresh when I arrive. Paul said it would probably just be me and the business crowd on Friday night. What's a red-eye?"

Fifteen hours later, Jimmy was more nervous than giddy in the car from JFK to Paul's apartment. He did not, in fact, feel so fresh after zigzagging across the country all night, but the driver with the sign waiting for him at the airport buoyed his spirits.

But how much more New York there was than San Francisco! Taller, more buildings, more bridges, more everything. This sort of hubbub could fill your sails or knock the wind out of them. The driver was personable. Once he learned Jimmy had never been before, he dug out a relaxed banter.

"Aw, I get all types, all types." He slouched, realizing his passenger was no one special. He had neck length hair, not greasy or gross, but a drift of dandruff on one shoulder suggested he had begun to brush it off on the right but forgot the left. "You watch TV?"

"Not so much."

"Yeah, me neither, but you get a lot of celebrities here, more than in L.A. even. Definitely more than Frisco. You watch that show with the girls? I think it's on HBO?" Jimmy did not get HBO. Jimmy had no TV. "Yeah, that's OK, me neither, but I drive some of them to their studio now and then, you know, the guys, mostly—they don't mind talking, but the girls, boy, you can't talk to them or you get reassigned. You can talk if they talk to you first, but if they don't talk, or they're on their phones, or they got your big ol' sunglasses on and looking out the window and hiding behind their lattes, you just keep your mouth shut, Tony—that's what my supervisor says to me." Jimmy admitted he liked talkative people, liked hearing other people's stories. "Oh yeah? Not so chatty?" Tony gawked sympathetically at him in the rearview mirror. "Me neither."

"Mr. Traywick, so glad to make your acquaintance," said the sugar-bowl-shaped man, shaking Jimmy's hand in Paul's living room. Dapper middle-aged men with their bowties and little round glasses—Jimmy could never tell them apart. Their dicks had more personality.

"Jimmy, this is Dexter Bash, owner of Bash Gallery on Fifth Avenue," Paul said.

Jimmy feigned delight, but he was so nervous he needed two hands to take his glass of champagne. Paul refilled Dexter's glass, though still half full—he would later tell Jimmy he had been nervous too. Dexter was famously candid in his criticism of artists.

"I think lunch is ready, yes?" Paul said, glancing at the caterer. He might not have as much on the line as Jimmy, but Dexter Bash was not the kind of contact whose patience he could test with frivolous introductions. The caterer nodded barely.

Dexter sipped his champagne, relishing the VIP treatment. "It smells divine!" He beamed unseeing at the young man ushering them into the dining room. The table was all white linens and peonies, more champagne, lobster bisque and three other courses—Jimmy could not remember what they had eaten the moment after the plates were removed, he was that astral. Dexter dropped names, Paul dropped better names. They laughed and ate and drank, excusing themselves to the bathroom together for a few minutes before dessert while Jimmy waited alone at the table.

"I'm so glad Paul invited me over," Dexter said to Jimmy when they returned, sniffling. "I do have some observations."

"You looked at my paintings already?" Jimmy asked.

"Oh yes, I insist on seeing any artist's work on my own, without the distraction of long explanations and fretting—Paul knows—that's why he invited me over early." Dexter winked and smiled archly at Paul.

While Dexter stepped out onto the terrace for a cigarette, Paul insisted Jimmy go splash some cold water on his face. "You look like you're going to faint—for real. Deep breaths!" Dexter swept in like a duchess when they convened in the library.

"Yes, well, shall we get started? First, let me say, James, I was not over-thrilled to do this favor for Paul, having seen some of your work several months ago now, wasn't it?" Jimmy's heart sank. "Oh yes—I remember now, you had those 'dreamscapes' I think you called them, and the landscapes, haha! Oh dear, yes! It's all coming back to me." Dexter guffawed grandly and swung round in his mirth to bray directly into Jimmy's face. "Yes, no 'dreamscapes' need apply! You are over a hundred years too late to be an Impressionist, dear boy. Let me put it this way: people can tear their eyes away from a sunset after a few minutes—it's a nice background for a romantic dinner, perhaps, or a suite in the Bahamas, but the world moves on rather quickly." His laughter simmered down to a pinch and stopped as his eyes came to light on a generic landscape over Paul's fireplace.

He continued. "What you want nowadays is a car crash. People will stand around all day watching that. It's the same for painting. But a good lunch greases many wheels, and Paul does have a legendary caterer, so..."

"So let's put the poor boy out of his misery, Dex," Paul said. "Don't be a cock tease..."

Dexter giggled. "Quite right—I'll sing for my supper now, shall I? James, let's get the bad news out of the way first. These three here," he pointed to the *Ghosts* paintings Jimmy had snuck in with the shipment. "I confess I was not interested in this series—I don't believe I saw these exact ones, but I think you have altered them recently, too—am I right? What is this sandy material—actual ground glass? And these pins and needles? Interesting. I see now how you have scratched and carved into the paint, and the color shifts—none of this was clear in Paul's pictures. I'm on the fence—for the moment I must exclude these from any possible arrangement we might consider."

"I understand." Jimmy looked falteringly at Paul, who gave him a little nod and a wink. "That's the bad news, you said."

Dexter rubbed his hands together. "Yes—but now we move on to these next four figures." He stood before the *Ramon and Oscar* group. "Here we have something quite different. The composition is interesting—the additional limbs, some of them broken, truncated—the kaleidoscopic quality, the eroticism—it's strangely angelic, and yet rendered in black, like a photographic negative. These are entirely different—an altogether better direction than your earlier work, if I may say. What I was not seeing before was a mature artist working through an aesthetic question, more of a technically proficient student trying on styles. Oh, I suppose it was good to see your earlier work and your progression. But here is a true vein of inquiry. I would encourage you to explore more in this line—and of course, the use of black..."

"Yes?"

"I'm afraid the only reason I remarked about what Paul calls—I can only hope facetiously—your leather painting? In that first group he showed me—there was so much black—I didn't love the painting, but I do like black—ridiculous, I know. Trite but true: black is the new black—and you can take that to the bank."

"So you didn't even really like that first painting, you're saying?" Jimmy asked, trying to keep a note of incredulity out of his voice. "Then it was nice of you to come today at all." He stepped back and bent slightly as though about to excuse himself.

Dexter chortled again, on a roll. "Dear boy, how could a lonely child daubing in an attic in—Albany, California? Heavens, I didn't know there was another Albany, as if one wasn't enough! But how could you possibly know what we—New York, that is—consider good? Not your fault. But you had the good fortune to catch the eye of one of the very few lay people I trust to introduce me to budding talent—and you have risen to the challenge, yes quite. I like these—on their own I would not consider them enough to hang a show around, but then we move on to this next group, and here I think I can hazard a little excitement."

"The *V*s?" Jimmy asked.

"Is that what you call them?" Dexter arched an eyebrow. "Oh, we might consider changing the titles, certainly. In any event—bravo! These, dear boy, are good—without question, this work captures a fresh angle I would most certainly include in my upcoming group show. I'm quite excited, actually—THESE are your car crash...!" He paused, inhaling deeply as though about to scream, his eyes growing wide and bright, but then he only exhaled and shivered violently.

Paul didn't seem to notice, and clapped Jimmy on the back. "And here we go..."

"So you like these?" Jimmy asked, slightly alarmed.

Dexter went on. "Oh yes! Quite aside from the subject matter, which is interesting—I'm not sure how many recognizably trans models are featured in figure painting lately, it's worth investigating, leave that to me. But, no, there's an attitude in the execution, in the brushwork, in the emotion you've brought out that does seem to capture both a reluctance and an attraction at the same time—forgive me for saying so, but a feeling many people might have to the subject itself."

"Themself," Jimmy corrected. "They're non-binary."

Dexter ignored him. "And Paul tells me you executed all of these in just a few months—it's possible the time constraint freed you to check that self-consciousness so evident in your previous work, let loose your muse—or perhaps you simply found a muse in your model." Jimmy admitted he had started to trust himself more. "So common for young painters to agonize over every brushstroke, every color, this detail or that—they get in their own way, half the time—and sometimes they do need someone cracking a whip."

Paul preened at this. "I knew you had it in you, Jimmy—just needed a kick in the pants."

"There is a sensuality to these, too—I think you've hit the right note, but we'd need to see more, and some bigger, is that possible? It's beastly but even serious collectors just need something to hang over their sofas—and you can ask for more when it's bigger, it helps to nudge your price point higher."

"More, bigger, yes." Jimmy nodded.

"I never feature a new artist in a group show without a minimum of nine works, ideally more, if things sell we like to hang new things in their place, keep the curation up to snuff—it's partly to do with the size of the gallery really, if we are going to fill it up, assuming your new work were to be as persuasive as these. We'd need to polish your story, of course—and maybe weave your model into the mix. Do you have a client list?"

Jimmy's voice cracked as he lied about the only Mission local he had ever actually laid eyes on. "Tracy Chapman bought one of my paintings."

Paul's eyes pierced Jimmy for a moment, then darted to Dexter. "He's new, Dex, I told you—unmolded clay. You'll have to sort all that shit out."

"How interesting. I'm thinking: Outsider artist, with a picture or two of you—couldn't hurt, you are delicious, James—you haven't done any porn? No? Oh, good—all mine, then. Social media?"

"No."

"Dear me. So young to be a Luddite."

Paul interjected. "Outsider artist? Are you kidding? This is the whitest boy on the planet!"

Dexter corrected himself. "Neuve invention," he pronounced, "it's a subgenre, to explain your naiveté. The group show is centered around millennials, and I've had a drop out—OD, very sad. You can have something before the end of the year for a show next summer, James? Obviously the publicity won't be able to feature every artist, but there's always a stand out who captures the most attention and we like to be prepared. Fresno? Good lord. Do you surf?" Jimmy explained that Fresno was hundreds of miles from the Pacific. "More oranges, less waves then—sun-kissed—no matter. Do you know I have never had the slightest desire to visit California—well, Los Angeles of course, but that's a world unto itself."

"I'd like to keep these seven," Dexter said, pointing to the three of Vic and four of Ramon and Oscar, "and see what my marketing girl can make of it, do some research on comparables and valuation, etcetera. I'll have a contract drawn up next week. I really must be going—so nice to have met you, James—lots of homework for you! Talk soon!" Dexter Bash flitted out the door before Jimmy could say thank you.

"What's a Luddite?" he asked.

NINETEEN

Paul had promised to take Jimmy to the new Whitney Museum after they finished with Dexter. "I know a guy who gets me free tickets."

"Fuck the sights, if you want to make it in this town, we gotta polish you up a bit, expose you to some culture. And your clothes, well..." Jimmy blushed and glanced into the front seat of the cab to see if the driver was listening. He had bought a new shirt with a pattern of Japanese blossoms at Ross especially for the meeting with Dexter, and a new braided leather belt and loafers. "Anyway, your education starts now."

Barely twenty minutes into their visit, Paul was talking a mile a minute, rattling nuggets from his catalog of facts about each painting, then dashing on to the next. When Jimmy tried to linger at one piece that caught his eye—hot boys cruising by the sea—Paul sniffed, "That also-ran," and pulled him along by the arm. He kept glancing at his watch. Finally Jimmy asked if everything was OK.

"Yeah, sorry, I don't mean to rush you, I was just here at the opening gala. So listen, I've got a meeting with my editor at four, he's heading to the Hamptons for three weeks and I need to check in with him."

"Hamptons?"

Paul rolled his eyes. "Anyway, how about I let you take this at your own pace? Walk around the Village for a bit if you like, and then I'll meet you back here in front—I'll text you."

Jimmy missed the torrent of helpful trivia—he was always a little in awe of the work of famous artists, always a lot bewildered by the imagery and styles. Mrs. Stacey's slideshows had been helpful, but somehow, making his own art, knowing his own process, left him more perplexed not less. Was he missing something? Many works inspired no reaction in him one way or the other. As he stood and examined several pieces in a row, large works on adjacent walls, piles of objects here and there, he thought of cruising at the bars, all so many cardboard cutouts—opaque, flat, dumb to his understanding. Just the fact of their being collected in a museum must mean someone thought they were good, right? He did not speak this dialect though he felt he should. Instead of going on, he circled back to the artists Paul had been explaining.

Was he creating art to understand art? From idea to bones to flesh and hair and clothes? Would he someday begin to see beyond the impenetrable surface? He wandered back through the galleries and came again to the painting Paul had dismissed earlier. An older woman, tall, with a kind face and enormous candied glasses, stooped to murmur in the ear of her companion, an ancient, glaze-eyed woman who appeared as groggy as Jimmy felt.

"Look at the baguettes," the tall woman was saying, "phallic symbols obviously, but treated differently, you see? Here, trapped under the woman's arm—the old guard, chaperoning the beleaguered veteran, the man in his prime, the young object of their interest. But here, another loaf held frankly by another youth, free of the knot of society, guiding the bicycle seat toward his buttocks, you see? And the object of his interest beginning to undress—just a gesture, his near nakedness emphasized by the tan line." She pointed as she spoke, careful to hold her beringed fingers some distance from the canvas. The other woman looked but did not speak, nod, or move at all. Jimmy almost laughed to think she might be a statue, another piece of art intended to deceive the patrons, but then at last she turned and shuffled stiffly away as her companion remained gazing at the picture. She glanced down at Jimmy and offered a faint smile.

He smiled back up at her. "That was very interesting—thank you, I hope you don't mind my listening—I'm not sure I would have picked up on any of that. I'm feeling a little lost."

"Not at all, dear. Is this your first time at the new Whitney?"

"First time in New York—and I just have one day."

She commended his choice of museum. "I try to come every month on the free day, you know, but my friend is in town so I splurged. And where are you from?"

"San Francisco."

"Oh you have some very good museums." He admitted he had been a couple times to MOMA but always found himself feeling tired and overwhelmed after an hour or so. "Museum brain." She nodded. "That's why I try to come often—like meditation, you know—you get more out of it with small regular bursts than a single big gorge."

"What a good idea. Like a weekend getaway."

"Yes, that's it—a weekend in Vermont rather than an around the world tour." She smiled demurely. "Or maybe Fire Island?" He did not take her meaning.

"Do you really think the lady in the hat is trying to keep those men away from the blond boy?"

She turned to look again. "Why not? It seems like they might have had some fun if she hadn't shown up. Why else the bread?

Maybe just lunch." She simultaneously nodded her head and bounced her shoulders with a smile, as though laughing with her whole body. "Maybe the artist was hungry when he painted it, or maybe he was horny—or maybe both? Do you always know why you paint?"

Jimmy was caught off guard. "How did you know I'm a painter?"

She reached down and took his hand, holding it up to examine the intricate spatterings of paint never completely washed away. "I don't read palms, dear, but these are an artist's hands." She held it for a moment longer than necessary. "But what do you think of it?" she asked, nodding at the painting.

"My friend called it an all so ran—I have no idea what he meant."

Her face screwed up for a moment in confusion, and then she shrugged. "What an odd turn of phrase. But I mean, you dear, what do YOU think of it?"

"Pretty sexy, I guess—but now that I heard what you said I'm starting to see other things in it too—that girl, why is she writing?"

"Yes! Why IS she writing when there are so many handsome men standing around? It takes time to see," she said, bowing her head closely toward him, not unlike she had with her friend. "I never had the time when I was working and raising children and looking after a husband. Now I'm retired, my children are grown, and I'm a widow—I have all the time in the world—or do I?" He looked at her cautiously askance, but she winked. "The end of the world," she continued and then laughed when he nodded blankly. She pointed to the title on the sign next to the painting. "That's what that means, in French. I better catch up with my friend, dear—see you next time?"

Museum brain. Probably not fatal. After staring at the picture for a few more minutes, seeing all the things she had pointed out but drawing no further conclusions, Jimmy decided to head to this village Paul kept talking about—how far could it be? He pictured windmills for some reason.

As he walked out into the street, he was reminded of South of Market. He would not consult the map on his phone but wander around by instincts alone. Greenwich Street seemed a good bet to find his way to Greenwich Village, and he turned right, wanting to wander and soak up as much of the city as he could. In less than two hours they would be on the way to the hotel, closer to the airport, Paul said—no time to see Central Park, or Times Square, or the Statue of Liberty.

The majority of his impressions of New York came from September 2001. He was almost ten, and the school had sent word that everyone should stay home.

"It's war, then," James Sr. had said flatly, retreating to the family room to watch old recorded golf tournaments. His mother cried—the first time she had ever cried in front of him, and the last until his father died. He comforted her the only way he knew how in those long hours in front of the TV, with plates of cinnamon-sugar toast, microwave popcorn, and a Snoopy mug full of jellybeans from his father's secret stash in the pantry.

"Good grief, what's this?" she said. "What a feast! Thank you, sweetheart." She held him so tight he had a hard time breathing. Frequent refills of her wine glass stemmed the tears—thank god the rosé was a screw-top.

His ten-year-old impression (never replaced by any other) was of a tall city not so much on fire as on smoke—gray, dim, desolate, haunted by dusty people stumbling around in ashen suits, clutching bags and briefcases like half-forgotten rag dolls dragged on the ground.

At least the gray October sky over this neighborhood of low brick buildings seemed less fraught as he walked, though neither a village nor any New York he had ever seen.

As Greenwich Street bent to the right, a lone skyscraper loomed into view like a twisted, square syringe, almost certainly not the Empire State Building, that much he knew at least. He had expected more glass and steel, more people. This suburb (it must be) seemed almost humdrum. By the time he reached Christopher Street he was thinking he must have turned the wrong way on Greenwich, that the village must have been in the other direction. On a whim he turned left on the street with his name—his middle name anyway, his almost name.

Marlys had implored him to introduce himself as James when he told her he was flying to New York for an interview.

"Opportunities like this don't grow on trees, James—you're not a child, I can say these things to you, and I'm telling you: do not continue with that ridiculous baby's name. You'll never be taken seriously."

"You know your cousin Jimmy Locke changed his name to Jim, and that was two years ago already, and he's a year younger than you," she had told him that same summer as the Filoli trip. He would be starting at the junior high in the fall, kids would think he was a baby for still calling himself Jimmy.

"But I don't like Jim, it's so short," he said.

Marlys decided to simply start calling him James, found reasons to call him by his new name in front of others. Inevitably, she had to explain when people who had always known him as Jimmy looked confused, and for a short time he became "Little James" and his father, "Big James." Neither he nor his father cared much for this new iteration. Jimmy disliked the constant reminder that he was so much smaller than his classmates, and his father, not an especially tall man, had gained a few pounds as he was approaching seventy and would just as soon have left his name and the word "big" at a respectable distance from each other.

Attempting to wrest control of the situation, Jimmy announced he should be called by his middle name, Christopher. He liked the association with Christopher Robin, and Pooh. His decision met with pointed silence at the dinner table. Henceforth, he was known as James at home—James Jr. if he and his father both answered his mother's calls from different rooms—Jimmy if his she was tired or tipsy, and by a small coterie of classmates who remembered his name was Jimmy before it was James.

Moving to San Francisco, he had reverted back to Jimmy, his preferred, true, original name, never having seen the need nor wishing to change it in the first place. Still, he retained a fondness for "Christopher," still had his tattered Pooh packed away somewhere, sometimes wondering whether his penchant for sweet and burly bears was not somehow related to the comfort and confidences they had shared under the covers in his childhood.

But where were all those skyscrapers he had seen from the plane? He walked a few more blocks—"Village Cigars"—he must be getting close, and then there was a park across the street. Crossing the three-way intersection, he entered the sliver of a green space, wrought-iron fence, four ghostly white figures, seated and standing, statues apparently. A tour group of ten or so people listened to a short woman nestled among them—he could hear a thick accent but not what she said. In a moment he was already through the postage stamp park and choosing the left-hand path back out to the sidewalk. Another statue, green with patina, stood further in a fenced area. "General Sheridan" had a most handsome mustache and looked every bit the macho man with his hat, uniform, and saber.

It was a nice little park anyway, lush. He noticed a building and a gaggle of people milling about taking pictures. The Stonewall Inn. A trio of bears in leather vests, beards wagging, seemed like they knew what was what, so Jimmy sidled up to the nearest of them, the oldest and roundest, touching his forearm hesitantly. The bear turned, looking down as though expecting a child at his sleeve, then raised his eyes to peer over his sunglasses quizzically.

"Sorry—I was just wondering," Jimmy started, "what's the deal with all this? Is it a Civil War monument, or...?"

The man grimaced, forehead wrinkling, head shaking in confusion. "Civil War? Of a sort, I guess. You're kidding, right?"

Jimmy pressed on. "I mean, there's that General statue. And Stonewall ... Jackson? I didn't love American History..."

The man pronounced clearly, as if he might be the one mistaken, "Are you really asking me if The Stonewall Inn is a monument of the American Civil War?" He began to chuckle wheezily and turned to his companions. "This child wants to know if this is a Civil War monument!" He almost screamed with laughter. The other two cocked their heads and looked round, mouths half open.

The biggest, burliest one said in a clear tenor, “This must be a joke—is it Candid Camera? Do they still do Candid Camera?” He clutched the first by the shoulder, looking around as though for a hidden camera crew. “What’s that new one? Dunked? Skunked?” They erupted in mirth as Jimmy blinked, now truly perplexed.

“Thank you,” said the baby bear, “but we don’t want to buy any cookies today.” They howled and floated off, Jimmy’s questions unanswered.

TWENTY

They drove out to Long Island City in Paul's Audi as the sun set, and crossing the bridge it slowly dawned on Jimmy. "So Greenwich Village...?" he said tentatively.

"Cute neighborhood, huh?" Jimmy's inner compass spun dizzily. "What'd ya see?"

"The Stonewall Inn?"

"Ha! Good for you, you get a drink? Shit, you know I've never even set foot in the place—it's like one of those things a good gay is supposed to do..."

Dammit! He could have had a drink.

Parked and checked in, they went up to the room and Paul set about playing bartender on the desk

"Bolli Stoli?" he asked, and to Jimmy's blank look he said, "Champagne cocktail?"

"What?"

"AbFab? Bolli and Stoli? Seriously?" He pulled bottles out of his bag, Bollinger champagne and Stolichnaya vodka. "I'm too old for this shit," he said under his breath.

Jimmy poked around the room. Ultra-modern and chic, the floor was bleached, distressed, maybe a laminate, but the headboard and linens were crisp, expensive, and new—exotic woods, plush pillows, snow white terry robes. He played with the dimmer on the old-fashioned lightbulb fixtures—Paul looked up from mixing drinks as the lights lowered and raised again.

"That's handy—turn it down nice and low, kiddo—for your sake as much as mine." Jimmy turned it to a soft glow as he looked at Paul—he was handsome, yes, but yes, also old enough to be his father—shit, maybe even grandfather. Seeing his own tattered duffel sitting next to Paul's black and gray Louis Vuitton, he felt a sudden embarrassment—the hotel, the flight, the introduction to Dexter—everything.

He drifted to the huge window wall, the city view across the East River sweeping as far as he could see in either direction. Where San Francisco was bite-sized, here was the whole buffet. Through the window, he examined individual buildings in the skyline. There was the syringe-shaped building he had seen earlier far off to the left. Paul joined him by the window with their drinks.

"Well, cheers boy!" he said. "You're on your way! It went better with Dexter than I hoped—it can't hurt you're so cute." He leaned down and gave Jimmy a deep, sloppy kiss. "I wasn't a hundred percent sure he was going to feel your vibe, you are so not New York..." He trailed off and turned to look out across the river, his arm around Jimmy's neck. "Nice view."

"That there...?" Jimmy said, pointing to the syringe.

"Freedom Tower."

"The one that replaced the World Trade Center?"

"The very one."

His eyes tracked uptown. "So that's the Empire State Building."

"Yes, and the Chrysler Building there," Paul went on, pointing, "and Trump Tower, Rockefeller Center..." He sipped—Jimmy gulped. "I was there the day Trump came down the escalator, back in June—I wrote a blurb about his announcement. You know I think he might actually do it—Hillary's got so much baggage, not that Trump doesn't, but he's got charisma, and she's got a pussy, so ... don't be surprised if he wins it." Jimmy said nothing but noticed the tinge of admiration in Paul's voice. "My money's on Trump anyway. Seriously! I've already got three grand on him winning with a buddy of mine—he gave me crazy odds but I've got that feeling—if he wins it I make a fucking mint!" He chewed gently on Jimmy's neck, then took the empty glass from him. "Take your clothes off, boy—I'll fix you another."

The reasons for spending the night in the hotel had come fast and easy. Close to the airport—Jimmy had an early flight (at one in the afternoon). He got a great deal on this hot hotel—newly renovated and look at the view (again). And there were the perks from his club card; if he spent just one night every month in a member hotel, he got free gym access all month, weekday rates and free upgrades on car rentals. He traveled so much for work it was worth it to spring for the odd night on his own dime. Also Paul had a big surprise for him—a friend with good drugs and an enormous cock.

"Oh!"

And, last but not least, his neighbor across the hall was a notorious gossip, the old biddy with the Pomeranian and permanent bitch-face.

"I'm not worried about you, of course," he assured Jimmy, "but Nico, you know—let's just say he looks the part."

"Part?"

"You'll see."

By nine o'clock, the champagne was gone and most of the bottle of Stoli too. Jimmy's ass was humming—Paul took a

Viagra before they got started and had gone at him for an hour. But when Jimmy was ready for more, and Paul was feeling eager to get the real party started, he pulled out a little baggie and offered a tiny bump from the end of a key. "Ever try K?"

"No, but—"

"You'll love it."

And he was right. Jimmy dissolved into a slurry. "You know Paul I never have thanked you properly for all your help I mean this deal with Dexter this could be it this could really be my big break sometimes I wondered if it would ever happen if I was maybe just kidding myself and then along came you and you swooped in and really believed in me and you're so nice just a really nice guy and sexy too I mean I like older men anyway but you really are special and handsome you know that picture I took of you I used for the portrait I mean wow you look like a movie star or something I'm so glad you like it I think it did turn out really good probably the best one I've ever painted so I'm glad it was yours because you really deserve my sincere appreciation and I still haven't thanked you properly..."

Paul held up the key with another bump. "That's what tonight is all about, kiddo—have another."

In the eons that passed that night there were a few crystalline moments. The knock at the door rolled like a throbbing bass drum over Jimmy, announcing the arrival of a Greek one hundred feet tall, a warrior arrayed in black leather armor, hands as big, rough, and strong as charging wild boars. Jimmy was spun around head over heels over face down, now his ass was the drum, now an icy wind flushed across his backside—York Peppermint Patties in D minor and scarlet—he wiggled his ass to the beat. The Greek growled and snorted.

An angel giggled from the armchair with delight. Jimmy cocked one eye open as Paul bent over a pile of snow. He wondered where on Earth a body could buy a snowmobile small enough to plow such tiny straight lines. Paul and the angel laughed, side by side, one in each eye and each ear, and then he realized, of course. Of course! Paul was an angel, he really, really was—now offering him the key with another puff of cloud balanced on it.

The Greek bent down to look him in the face, his beard immaculate and the close-cropped furred helmet on his head. Jimmy wished he could grow a beard half so handsome. The Greek's muscles rippled endlessly up and down, a shimmering bronze carapace. He stood back and slowly pulled from under his loincloth a trophy—a creature from the depths of the sea, his pet kraken wet with brine, bulging and bucking in his caressing gauntlet.

So this was his life now. Now he had been taken captive. This, his new master, a son of Poseidon. Anyway, he had Paul with him, that was comforting. He shut his eyes tight.

A bass horn trumpeted. "Been hanging around the playground again, Paulie? Fuck that is a sweet piece of ass—I'm gonna rape the shit outta that hole..."

The angel replied. "Later, babe—me first."

Rough seas, for sure—sometimes Jimmy felt the pitching, rolling waves, other times he was the waves, slapped and tossed by a maelstrom threatening to split him open. Finally, he sloshed into some gently tumbling chambered cavern, all steel-pink opalescence and sweet slimes. He would be tossed, rubbed and polished away into oblivion, slowly, gratefully—a shard, into sea glass, into grain, into nothingness.

It was OK. He was so fucking tired. He let go.

Hello Eternity, you seem nice.

The tide gurgled. “He may look like the wreck of the Hesperus but that boy is going to make a big splash. He’s a really good artist. I know a guy, he’s going to polish him up—not too much—try to sell him as a white-trash Basquiat. It’s a long shot but the guy likes to throw spaghetti at the wall with these group shows, see who sticks.”

The sea murmured in reply.

“It was a poem, about a ship—never mind. Hey, you free to come to Atlantic City weekend after next?”

The sea seemed amenable but began to rumble again.

“No babe, my ass needs a break—use his.”

TWENTY-ONE

"Bowling. Really?" Jimmy had doubts as they walked to Albany Lanes. Vic wanted to see the old place one more time, before—

"Parenthood." Vic had decided. "Definitely not motherhood."

The old bowling alley was a couple blocks down San Pablo, and Vic was feeling feisty—baby hormones, they said. Back in high school, students could bowl for P.E., so Vic and their friends had availed themselves of the novelty to smoke a joint on the drive from school.

"Those were some fun times," they said, a bounce in their step. "Let's see how bad my game has gotten—I haven't been back since I graduated!"

Meanwhile, Jimmy had never bowled in his life.

"What if I suck? I'm scrawny. I got hollow bones."

Vic scoffed. "Oh stop, dingdong—I used to have a one-forty average, smoking dope."

Still, Jimmy had doubts. Balls were not his friends—throughout school he had been a well-known sissy picked dead last every time for sports of all flavors. No, he had been a jump rope and swings kinda kid until junior high, then intramural tennis. Even the tennis racket used to make his wrists creak. "Bird-boned" his father had called him, the bookend to his other favorite phrase, "Like a girl." But he felt no need to put on a butch show with Vic.

They were settling into friendship smoother than they had become lovers. Certainly Jimmy liked Vic as a person more than he wanted to be his boyfriend, and apparently the feeling was mutual. Vic had been on a date already—no looking back at their swing and a miss—though the guy disappeared the minute he found out Vic was pregnant. Literally the minute: he walked out of the bar without a word when Vic explained why they were fine just drinking a Coke.

"Typical, huh? 'Loves me some freaky non-binary sex, but fuck that baby shit—too real!'"

That they felt comfortable sharing with Jimmy was a happy sign. The feeling they had crossed a threshold to a bond which might last through some ups and downs was new and welcome.

And then there was Feo. Jimmy had held off telling Vic about him until they were back solid after their blowup.

(Meanwhile, Dee was thrilled they were now a couple.

"He is a GREAT guy!" he gushed as the weeks wound on, when the calls and the dates and the sweetness and especially the sex kept going. "I mean, I have never seen him angry—he's always sweet as pie, and generous? His customers LOVE him—have you seen the Yelp reviews for the restaurant? He helps the old lady on the third floor with her groceries—Ha! That's me!—and so big, and handsome, and manly, and big! Oy! But what an odd couple you two make. Like a chihuahua and a Saint Bernard. It's obscene."

"Yes, it is," Jimmy gloated.

"Marry him the minute he asks you, Mamie!")

Jimmy supposed Albany Lanes must make its money on the weekends. Definitely high schoolers only bowled if they were getting credit from the school, but Vic had guessed they might at least find an afternoon seniors' league playing.

"Wow, I've never seen it this quiet," they were saying just as someone hit a loud strike to cheers in the far lane, the only one occupied. They got shoes and Vic tried to explain the scoring, but Jimmy pooh-poohed it all away.

"Absolutely definitely never going to have to keep score myself—can we just toss the balls around a bit? Oof! These are heavy!" The rack of balls behind the lanes looked to him more like equipment for some prehistoric pastime. "Do they have any lighter ones? Jesus, I can hear my wrist popping—listen!" He popped his wrist by Vic's ear and the clicking was in fact audible.

"Yikes! Well, they have to be a little heavy or they won't knock the pins over, girl—here, try this one, I use the lightest ball too—almost the lightest." Jimmy lifted the suggested ball—it was lighter, if not actually light. And pink.

"Alright, we'll see."

Vic stepped right up to the lane, taking their starting pose. "Watch me—we won't start a game yet, I'll let you throw a couple practice balls while I get some drinks. Watch! Stand, aim, step, swing, release—so easy, my abuela can do it—she ain't half bad." They took their shot and left one pin standing. "Shit—I got some practicing to do." When their ball came back, they took the second shot and got the spare. "See? No problem—you go—don't step over the line, and don't forget to breathe."

"Step, swing AND breathe?" Jimmy was far from convinced. He took his shot. The ball went straight in the gutter and barely made it down the lane.

Vic stifled a laugh. "Oh dang! At least give it some oomph, huh? If I have to walk down the lane to get your ball I'll die of shame. Keep practicing! What do you want to drink? I'm having Coke, obviously."

"Something manly."

He threw a couple more shots, both in the gutter, while Vic was at the bar. He imagined abuelas averting their eyes. The place was mostly empty, thank god, and in the end, they never kept real score. Vic made a couple notes on their own and seemed pleased with their progress.

"All things considered..." they said. "Pregnant AND out of practice, I'm still better than you." Jimmy downed the rest of his drink, and over the next two shots, knocked down four pins. "I think you're just nervous—go get the next round, maybe you'll loosen up." Jimmy went up to the bar half-hoping Vic might be right, half-hoping that if he was bad enough he would never be invited to play again.

The lady bartender was nice, her face a mandala of eye-shadow and pores.

"What'll you have, sweetie?" He ordered and leaned against the nearest stool. At the far end, in a shadow where one of the fluorescent lights had given out, a man hunched over the bar, beer mug in hand, empty pitcher at his elbow, looking at Jimmy. Ramon. Fuck.

There was no ignoring him—Jimmy had already stared for several seconds before realizing who it was. He nodded and ambled down the bar.

"Hey, how are you?"

No answer, no movement at all, just glazed eyes and slack face. He was hammered, staring into the distance down the bar. When his eyes finally swam toward Jimmy and focused, he gave an exaggerated sway of his whole body and threw up an arm in greeting.

"Hola!" he slurred loudly. "Jimmy, my best friend!" He pushed at the stool nearest him to make a space for Jimmy, but too hard, and it fell over with a clatter. The lady behind the bar looked around briefly. She put the drinks on the bar at the ordering station rather than bringing them down to him as Ramon waved to her and held up his empty pitcher. Jimmy picked up the stool. No hug, and definitely no sitting down.

"Oops—it's cool." He clapped Ramon's shoulder as he stepped away toward his waiting drinks. "Hey, all good?"

Ramon nodded, seemed barely to have noticed the stool falling over and held the pitcher up again. The bartender ignored him. "Yeah—good. You good?"

"Yeah, real good—playing with my friend, yeah? OK, see you later!" He was inching away, waving at the lady—be right there—but Ramon gestured for him to come closer. He took a half step back in, afraid to be rude, and lowered his head as though to catch a whisper, hoping just a whisper, not more commotion.

"That your friend?" Ramon asked, squinting toward the lanes. "Your good friend, huh?" An unnerving intensity cut through the drunkenness.

Jimmy nodded his head. "Yeah, my friend—I gotta get back—take care now."

"You like that?" Ramon asked. A darkness came over his face as he stared at the distant figure of Vic—a slight grimace, a hard look of disgust. Jimmy took a step away.

"Sé lo que te gusta, puto." Ramon brandished his stump and poured the dregs of his beer over it.

Before it could go any further, Jimmy turned abruptly, no looking back. "Hey, say hi to Oscar!" he said loudly to the room, hoping it sounded final, and this time when he heard more mumbling behind him he did not turn around. He paid for the drinks and gave the lady a big tip.

"Thanks, sweetie—don't worry, he's mostly harmless," she said.

"I know, he lives in my building—it's fine—thank you!"

When he got back to the lane, he handed Vic their Coke and slurped his own. "Drink up. We gotta go."

Since they cut their bowling short and Jimmy had an hour to kill, they hopped over to a bar a few blocks from the bowling alley. Most of the other customers at the Topsy Turvy Pub were nursing beers around a game on the TV above the bar. Jimmy and Vic sat in a notched and worn wooden booth.

"Maybe I should reach out to Oscar, see if he needs to talk—you're a little close to the situation..." Vic was saying.

"I don't know—he'd know I told you what was going on, and I just don't want to deal. I feel really bad for him, but he says he can handle it. Ramon pretty much leaves him alone now I guess, so..."

"Alright, let me know. Hey, wanna see the flyer for Dee's Halloween show?" Jimmy flipped through the pictures on Vic's phone. Dee had a new costume—a witchy hat, puffed orange sleeves, striped stockings, and a blacked-out tooth.

He read the headline. "'Oranges Whoranges'...?"

Vic laughed. "Some kid show from the seventies. It's a song."

"Yeah, H.R. Puffenstuff. He made me watch it on YouTube. Pretty sure it's poranges."

"Shit—did I get it wrong?"

"Nah. Whoranges rhymes too."

Vic sipped their Coke and looked at Jimmy over the rim of the glass. "So what's about this Russian guy?"

"Goddamn Dee!"

"It's cool! Did you really expect him to keep it quiet? Secrets are to Dee like hairballs are to cats."

Jimmy handed back the phone. "That's who I'm having

dinner with later. And I was wondering if you would maybe want to join us? It's pretty new, but I think it could be serious."

"Oh." Vic's eyes wandered toward the floor. "Where are you going?"

"Emeryville. I'm dying for some fish tacos."

"Blondie's? Tempting—they make better fish tacos than my mom."

Jimmy cocked his head. "That's not a yes. Are you OK with this?"

"Yeah, yeah. I mean we haven't much talked about next steps, I wanted to give you time to process the whole papi thing. No promises, but I sorta thought about asking if you wanted to find a place together maybe, if you wanted to be more hands on. I mean, just co-parenting, but I don't want to cramp your style. Does he know about baby makes three?"

"Yes. He says he loves kids."

"Do you love him?"

"I don't want to jinx it."

"Then I better meet him and talk you up." Jimmy texted Feo they'd be having another guest, eating for two.

After dinner, and a playful evening that ended with Vic's enthusiastic thumbs up and a whispered "Fantastic!" as they dropped them back at their car, Feo pulled in front of Jimmy's building, backed expertly into the driveway next door, and turned off the engine. He pulled Jimmy close for a kiss. It was cold, but Bay Area-autumn cold—light jackets and shorts.

"Wish I could stay, cricket," Feo said.

"Wish you could too, but you know—work, and I got some shit to think about." Jimmy pulled away and turned in his seat. "Vic really liked you."

"I like Vic," Feo replied. "They're cute, huh? I think that baby will be adorable." He cracked a smile, but Jimmy was intent.

"So. Are you serious about being OK with the baby, and wanting to stick around, and..." He trailed off.

"And loving you?" Feo said. "Is that what you really ask?"

"I mean, we've only been going out for a bit—but it's a big responsibility, I'm not sure I'm ready myself. We can keep it casual too, I guess."

"OK, then I tell you now it may be only a little while, but it's not a little love I feel for you, cricket. Maybe you forget I'm alone too. Oh yes, friends—oh yes, uncle and cousins and good times at the restaurant. But I go home to empty bed. Maybe even a bear like me wishes for someone next to me when I fall asleep, and when I wake up. The night is a big lonely place. You're mine now—if that's what you want."

"I do want," Jimmy said.

Had he forgotten to lock the top bolt on the way out? Nothing seemed amiss in the kitchen, his laptop and digital camera on the counter where he left them.

Nothing out of place up in the studio. He threw his jacket on the bed as he turned on his bedside lamp and saw the dark spot on the bed. He picked his jacket back up off a wide circle on the bedspread. He touched it—undeniably wet. He sniffed it. Piss, cold, at least an hour or so old. What the...?

Someone with a key had come in while he was out and pissed on the bed—in anger, in spite, in a drunken rage. But not "someone."

His heart pounded as he stripped the bed. The stain went straight through into his new mattress, a big, soaked puddle over half the bed. Not a little squirt but an all-out pitcher of beer piss. He had been meaning to get an absorbent mattress pad. Towels had no effect. He dabbed at it with a wet cloth, but he would have to get some upholstery cleaner in the morning. In the meantime, he was sleeping on a wet spot tonight.

He went ahead and poured himself a big glass of vodka and sat on the window seat, staring down at the dumpster in the alley. No cigarette burning in the dark, no cloud of smoke. It was ten o'clock. Kitty was a night owl. She would want to know what was going on.

He had had his suspicions for a while. It was no ghost, opening doors and drawers he'd left closed; no poltergeist leaving tissues in the bathroom wastebasket he thought he'd emptied; not himself moving things to odd places during one of his blackouts. No wondering anymore. Not someone. Ramon. Motherfucker had been letting himself in, who knew how many times. He downed his glass and decided, yes, time to talk to Kitty, she was the landlord after all. She could have the locks changed and keep the key herself for emergencies, not give Ramon a copy.

He patted his empty pocket for his cellphone on the way out the door and turned back to look for it on the counter—he wanted to text Feo real quick. A figure lurked out of the corner of his vision as he stumbled through the doorway. He startled and cried out as he jostled up against someone waiting just outside his door.

Ramon grabbed Jimmy by the wrist as though to steady him but twisted it sharply.

"What are you doing!"

"What the fuck you doing?" Ramon spat back. He had a mock-friendly smile on his face, his eyes unfocused but hardened. Jimmy squirmed sideways into the hall, wanting to get past him down the stairs to Kitty's. He kept trying to break free, but Ramon's grip was solid.

"I'm gonna talk to Kitty about you, Ramon—I saw your little gift—it's done, we're done! I was trying to be nice but we're done!" He tried to sweep past.

"Eh, you want loca travesti, huh?" His grip was crushing.

"Let go!" Jimmy yelled. He wrenched his arm out of Ramon's grasp hard enough to knock it up against the corner of the wall and jammed the same wrist he had hurt before. He yelped.

"Puta!" Ramon growled.

Jimmy backed away. "No! No!" He kicked at Ramon's shin but that only brought a derisive chuckle. He bolted down the stairs. In the small of his back, a forceful kick from a boot sent him careening down to the landing between floors. He slammed hard up against the wall face first trying to protect his wrist. Ramon thundered down the steps after him.

He would run downstairs, out of the building, get away—Feo! He started down again, but Ramon yanked him by the hair backwards. He fell half on the steps and half on the landing. On his back, eyes closed, he flailed with his arms, trying to hit or scratch at anything, yelling.

Ramon lurched away. At first Jimmy thought he had fallen down the stairs in the tussle. By the time he righted himself, though, someone else loomed over Ramon on the floor.

Oscar, fist raised and ready to strike, screamed at his father. "You stupid piece of shit! Stay down!"

There was no contest. Oscar had at least a hundred pounds on him and was used to knocking people around on the football field. They glared for a long moment. Finally, Ramon crumbled and rolled on the floor, thrashing and moaning. He pounded his fist on the floor in a fury.

Oscar picked Jimmy up and stood him on his feet.

"Are you OK?"

"I'm sorry," Jimmy whispered hoarsely, fleeing upstairs.

[Interview transcripts edited for clarity.]

You mentioned you felt like you wanted to make amends to Oscar when we first spoke.

I've never really forgiven myself for how I handled that situation. I should have said something, called someone—anything, really, but he begged me not to and I just wanted to move on with things. I had so much else going on—a baby! Feo, my show—I was being pulled in a million different directions. And there was a part of me that didn't want to spoil it, I guess, even after I found out how old he was, I didn't want to burn any bridges. Things were still new with Feo, what if it didn't work out? I had a history with Oscar, I knew we had a connection, I didn't want to just throw it away.

Did you love him?

I'll never forget what my old roommate Vern said to me one time, it might have been the night I was painting him and we were smoking meth—he started wondering out loud why we had waited so long to hook up, and I was like, "Dude, because we're both bottoms?" He seemed disappointed for a minute, and then he was like, "Yeah, yeah, stupid, sorry. You know how many times I've fallen in love with a trick after fifteen minutes? Every single time."

I've been there…

I know, there's an element of truth to it, right? You like someone, they're nice to you, you have great sex—thank you, tina, or vodka, or whatever your poison—but that's the easy stuff.

You're right, more relationships end because the people can't get along than because the sex is bad.
Exactly. For weeks, Oscar was still coming upstairs—this is while I was dating Feo, meanwhile, I mean, we still have an open relationship, most gay couples do—and the fact that I had ended things with Ramon, I think, made Oscar feel even more special. I'd be horny, I'd be drunk, or vice versa—he'd text me, I'd spent all day working and then coming home to paint, I deserved to feel good, come on up. But it's like a summer thunderstorm, you know, everything is hot and heavy and coiled up like a spring, and then the clouds burst and dump a bunch of rain, and it's over. Every time Oscar left I was back to that feeling that it was wrong, he was too young, I was using him. And the problem was I would say things back to him, you know, he was trying to start a real relationship, I suppose, or maybe we already were in one. Damn. I still get all churned up when I think about him.

It's OK, take a minute if you need to—
Anyway. I made the mistake of telling him that I would have kept dating him if it weren't for his dad. I didn't tell him about Feo, I just wanted to keep it all separate, you know? I had feelings for him, I might have considered a longer term thing with Oscar if Ramon was out of the picture.

TWENTY-TWO

A strange man's deep, sonorous voice on the phone—not an unfamiliar situation to Jimmy first thing in the morning.

("I have a husband, by the way. And a kid."

"I should have told you I tested positive for chlamydia, sorry."

"I'm on the down-low—if you see me with my wife, I'll kill you if you say anything.")

"Mr. Traywick? Harold Fisher, here, attorney at law, New York. Paul Allenson asked me to give you a call this morning, I hope it's not too early there. You're in California, is that right?"

"Paul? Yes. No. Yes, California!"

"Sorry, is this a bad time?"

Jimmy sat up in bed and tried to shake the sleep from his voice. "No, it's fine—I'm sorry I wasn't expecting anyone to call so early."

"Forgive me—well if you're sure, I wanted to cover a few details about a contract from Bash Gallery I received this morning—at Mr. Allenson's request—he said you might need representation on this, it's your first time entering into a contract with an art gallery I understand?"

It was all rushing at him pretty quick. Jimmy stood up and wrapped his sheet tight around his waist—business casual, or close enough.

"So, you got the contract from Dexter already? And Paul asked you to call me?"

There was a pause on the other end.

"Yes, as I said ... Sorry, Mr. Traywick, can I ask—have you been drinking? No judgment—I just want to be sure you understand and remember everything I say. If I am to represent you in this matter, I don't want any misunderstandings."

Now why would he ask a thing like that, Paul?

"I'm sorry—I'm just a bit groggy, I was fast asleep—this is my day off. Lay it on me."

"Right then, let me make it clear that everything you tell me, everything we discuss, is completely confidential."

"How discreet of you," Jimmy said.

Another pause. "Yes. Anyway, I say this for several reasons. Full disclosure: Mr. Allenson is a social acquaintance—he's referred a number of people to me for legal services, but he is himself not a client and receives no compensation from me or my firm. Also, he's asked to be a party to the contract between yourself and Bash Gallery, to the extent that he's asked for reimbursement of expenses he incurred to help connect you with Mr. Bash and his gallery, ship your artwork from California to New York, airfare and accommodations for your recent business trip to meet Mr. Bash and discuss your inclusion in an upcoming group art show, a catered lunch, etcetera."

"Oh really. Alright then."

"He would also like to be paid a commission as a referral on any sales which occur as a result of the upcoming show in May. It's all quite standard, Mr. Traywick—he's provided receipts for the expenses, and he and Mr. Bash have engaged in referral agreements in the past. Meanwhile, he is also offering to pay the one-time fee for my service in the amount of fifteen hundred dollars to review this contract and suggest any changes, as well as the additional shipment of paintings in accordance with terms of the agreement with Mr. Bash."

"So let me get this straight," Jimmy started, "I have to pay him back for everything and a percent of anything I sell in the group show?"

"Yes—now don't panic. Can I call you Jimmy?"

"Yes, please."

Harold Fisher's voice softened as he struck a warmer manner. He sounded like a big man, a salt-and-pepper teddy bear, or so Jimmy liked to think.

"OK, Jimmy—this is not a big deal—it's pretty straightforward, and I'll say again—if we move forward, I represent you, even if Paul is paying my fee this time—he is not my client, you are, and I will not discuss or disclose anything to him unless you tell me to. Also, you can say no to any of these terms—apparently you had no agreement, verbal or otherwise, that he should be reimbursed, and so it's an ask on his part, not a demand. OK?"

"OK."

"First I'm going to suggest some changes in the contract. It should be non-exclusive outside of New York, and within New York, a term of no more than nine months. I understand you are a new artist and Mr. Bash is taking on a certain amount of risk, that's understandable, and one can hardly fault him for trying to secure exclusive three-year terms: he is a businessman, and he's hoping you will be a success, but Mr. Bash hasn't committed to market your work beyond this show, so more limited terms protect you."

"Makes sense—I agree," Jimmy said, imagining Harold Fisher with big strong hands.

"The split on sales is a standard fifty-fifty, no problem there, but I am also going to suggest Mr. Bash split the expenses Paul is asking to be reimbursed—he can deduct those as business expenses anyway, while I am guessing you probably cannot. Also the photographer fees..."

"Photographer?"

"Yes, I understand Mr. Bash will be contacting a photographer local to you for some head and studio shots for marketing—he should pay for those, not you—marketing is his job. Finally, I will offer a lower commission than what Paul has asked for, also to be split fifty-fifty between yourself and Mr. Bash, and that the reimbursement only be paid if the amount of the commission covers the expenses. In other words, if his commission on your total sales were only a thousand dollars but his expenses one thousand and one, he would only receive one thousand. Does that make sense?"

"Yes," Jimmy said. "Damn, am I going to make any money out of this?"

"Look at it another way, Jimmy—if it doesn't work out, you neither lose nor owe anything to anyone. Paul gets it—he told me he's happy to eat the costs if he's wrong about your prospects. If it does work out, you have Paul to thank for helping launch your career. He's done this a few times I know of, and a couple of his bets have done well. He and Mr. Bash both are motivated to ensure your debut is successful—and I am here to make sure you get your fair share. Do you have any questions?"

"What happens next?"

"I'll make the changes to the contract, email it to you and we'll have a brief call to review the final version. Then we'll need to arrange for you to sign and return it. No big deal, like I said—and call me if you need anything. Goodbye." Fourteen minutes and thirty seconds flat—Harold Fisher billed in quarter-hour increments.

Jimmy stood naked in front of his current canvas, just headphones and ambient chillout, trying, almost succeeding, to capture the evaporating memories of New York and Nico the Greek—DJ, personal trainer, bodybuilder, fitness model, escort, Renaissance man. Actually not Greek but Italian American from the Bronx. Nico had several websites with menus of services, fees, and galleries of pictures featuring varying degrees of nudity, including a members-only area with live-streaming and private chats should one be inspired. Along with some of Nico's free pictures saved to his laptop image file, for inspiration Jimmy set a slideshow flipping of ecstatic Japanese women with octopus lovers and other erotic curiosities.

Feo dozed on the bed, snoring. He choked and coughed, woke himself up for a moment, long enough to squint and mumble, "My cricket," before falling back to sleep. He had rearranged his schedule to allow for more nights over at Jimmy's, since the incident with Ramon on the stairs.

"Very sexy," he said when he first arrived, examining the work in progress and flipping through the slides on Jimmy's laptop with the space bar. "Scary sexy, yes? That's what you hoped? Yes. Success."

"It's getting there." Jimmy added a bit more green-gold tone to Nico's skin. It took a few tries, but he had settled on three metallic hues for a kaleidoscopic effect.

"Someone you know?"

"That guy I told you about—in New York—Paul's friend." He had not told Feo absolutely everything.

"Ah! The hooker! Yes. Whoa! Big stud! Bigger than me."

"Well..."

"Bigger dick—yes, that's OK, now I know where are all your secret buttons to make you squeal, I don't worry." He settled onto the window seat.

"You sure you're not jealous?" Jimmy put down his brush and slid onto Feo's lap.

"No, no! It's good you had fun, I had some fun too that weekend. Filthy little whore, I told you."

"Filthier than me?" He started to unbutton Feo's fly.

"Impossible."

Nico I was a gorgeous mess Jimmy slapped together the day he got back from New York, still a little high. Sleepless and nervous one night at ten p.m. working on *Nico II*, there came the familiar half-scratching, half-tapping downstairs. Jimmy answered the door in his robe.

"Oh honey! I hope I didn't wake you," Kitty said.

"It's cool—I was working on a painting."

"Do you have a minute, I wanted to ask you—"

She made as though to invite herself in, but Jimmy stopped her with a flap of his hand toward upstairs, whispering, "My friend is sleeping." She seemed taken aback to be denied entry, but he smiled brightly and stepped into the hall, closing the door behind him. "Sorry, my dear, what's happening?"

She nodded, appeased. "I just wanted to ask you—you've gotten real close with Oscar and Ramon. See now? I'm trying to remember to call him Oscar. It's just so nice they found a friend, you know, but I guess Oscar hasn't been at school for the last week or so. The school called me when they couldn't reach Ramon, and I had no idea—I just wondered if you knew he's been skipping school...?"

"Oh, no, I didn't. I'm sorry, I haven't seen them much lately, I've been super busy." He and Oscar had agreed not to tell her about the scuffle on the stairs. "Did you hear I'm going to be in a show in New York?"

"Oh, yes! I'm so happy for you, hon—what great news! You can tell us all about it at Thanksgiving, if you'll come—that's why I'm really here, I just wanted to ask. Ramon and Oscar and me, and you, if you can make it?"

"Oh, Kitty, I'm sorry—I can't." He was mortified on her account, but glad not to have to lie. Feo was going with him to Vic's mom's, Dee too—he had a show Friday night while Ricardo headed to Disneyland with his sister's family for the long weekend.

He was genuinely sorry to disappoint her, despite the problems with Ramon. "I already told my friend I'd come to their mom's house."

She was crestfallen but recovered quickly, peering over her glasses at the bruise on his face from smacking against the wall. He tried to head her off.

"It's nothing—smacked myself in the face with a door."

"OK, that's OK—there's always Christmas, and New Years too! And your friend is welcome if you ever want to bring him—we'll talk later honey, I won't keep you."

The invitation from Vic's mom had extended to Jimmy's own if she wanted to drive up to join them, but Marlys flatly refused. They were not the kind of people to bother with relations who lived more than twenty minutes away—she had cousins who moved to Lancaster in the eighties and were never heard from again, though lambasted for their defection every year.

"Then what is your plan, mother?"

Groan. "Oh. Well, I really haven't given it any thought, dear, you know since your father died I'm not much for the holidays. But if your plans fall through I suppose I could nuke a couple of Lean Cuisines for us, I practically live on them anymore. The Roast Turkey Medallions with Cornbread Dressing aren't half bad, and you know I love those cinnamon apples. I could even splurge and make two for each of us—I think I have a coupon—what are they, two hundred and thirty calories? So two of those would be, what? Four hundred and sixty calories? That's not too bad. We could put them on plates and put the apples in my fancy pudding cups with a scoop of vanilla ice cream."

"Real plates?"

"Don't be ridiculous. Paper plates. Honestly, James, you know I can't stand the fuss of dishwashing—I'm not your maid."

Dexter's publicist called a few days later to talk about the upcoming photo shoot and ask about biographical details, all business. More interrogation than interview, Jimmy was unsure if she was pleased or perturbed.

"I guess that covers all the basics, James," said Siobhan finally. She drummed her fingernails on her desk loudly enough for him to hear over the phone. He pictured Jungle Red nail polish. "But what's the real story? Give me all the sordid details, the juicier the better."

"Please, call me Jimmy."

"Mr. Bash has insisted we say either Mr. Traywick, or James—Jimmy is a bad habit."

"You flatter me."

"Excuse me?"

"Nothing."

"Let's see—your family is from Fresno—any notable ancestors? A mayor, perhaps? Prominent Traywicks in history?"

"My dad was a water system salesman, and my mother was a cafeteria lady—no hair net, though." Long pause.

"Any artistic traditions handed down to you?"

"Gramma made ceramics at the retirement rec center until her arthritis got too bad."

Big sigh. "Judging from your picture, I assume you're not Jewish," Siobhan continued, her voice flat with growing irritation.

"Probably not—I was adopted."

"Have you looked for your birth family?"

"No."

"Any immigrants in your past? Mixed heritage?"

"My dad's family moved from Oklahoma when he was a kid."

"Oklahoma, you say? Fundamentalists? Snake handlers? Holy rollers?"

"Jeez, I'm from Fresno—I've never even been baptized."

Siobhan actually tsked. "Anything! Addictions. Mental illness. Famous lovers. Terrible accident that left you clinging to life. Suicide attempts."

"Not that I'm willing to admit. Just gay white male."

"HIV positive?"

"No, thank god."

"Ugh. Alright, we'll think of something."

After much wheedling, Dee convinced Jimmy to let him play stylist for the photo shoot and use make-up to cover the not quite faded bruise from the tussle on the stairs. It all started simply enough.

He was in the middle of blocking out a new canvas when the bell rang.

"Was your hair always this color?" Dee asked, bustling in two hours early with enough luggage for a long weekend.

"Blond?"

Dee squinted, rummaging through his wonder of a make-up box, big as a small trunk, with tiers and compartments and multiples of every imaginable concoction. "No—I mean ... it's gone a bit dishwater, as your mom would say. Didn't it used to be a bit fresher?"

Jimmy huffed. "Yeah? Once upon a time you were a size eight."

Dee pouted. "Twenty-two on top, fourteen on the bottom, thank you very much! Anyway, I'm not the one doing a photo shoot."

"It's just some publicity photos for the show and I'm not even the only artist. If I'm lucky there might be two pictures, a headshot and one of my studio on an info sheet."

"Whatever." Dee pulled a wife-beater out of his bag, a size too small. "Put this on."

"Why?"

"Just do it." Jimmy put the t-shirt on and Dee grabbed the wet brush from his palette, flicking and dabbing smears across his chest and stomach.

"What the hell?"

"Local color!" Dee declared. "Now you look like a painter—alright, take that off and let it dry, and we'll work on that bruise. What a lovely shade of green."

Dee took the full two hours to fix Jimmy's look. The moment of truth in the mirror—he was afraid it was too much fuss, that he would end up looking like a drag queen, but he looked good.

Damn good. The change was subtle, highlights and lowlights, like underpainting. And the bruise was gone.

The photographer's eyes popped when Jimmy answered the door. JT—all dreadlocks, sleeve tattoos, indeterminate accent, and brilliantly white smile—cultivated a mysterious Oakland-Tokyo vibe.

"Wow! Look at you! Jimmy? Are you wearing make-up?" They went up to the studio.

"I'm afraid so—my friend, Dee..."

"JT. Charmed," Dee started in. "David Dennis Waters. Stylist, Make-up AND Performance Artist."

"There's a name," JT said.

"It's real—and so are my tits!"

Jimmy had to laugh as JT struggled not to glance down at Dee's chest and failed.

"Ha! Made you look!"

JT shook his head with a chuckle. "You got me, you got me. You did this?" he asked, pointing to Jimmy and examining him more closely. "Damn, you look hot, boy—Dexter told me you were cute, but ... wow. I can't wait to photograph you."

There were pictures of Jimmy standing at his easel, from the back and from the side—pictures of the studio itself, all the paintings hung and stacked against the walls, his paints and palettes. They spent a good while on headshots, JT setting up a light and Dee holding a big reflector this way and that. He used two cameras, one digital and one film. At one point he peered up close at Jimmy's cheek.

"Is that a bruise? I didn't even see it until we put the reflector on you." JT paused. "Do you mind..."

"He does not mind," Dee declared, "whatever you're going to ask..."

"I like this one," JT said to Jimmy, "she's audacious."

"That's one word for her..."

JT thought for a moment, then said, "Do you mind wiping off the concealer so I can see? I have an idea."

Dee spit on a Kleenex.

"You will NOT...!" Jimmy hollered.

"Ha! Relax, Aunt Jemimah." Dee pulled a baby wipe out of his bag and wiped away the make-up on the bruise.

JT continued taking pictures, directing Jimmy to look here and there, stand up, sit back down on his stool, feet down, feet up, barefoot. "Do you have some boots? Don't lace them." After another ten minutes, he finished and stood flipping through some of the shots on his camera.

"Lemme see, lemme see!" Dee sidled up to peek. "OMG. Gutter chic! Oh yeah! Why have I never pimped you into porn? I coulda been the new Chi Chi Larue."

JT looked thoughtful. "So, would it be OK if I sent a few of these to a guy I know down in L.A.? You've got a great look—especially in print and online, but even on runways nowadays, little guys like you are getting modeling gigs—you'd be surprised."

The moment JT left, Dee started screaming.

"WE'RE GONNA BE FAMOUS!!!"

TWENTY-THREE

The moment he buzzed Feo in the front door, Jimmy decided his attempt to recreate a little of the glamor Dee had managed for the photo shoot was ill-conceived. The bruise was gone anyway. The barest frost of eye shadow, a blush of cream bronzer, a clear lip gloss from Dee's gift bag full of samples—not working today.

"Use it wisely, grasshopper—you may be an artist, but I ... am a sorceress!" Dee had proclaimed, but without his drag magic, maybe too K-pop for Thanksgiving. Before Feo could climb the three flights up to his door, Jimmy had jumped back in the shower, scrubbed his face, toweled off, and slapped some gel in his hair.

Feo examined the painting he had been working on all week, a gift for Vic and their mom.

"Very nice," he said, peering close, then standing back. "This is new? Smells new."

In the stacks of canvas piled around the studio, Jimmy still had far too many of the old landscapes from his Fresno days. Despite Dexter's merciless appraisal, he would not apologize for the poppies—they captured the brilliance of those springtime hills and reminded him of his original impulse to become an artist. Anyway, he thought a new work might be a more meaningful gift for Vic, so on one of the poppy-smeared hills, he created a new ghost composition of landmarks seen from the East Bay—bridges, city skyline, Twin Peaks, Albany Hill too, in pale creams, corals, and rusts. Central Valley meets Beach Blanket Babylon. It turned out better than he'd hoped.

Mouth full of toothpaste, Jimmy croaked, "New painting on an old one. Don't you look sexy!" Feo wore his new black suit from Big & Tall with his new black shirt and black shoes, and a pocket square in the latest shade of black.

"Look who talks, naked." Feo grabbed for him but ended up with a handful of towel.

"My birthday is the only suit I own. You look super sharp and I'm going to look like a slob."

"No. You're my star, always. I have to dress up to look good enough to be your boyfriend."

While Jimmy dressed in his skinniest jeans, a pearl-gray sweater, and his new loafers, no socks, he tasked Feo with wrapping the painting in brown paper, a clumsy affair on the unmade bed. Skipping down to the kitchen, Jimmy poured himself a vodka to steel himself for the party.

"You want one?" he called.

"No, no, just wine tonight."

Jimmy brought his glass back upstairs.

"So, I ask you something, cricket?" Feo, propped on his side on the bed, patted the space next to him.

"Anything." Jimmy sat.

"Why you drink so much?"

Jimmy grimaced and screwed his eyes shut. "What a very good question. Why are you asking?" He stiffened as Feo tried to pull him closer. "Are you going to break up with me if I don't quit?"

"No! Don't say that."

"I'm joking, mostly." Jimmy pouted, trying to diffuse the sudden turn of mood. "Dee said you never got mad."

"DeeDee has good heart, but he doesn't see everything."

"Please don't be mad."

"I only ask why you drink, is not judgment, you see me, I drink—but I worry, for your health. I know guy, beautiful boy, got too drunk and went down basement stairs—boosh—broke his jaw, and knocked out his teeth. They fixed, but not the same. Lots of pain. So ... I worry."

Jimmy relaxed and let himself be engulfed in lap and beard. "Do I have to answer that today?"

"Are you afraid I walk away from you? I think lots of people have—you are strange."

"Yes."

Feo squeezed him tight, then set him on his feet and smoothed his sweater. "You'll see, cricket. We should go." They collected keys and phone and bottles and painting. "Also my uncle is retiring—did I tell you? I'm taking over Volga Restaurant."

"What? That's great! Isn't it?"

"Yes, I buy him out, is not cheap but I told him I break his legs if he doesn't give me good price..." Jimmy's eyes went wide. "No, no, is good deal for both of us, but I have reason to work less, now—and I will hire new cook—Ludmila, my cousin! Oh, she's wonderful cook, but she doesn't get along with my uncle so much. But now—no problem—her kids are grown, off to school, she wants to get back to work besides just mama. So now, I have more free time. Just a little."

"I thought you said Ludmila had a baby, Ludmila ... Junior," Jimmy said as he locked the door behind them. "She knocked out your tooth."

"Ah. No. Other cousin Ludmila."

They reached Vic's mom's house—past the cemetery, up a winding drive into the hills of Kensington, just over the crest and barely back down the slope toward the canyon—tucked up a private driveway. "Nothing fancy, just a wreck when they bought it," Vic had said, but they found a gingerbread and cedar-shingled cottage glowing with lanterns and Christmas lights.

Dee opened the door as though he lived there, rushing them into the front room, all turquoise and pinks, awash with pots, plants, and figurines. "About time, you bitches!" he hissed. "I've done two Dolly Partons for Abuela. Were you fucking? I smell sex."

Jimmy pecked him on each cheek. "That's your breath. Let me guess, *Jolene* and *I Will Always Love You.*"

"*Nine to Five* and *Texas Has a Whorehouse in It*, as it happens—well, that last one's only Dolly-adjacent, but it's a favorite."

They greeted Vic and a snuffling Trixie with *Heys* and *Happy Thanksgivings*, kisses and scampering feet and jackets. Jimmy hid the painting behind a chair by the front door.

Feo scratched Trixie under the jowls. "And how you, Miss Davis?"

"Ma!" To Vic's call, a short, round woman—followed by an almost identical woman in a slightly smaller, apple head doll version—came hustling in from the kitchen. "This is my mom, Florencia."

"Call me Flor." She swept aside Jimmy's extended hand and grabbed him in a she-bear hug. "How wonderful to meet you!"

"And this is my abuela," Vic said, ushering forward the doll, "she understands English, but she won't say much—if she does, though, you better do what she tells you." Jimmy stretched out his arms, and only then realized Abuela had extended a hand to shake (so awkward, again!) but when he put his out, she slapped it away with a snort to hug him.

"And this is Feo!" Vic boomed in a voice to match Feo's bulk. No shrinking to match the company—Feo stood tall and hugged both of the ladies to his belly.

"Is an honor to be invited to your home!" he cried.

"Ese no es su nombre. ¿En serio? Gigantesco, si—pero no feo," Abuela mumbled from inside the folds of his jacket. Once she escaped, she looked again at Jimmy. "¿Estos dos están juntos? La calabaza y la grano de pimienta."

Feo beamed. "What she say?"

"She says you're a cute couple," Vic translated.

"We've got a little while," Flor said, "show Jimmy and Feo around, V—Dee come back and stir the gravy when you get a chance." She and her mom headed back to the kitchen.

"Don't let all the crosses fool you," Vic said. There were a fair few, mostly painted pink, candy striped, or bejeweled—more of a collection than a religious observance. Snapshots and school pictures lined the walls, but Vic was quick to distract. "Don't look there! Lookie here: Mom's a big reader!" They pointed to the bookshelves, lined and stacked with medical books, cookbooks, Mexican history, gardening, knitting. Every chair and seat had its doily, every table a lit candle, and on an altar in the corner, incense burned and an electric Virgin Mary shimmered beatifically.

The dining table was set with three different cloths, five different kinds of cutlery, two glasses—wine and water—and another flickering votive for each place. Pine cupboards with stacks of pottery, bowls, pitchers, vases, and more crucifixes—all the good silver ones—stood collected between Mexicolored mirrors.

"Mom's room," Vic indicated on the left as they led the way down the hall—"Abuela's room"—on the right, a lace confection. At the end of the hall, a Dutch door led out to a big porch and riotous garden, petunias spilling from pots on the steps down to beds of primrose and impatiens edging the path of a gentle ravine up the hill. Off behind a stand of young redwoods, a second smaller cottage hugged the slope.

"This is me." Vic walked them down the short path into their studio. "This used to be a chicken coop—can you believe it?"

There were two rooms on different levels—a living and office combo, and a bedroom—lots of tall windows, and a spartan bathroom beyond. Through the windows in the dusk, lights by ones and twos peeped through the trees. "No kitchen, but look! Tilden Park—best view in the house. Great light in the morning."

"I've seen this show already, I'm just going to pop back and tend the salsa." Dee headed back to the house with Trixie.

"It's so homey," Jimmy said, "I didn't have anything like this when I was a kid."

"No, nothing like this," Feo agreed, "a real home."

Vic opened a pair of French doors. "Salvaged— cool, huh? My dad was a contractor." They sat on worn velvet chairs as the evening air brushed in around them. The plink of cutlery and plates carried from the kitchen window. "I didn't move out here until I was in high school, this was originally my dad's workshop and man cave. What's it like at your mom's house?"

"No knickknacks, that's for sure," Jimmy said, "nothing to collect dust. Marlys vacuums twice a day even though she never stops complaining about housework. She'll deny it, but she gets down on her hands and knees and cleans the carpet with a toothbrush and hydrogen peroxide."

"Holy shit, what color is it?"

"Whiter than teeth. I think it used to be tan."

There was silence then as the darkness gathered outside. A night-light glowed by the doors.

Jimmy put his hand on Feo's arm. "Can you give us a couple minutes?"

"Yes, of course—I think I not kissed Trixie not nearly enough." He lumbered out.

Vic smiled, nothing rueful in it. "You guys seem happy."

Jimmy nodded slowly. "You know, I'm starting to think it's OK for me to feel that. Happy. Why not? Enjoy it while it lasts, anyway."

"You never know..."

"So what's the plan, Vic?" Jimmy asked. They had avoided talking in much detail as they fell out of romance and into something else, but there was no getting away from Vic's emerging baby bump. "How do you want this to work?"

"I've been talking to my mom—she wants to retire—been at the hospital for thirty years, can you believe it? She's got her pension and all that, she's been thinking about it for a while now."

"What about you?

Vic stared out into the canyon. "You know what? I don't know. Is it OK if I don't know yet? I wasn't ready to be a parent—someday sure, but hell, if everyone waited until they were ready, we'd probably be extinct. I've been wanting to pull out of the art store and focus more on my own stuff—Dee says he'll keep using me for all his graphics, and I've been picking up work from some other bars and clubs too. I already ramped up online since I moved back from the City anyway, and I can still get over there when I need to if mom or Abuela can take care of the baby. Or you."

Jimmy hedged. "I can help, I want to—but my resources are limited. You know our health insurance is just so-so. My rent isn't a lot, but you know I don't make a lot. And I don't know what's going to happen with this New York thing—it's just a group show. I gotta get my shit together."

"It's cool, I mean, I'm on my mom's insurance, it's a lot better than ours, and she gets extended coverage for me. She checked, the baby would be covered too since I'm living at home—thank god for unions, huh? Money's not a problem, really..."

Jimmy shook his head. "But I don't want you to think of yourself as a single parent."

"I'm prepared to, though. I'm not worried about having enough, OK? I was raised by those two ladies in there—we've been lucky, and now there's three of us plus you for this little peanut—hard work and a lot of love is the name of the game up here."

"OK..."

"So what then? I don't feel like we need to start hiring lawyers and shit, I mean—I would have been scared to say this when we were fooling around, but—I love you, man—I really do. I'm glad to have you in my life."

Jimmy's voice caught in his throat. He was overcome, but finally choked out, "Yes." He breathed deeply, letting the knot in his chest pass. "The family you choose, right?" he whispered.

"Aw, cariño. So. Next steps?"

"Can we start with dinner?"

Flor was yelling from the kitchen, "You guys hungry?"

They trooped the feast into the dining room—turkey stuffed with jalapeño dressing, enchiladas, sweet corn tamales. Candied yams were the star.

"You'll die," Vic told them—"Die!" Dee echoed—"she puts cinnamon and Mexican chocolate in the yams, it's better than dessert…!"

"Now, Jimmy," Flor said, "you sit between me and Abuela, and Feo on my right, and Dee and Vic wherever."

"What?" Dee cried. "I used to sit between you and Abuela—there's a new prize pig at the fair, I guess." He stuck his tongue out at Jimmy.

"You can sit on my lap, but no bouncing like last time," Feo offered.

Somehow the turkey ended up in front of Jimmy, and he picked up the knife hesitantly. "This could be a disaster."

"Oh no, honey, I'll do that," Flor said, "but first…"

"We say grace," Vic whispered. "Just follow along, it gets a little kooky."

When they had all sat and taken hands, Flor began.

"We thank you, Blessed Virgin, for all the gifts you bestow on us, for each new morning with its light, the sun and moon that shine so bright, for rest and shelter in the night, oh Heavenly Mother with loving might for family and friends, your grace transcends, for everything your goodness sends, bless our happy home! Amen."

Feo clapped. "Amen! Ach! Beautiful!"

After dinner, the baby came up. Dee felt it necessary to defend his involvement.

"Don't blame me! I may have introduced them, but not in one hundred million years would I have imagined James Christopher Traywick would actually—I can hardly say the words—actually TOP somebody! In the vagina! Jesus Honoria Christ, what next?" Abuela tittered behind one hand as she crossed herself with the other.

"Pumpkin flan!" Flor dumped a gravy boat of brandy on top of the dessert and sparked it with a long barbeque lighter. Ooos. Awws.

"Speaking of flaming—do you know," Dee announced, "that Jimmy's father is the source of my alter ego's name?"

Feo took the bait. "What? It can't be. DeeDee?"

"Not DeeDee, technically—Dusty Davenport. Dusty "Double-D's" Davenport drew inspiration from the sofa in Jimmy's parents' family room—on the davenport, as your dad insisted on calling it for some reason..."

Jimmy groaned. "If you're about to announce that you blew my father in the family room, so help me god..."

"For chrissake don't interrupt—but the sofa..."

"It was the sofa they brought with them from Oklahoma," Jimmy interrupted.

Now Dee was interested. "What? In the Stone Age?"

"My mom had it reupholstered when they got married, but yeah—they brought it in the back of their pick-up truck when they moved from Oklahoma, Grandma's old davenport, almost brand-new and she didn't want to leave it behind. She was from Massachusetts originally, and that's what they called it—only stick of furniture they brought to California. The kids sat and slept on it on the drive out. During the Dust Bowl..."

"And that—thank you Jimmy for almost ruining my story—is the inspiration for Dusty. Somehow I got wrangled into sitting on the davenport in question waiting for Jimmy to come home one fateful day while his father lectured me for a good half hour about when he was a kid, and how awful it was, the Dust Bowl this and the Dust Bowl that, and how life ain't no goddamn bowl of goddamn cherries goddamnit..."

Jimmy rolled his eyes, remembering. "You're channeling him..."

"Exactly. And it came to me then as I was glazing over—Dust Bowl, Dusty, Davenport, of course…!"

"Genius," Jimmy said.

"Quite. But do you know what that old coot said to me then and there? Did I ever tell you this, Jimmy?"

"Oh jeez. What?" He braced himself for a bombshell.

"Thinking myself funny, just to be audacious, I batted my eyes and lisped to your father, 'Good Lord, Mr. Traywick, what a trooper you are—if I knew today that my life would turn out as full of trials and tribulations as your own, I would probably kill myself.'"

"Oh fuck."

"And you know what he said? This is why I never told you—but the old bastard is dead and gone, now—pardon me, Flor, Abuela, but he really was awful"—Jimmy nodded—"and he said to me right then as we heard you coming in—we heard the front door open, and he turned and looked me square in the eye, and he said, 'If I'd known then what I know now, I probably woulda killed myself too.'"

The room went quiet.

"Thanks, Dee—another heartwarming holiday story," Jimmy said.

"Oh!" Dee cried, "Was that bad?"

"No, that's probably exactly what I needed to hear."

"Oh good. You know, I never understood why you cried so hard when he died—he sobbed for like twenty minutes straight, no joke, I had to change my blouse."

Jimmy scowled at his empty glass. Flor picked up a plate to start clearing, but put it back down and stood behind Jimmy, hands on his shoulders. "Don't you worry, there's enough love in this house for everyone." She kissed him on the top of his head. "Dee, play us a song?"

Dee retrieved his banjo and shushed the room. "Don't. Speak. Don't. Please. No." He held up a braceleted wrist and struck the strings ferociously, singing, "Hot ginger and dynamite! That's all there is at night, back in Nagasaki where the fellas chew tabaccky, and the women wicky-wacky woo...!"

After a few more show tunes, Vic took Jimmy out to the porch to finish their conversation. They sat on a chair swing in the crisp night facing the garden and the ravine. Storm clouds had gathered, bathed in an orange glow from the bayside city lights.

"Looks like rain," Vic said.

"What a great house to grow up in," Jimmy said. "And your mom..."

Vic nodded. "Yeah I got lucky, she's the best person I know. We've missed my dad, of course, but he's been gone a long time—he died when I was nine."

"I'm sorry. How did he...?"

"He got shot."

"Oh my god, what?"

"He was at a convenience store up in Richmond buying a Coke and a sandwich and this guy tried to rob it—of course my dad tried to stop him. Dude shot him in the chest, bam, just like that. Dead before he hit the ground. My mom, you know, she was devastated, but she held it together for me. That's when her mom came to live with us. House full of girls—I think my brain jumped ship and decided that was enough big female energy."

Jimmy struggled to find words. "I'm ... shocked. That's terrible." They fell quiet, and more of Dee's singing drifted out to them—the Three Stooges' "Alphabet Song."

Vic laughed. "He's been practicing that for when the baby comes."

Feo wandered out to the porch and squeezed in between them on the swing. Vic and Jimmy held their breath as it creaked, but it was quadruple bolted. He settled his big arms around the two of them. "Cozy."

"And along came Feo," Vic said as they snuggled into his side. "Gee, you smell good."

"Old Spice, like me."

"Ha! What a dad smell! How old are you, anyway?"

"Dirty-six," Jimmy answered. Feo pinched him under the arm and he giggled.

"Perfect age," Vic said. "So what do you really think, papi? We're a fucking clown car, in case you didn't notice—and we haven't even got to the dirty diapers yet."

"I'm dirty diaper boss, no problem," Feo replied. "I'm not going nowhere." With a start, he jumped up and sent them careening on the swing.

"Hey now!" they yelled.

"We forget the painting!" he cried, rushing back inside. "My cricket painted beautiful picture for you! Look!"

By the time Jimmy and Feo groaned their way up the stairs to his apartment, bellies overstuffed, the skies had let loose the first good soaking of the season and revealed a leak in the studio roof. Luckily, the mess of plaster and dirty water missed the big stack of paintings, but it was still coming down pretty hard. Feo was supposed to stay over, but he insisted they go to his place and let the "janitor" take care of the problem.

"OK but what if we just leave a trash can underneath it and deal with it tomorrow?"

"This little bucket? No. It fills in an hour, even bigger mess tomorrow. No—call him."

"No I can't..."

"I call."

"No, please, I'll stay, I'll figure it out."

"No. I go to basement."

Jimmy relented and texted Oscar. In five minutes, he was clumping in the door with a giant building trash can, rags, mop, and bucket. He took one look at Feo towering on the staircase and dropped the bucket with a start. "Whoa—what'd you do, hire a bodyguard?"

Jimmy picked up the bucket.

"Oscar, this is my boyfriend, Feo."

"Feo?" He chuckled in confusion. "Boyfriend? THIS is your boyfriend?" He put everything down and straightened up tall as Feo descended to shake his hand.

"I am boyfriend." Feo knew the whole story. "Is nice to meet you, Oscar, Jimmy says very nice things."

Oscar's confusion persisted. "I thought you were dating Vic?"

"That was, you know, just—Vic and I are friends, and well—yeah, just friends."

As the situation became clearer, Oscar avoided looking Jimmy or Feo in the eye. He bustled upstairs, set up the bin to catch the leak and assessed the damage. "I can clean this up quick, but I can't really do anything about the leak until tomorrow. I seriously doubt it will overflow, but ... are you staying here tonight?"

Jimmy was too flustered to speak. Feo took charge. "We go to my place tonight—you check in a few hours if rain keeps going, yes?"

For the first time, Jimmy saw Oscar as a child—slouched, his old football jersey too small, shorts absurdly long; he looked dazed and sleepy as though just tumbled out of bed to ask for a drink of water. But when Feo put his hand on his shoulder and asked, "You OK?" as warmly as he could, Oscar jerked away as though stung.

"It's cool—you go, I got this—I'll take care of everything." His face was a brick wall as Jimmy threw a few clothes into his duffel, and casting one last pained glance, abandoned Oscar to his task.

TWENTY-FOUR

"God I love you." Dee spoke not to Jimmy, but to his second Bacon, Egg and Cheese Biscuit, Jimmy's treat for taking him to his first AA meeting in the basement of All Saints Lutheran. "One's never enough, two is too many—but since you're paying..." They sat in Mildred with their McDonald's, watching the early risers shuffle in. "What a dusty crowd you East Bayers are. You ready for this?"

"Not really, but I also don't want to end up like Ramon—I'm going to be a father for god sake."

Dee slurped his coffee and took Jimmy's unfinished hash browns. "And I'm going to be an auntie! A most strange and extraordinary baby, I just know it."

"If you have anything to do with it."

"Them."

"Excuse me?"

"The correct pronoun for a child is them, not it."

"So help me... You know I've got my dad's rifle, lady. Somewhere..."

"That pop-gun? Bitch, please—I've sucked dicks with more firepower. What's Feo got to say about you flirting with sobriety?"

"I haven't told him, I don't want to make any promises I can't keep."

"I wouldn't worry too much about that, he's head over heels for you, and he has experience tending drunks." This was new. "He didn't tell you about his dad? He died right before Feo came to the U.S. His mother died when he was a kid."

Dee lived for moments like these. "Yes, but here's how it really happened. When he was a little kid, like eight years old, he went out to play—his dad was at work, but his mom was like 'Go outside, come home for lunch.' And so lunch time comes around and he goes up and he can't get in and she doesn't answer."

"The door was locked?"

Dee did a perfect impression of Feo. "Ees Russia, all doors locked."

"Please tell me she didn't kill herself?"

"Don't try to guess the ending! So he goes back down to the playground, and he waits all day until his father gets home, and his dad's like 'Go to the neighbor lady's apartment and wait for me.' And sure enough, she died—heart condition—they knew about it, that's why they didn't have another kid, her heart couldn't take it. Feo said he always wanted a little brother."

"That breaks my heart." Jimmy handed the rest of his biscuit to Dee.

"I know, right?" Dee said, mouth full. "And then his dad drank himself to death over the next fifteen years." He guzzled coffee and rolled up his window. "Showtime."

"Alright, then, let's do this. Hell."

"That's the spirit!"

The rooms, Jimmy would find, were usually the same, some combination of folding or stacking chairs, fluorescent lighting, and sullen or earnest or jovial people. Some meetings' snacks were better than others.

"Ooo! Oreos." Dee made a beeline for the cookies. They took seats at the back of the three-sided arrangement facing a speaker's podium.

"Let us take a moment to remember the still-suffering alcoholic in and out of these rooms, followed by the Serenity Prayer," said the grandfatherly guy at the front once everyone settled down. "God..."

"Gandalf..." Dee warbled, to an eruption of laughter.

"Chocolate—I need chocolate, gotta have chocolate! I wanna go to See's Candy." Vic wheezed as they trudged upstairs.

Jimmy was straightening the studio—all of the new paintings for the show were finished. Some hung on the wall, others lined the floor beneath to snap some good clear shots for insurance, per Paul's suggestion. Everything would be ready when the shippers came for the remainder the week before Christmas.

They were supposed to go shopping, start looking at some baby stuff—a crib, clothes, and whatnot. Abuela wanted them to pick out the crib as a gift from her. "Something with some color. Not white—no offense," Vic said.

"None taken. I gotta get my laundry out of the dryer. Are you wearing make-up?"

Vic pouted. "A little. What? My skin was blotchy! And— And— And look who's talking!" Jimmy might in fact have started wearing a little clear mascara around the house to make his eyes pop. Vic flopped on the bed and buried themself in the tangle of sheets and comforter. "Chocolate..." they moaned from under the covers. "Shit!"

"What now?"

"Ow! The baby just kicked." They flipped back the covers and waved to come quick, but Jimmy shook his head.

"That's OK, I don't need to feel it..."

"For real? Dude, this is your kid too, you know. C'mon!"

Jimmy grimaced as he sat and let Vic position his hand, but the baby had quieted down and he withdrew after a few moments. "Nice try. I've got a boyfriend."

Vic slapped at his retreating ass. "I said 'CHOCOLATE!'"

"Jeez, crazy! Fine—See's Candy first, shopping second—be right back..." He grabbed the laundry basket and jogged downstairs.

In the foyer by the inglenook as he passed, a fresh Christmas tree gave out its piney smell, half-dressed with ribbons and lights and open boxes of ornaments strewn about. Ah yes, Kitty's little Christmas tableau—there was supposed to be a building mixer with cider and cookies next weekend, according to the card she had slipped under his door. She had probably run back to her apartment for her bottle of Bailey's—a mug of coffee steamed on the mantle.

Jimmy had a full load in each of the three dryers, plus another still in that noisy washer because he had been avoiding the basement for weeks. The dryers were running, less than a minute he guessed. In his haste to get his clothes done earlier, he had failed to notice how badly the wall at the back of the laundry room was disintegrating with the recent rains soaking through. Like his ceiling, whole sheets of paint had bulged and fallen away in tatters. Weeping ooze streaked through the powdery mess and rendered the drain in the corner a crunchy soup. He picked idly at one promising blister, and it came away in his fingers, releasing a trickle of moisture.

The washer made such a racket he only noticed the first dryer had stopped when its light turned off. He chucked his laundry on the table and pulled out a couple of t-shirts to fold them while he waited.

Might be nice to move—a place with its own laundry at least. Too soon to imagine moving in with Feo. Although they hadn't mentioned it again, Jimmy guessed Vic might also still consider the idea of their living together. Maybe not right away, but once the baby got a little older—Vic was going to be sharing their studio with it—them!—as long as they were living at Flor's. Well, one day at a time. Ugh. A father! Daddy? Or papa, or...?

He emptied the other two dryers into the basket, piled on top of the first. He slammed a dryer door, and it made a crazy loud bang, like a belt had snapped. Baffled, he opened it back up and looked inside, but nothing. The off-kilter washer spun down and stopped.

Then he heard the screaming.

From out in the hall, echoing off the cinder block walls. Yelling. Rage. And a high, hysterical howl—two men. It could only be Ramon and Oscar. He had never heard them yell at each other before. He clapped his hands over his ears in a panic. Then more screaming, louder, piercing!

When he heard the second sharp crack, he knew. The screaming stopped, but he was already pounding up the stairs, laundry abandoned.

"Kitty!" he yelled as he passed the foyer, still empty. He momentarily thought of heading to her apartment. "Kitty!" It occurred to him that if he had to barricade himself in with her, Vic would have no idea what was going on. He yelled for her one last time as he kept his momentum up to the third floor.

He slammed his front door open so hard the knob dented the wall. "Vic!" he tried to cry out, barely able to make a sound with his heaving heart and breath. "Vic!"

"What?" Vic came to the railing. Jimmy bent double at the door, frantically bolting it. "What's going on?"

"I heard a gunshot—I..." A great sob tore out of him. He nearly crumbled. Vic rushed to the steps. "Stop! Go in the bathroom—lock the door!"

"What the fuck? You're freaking me out!" And then came another sharp crack, loud, not right out in the hall, maybe down at the bottom echoing up the stairwell. This time even Vic heard it.

"Get in the bathroom!" Jimmy yelled. "Go! Lock the door!" Vic did as they were told. Jimmy took the stairs two at a time, punching 911 into his phone.

One, two, three rings.

A woman answered. "Nine-one-one, what's your emergency?"

He tried to moderate his voice but it shook wildly. "I heard gunshots, here in my building." He could hardly get the words out, gasping like he was drowning. He made it up to the studio and collapsed on the window seat.

"Sir, are you in a safe location?"

"I don't know." He spoke slowly, trying to take deep breaths. "I know the guy—it's ... I think it's my gun—he stole my gun..."

"Can you leave the building safely?"

"I don't think so."

"Then lock as many doors behind you as you can and stay down low to the ground—stay on the phone—what's your address?" He told her, and the click of her typing was both terrifying and reassuring. This was real. Help was on the way.

"I need your name, can you give me your name? Jimmy? OK, Jimmy, don't hang up—is there anyone with you?"

Vic cracked the door of the bathroom and poked their head out. "Was that a gunshot?"

"LOCK THE FUCKING DOOR!" Vic obeyed instantly, shocked by the harshness of the command. They slammed the door loudly and fiddled with the lock.

"Jimmy," the lady was saying when he got back on the line, "I want you to keep your voice down, but I want to hear you keep talking so I know you're OK. Do you know who is involved?"

"The janitor of the building and his son—I heard them screaming at each other downstairs and then—"

The bathroom door opened again and Vic came out, stiff and slow as though in shock, their face pale.

"Is it Oscar and his dad? Do you think...?" But even as they said it, they looked past Jimmy toward the stairs and their eyes grew big. An electric current shot across the skin of Jimmy's back as though he had plunged into a freezing cold pool, the wind sucked from his lungs. Like a drowning man, he feared to gulp in that last breath full of water. He turned.

Ramon stood halfway up the stairs on the landing, arms braced against the railing, Jimmy's own rifle aimed. His face was red and black, a bruised and bloody ruin—one eyelid swollen shut, the other a well of emptiness.

The phone fell from Jimmy's paralyzed hand, forgotten. He stood up in front of Vic, opened his arms wide, made himself as big as possible. He closed his eyes and turned his head away.

BROKEN SPIRITS

JAMES TRAYWICK

Bash Gallery is honored to present a collection of paintings on canvas by the young artist, James Traywick, in his first solo show. Along with an important series of recent work, this premier event represents an overview of his output from the last decade.

> *"Mr. Traywick's talent lies in his ability to rewrite narratives both intimate and communal, adding nuance and insight. He makes the legendary immediate, the ordinary strange again. Loneliness, alienation, eroticism, communion, and violence—these are the colors of his palette.*
>
> *We sincerely wish for his recovery after the recent tragic events that have already claimed three lives."*
>
> — Art Speak

> *"...Arresting. Captivating. Seductive. If this is it … it's everything."*
>
> — Times Supplement

> *"...hints of late Goya and Jay DeFeo. Compelling and provocative."*
>
> — De Profundis

Exploring themes of the Private vs. Public gaze, Taboo, Dominance and Submission, Objectification, Fantasy, and Grief, James Traywick has progressively confronted longing and fulfillment in diverse subject matter. Frequently overpainting earlier work to express new concerns and highlight epiphanies of understanding, his oeuvre can be seen as a series, vulnerable to ongoing manipulation and interpretation. Diptychs, unconventional materials, and repeating motifs provide a space to explore layers of meaning in the artist's largely self-taught lexicon.

Bash Gallery hopes for a positive outcome in Mr. Traywick's recovery due to the recent tragic events in which he was involved.

If you wish to make a donation on behalf of the artist and his family, please ask a staff member for information about our GoFundMe campaign.

Bash Gallery acknowledges the generous support of the Hopper & Allenson Trust for this exhibit.

TWENTY-FIVE

Marlys drove up from Fresno while Jimmy was still in surgery, and later that evening she got a few minutes with a camera crew outside the hospital. She had put on her full face and dressed up for the drive, just in case, and sidled up to the news van with the satellite dish and the "Black gal" reporter to inquire if they were there to cover the "Albany Massacre." What really ticked her off was not that they refused to call it by the name she coined—calling it simply a "mass shooting" as if these things happened any old day of the week—but that her part got pared down to eighteen seconds on the ten o'clock news. To top it all off, they credited her as "Marilyn, Victim's Mother."

She did visit punctually every morning from nine to noon but spent as much time in the cafeteria and out on the sidewalk smoking her Parliaments as sitting in the room. Flor offered Vic's studio to stay in, but Marlys insisted the Best Western in El Cerrito was just fine with her—she was not the kind of person to impose on others. Vic had been released after one night of observation for a superficial ear wound and monitoring the baby, but Flor was feeling protective and wanted them to stay in the big house with her for a while.

Feo unnerved Marlys.

She and Dee sat out in the hospital parking lot, Kenny Rogers on the Banana Boat's stereo. "There's only so much space by the bed," she said as she lit another Parliament. "Talk about the elephant in the room."

"I said something almost exactly like that," Dee remarked, turning up the volume to hear over her talking.

"Is that even English he's speaking! I can't understand a word he says!"

"I think it's love!" Dee yelled.

Meanwhile, Paul flew in from New York to assist in any way he could with the investigation, answer questions, support the family, and so forth. He was suitably dismayed, paying special attention to Marlys, who was utterly charmed.

"There's a tall drink of water," she whispered to Dee. "Is he married?"

"Bisexual."

"Oh. Oh!"

"Exactly."

She was relieved "someone with some clout" was looking after Jimmy's interests at least. Also, he urgently explained the need for her to assert her authority as next of kin while Jimmy was incapacitated, for his medical directives, legal, and business interests—Paul had contacts at his disposal, private investigators, lawyers, and such.

For example, authorizing the execution of the contract with Dexter. He impressed on her how very important Jimmy's participation in the show in New York was for his career. Some details had changed, but he provided copies of the original contract and an addendum. No worries! Paul would handle everything. They might move the show up to January featuring Jimmy all by himself—much depended on how soon the Albany Police Department released the crime scene. Also, it was a great opportunity to help raise some funds for his medical care.

"Hallelujah, at least somebody's thinking on his feet." Marlys signed the documents without bothering to read them. Paul left on the second day but promised to stay in touch, and unable to bear all the commotion, Marlys also drove home to Fresno but called Flor every day to ask if there was any news.

The doctors kept Jimmy in a medically induced coma for six days. For another couple days as the drugs dissipated from his system, he floated among currents of light and dark, blasts of noise and silence. He had the distinct impression of being encased but muffled, as though submerged in a deep-sea suit.

When he dreamt, he found himself struggling frantically without grip or footing—not chased but drawn down to fathomless depths by toothsome figures. Late in the evening of the ninth day after the shooting, he recognized Feo's voice, and felt the pressure of his hand holding his, was able to squeeze back. He had difficulty talking after all of the tubes and drugs, so he stayed silent but clung to Feo's hand until he exhausted himself.

Early the next morning, disoriented, he saw Feo slumped in a chair and his first thought—"Is that Vic?"—jogged his memory of the morning Vic had come over. He made a guttural croak, and Feo started awake. He managed to mouth, "Vic."

"It's OK, cricket—it's OK—keep calm now, don't talk." Feo soothed him with heavy hands. "You OK? You sure? OK, Vic is fine, the baby is fine—I wanted to tell you sooner but you were so out of it. He's at home with his mama." Feo pulled his chair up close.

"So I'm not supposed to tell you—the police want to talk to you once the doctors say OK—but yeah, they got questions."

Jimmy nodded. "You remember much of what happened?" He shook his head.

"So that crazy guy, the janitor, they think he got in a fight with his son, and he shot him, that poor kid, and then he went upstairs and he shot that landlady in the hall."

Kitty! Jimmy moaned, the shock of it snapping his stomach like a slingshot.

"I'm sorry, cricket! I'm sorry, I shouldn't say—my big mouth." Once he calmed down, Feo went on. "Your gun? That's what they say—your mom saw it, yes, your Dad's gun. Oh boy, she had things to say about that. So, then he let himself into your apartment—he had your key—and he shot you. The bullet went through your eye and out the side—shattered your eye socket, but thanks god, it missed your..." Feo choked up, and pet Jimmy's hand. He tried to start again, but his throat was full of gravel. They sat quietly, Feo resting his head on Jimmy's leg.

Another day went by before Feo, Vic, and Dee gathered around his bed to tell the rest of the story. The damage to his eye was permanent—his left eyeball was gone—it had required hours over two surgeries to repair the damage to his eye socket and face.

With a clumsy hand, Jimmy tried to feel the side of his swaddled face, then traced the still livid scar on Vic's ear, a tiny piece missing from the top. "You saved my life, boy," Vic said, taking Jimmy's hand. "If you hadn't stepped in front of me... He only took one shot—it just grazed my ear, lots of blood, but I like the chewed up look, kinda butch, huh? Like an alley cat." It was a lot to take in. "You fell back onto me, so we're both on the floor, and Oscar's dad, you know, he came up and he looked at you, and then he looked at me. I was so shocked I just grabbed onto you screaming. And then he noticed my baby bump and he just ... stopped. Just stopped. He stood for a minute like he didn't know what to do, then he turned around, and put the gun in..." Vic shut their eyes tight in the grip of remembering.

Feo finished. "He had blood alcohol level high enough to knock a horse on his ass, and his liver was advance pickled—that's what cops say. The kid was drunk too, empty beer cans everywhere down in their apartment, shit and puke all over, like someone real sick—they had it bad."

Dee was remarkably subdued until the story was told, but once Jimmy's eye settled on him he made an effort.

"One headlight now, my little wallflower," he cooed. "Now winking and blinking are the same thing—pretty cool, huh? Wink once for yes, blink twice for fuck you."

Blink. Wink.

"Aw, that's the plucky guttersnipe we know and love."

With Jimmy awake, Marlys drove back up but stayed only long enough to assure herself that he was on the mend. She expressed disappointment that Paul had not returned from New York, nor had she heard anything from him. Feo was on duty by Jimmy's bed every moment he could until she finally had to ask in a huff whether she might have a moment alone with her only son.

"Of course I'm glad you're alright, dear, but my goodness, I just had a feeling something like this was going to happen. I don't even want to know what you were doing with that boy and his father, I told the officers I simply couldn't bear to know any details—they were welcome to ask me anything they needed to, but I was not interested in the outcome of their investigation, I mean, the guy is dead, and that's that."

Jimmy tried to turn his head away, but the bandages made it awkward and he settled back into the same position again, fixing her with a stare. He tried to say "enough" but his throat was still raw. Marlys held up a cup of water with a bendy straw but he waved it away.

She went on. "It's too bad about the son and the aunt, of course, just awful, but what do you expect when alcohol is involved, and..." She stopped, glancing at him, shaking her head primly. "Anyway, like I say, terrible, just terrible, but not unexpected, thank goodness it was just the one eye, and your ... friend escaped with just a little scar on her ear. Could have been worse—much worse. Lesson learned..."

Jimmy pushed the call button for the nurse's station as Marlys explained how tactfully she had complained at her hotel about the housekeeping staff. "I actually found a Cheeto under the bed!"

The nurse explained that visiting hours were merely a guide as he ushered Marlys out fifteen minutes early so Jimmy could rest. Preoccupied with her wounded pride as a now-minor player in her son's life—and the discomfort of knowing he was sleeping with the alarmingly large and incomprehensible foreigner—Marlys departed the next day in the Banana Boat, a flotilla of resentments.

Once Jimmy got the sign-off from the doctors, and a thorough debriefing with Harold Fisher over the phone ("You've done nothing wrong, Jimmy—just be one hundred percent honest,") the police came to interview him. Feo fretted, but the partner of the lady detective who went in alone was a hunky blond, so he agreed to wait outside the door and chat with him. The investigation had been largely wrapped up before Jimmy woke from the coma.

Details about the stolen gun, the order of events that day, his relationship with Ramon and Oscar and Kitty—these were mere confirmations of information the detective already had, but she gave him free rein to talk.

"We have the text exchanges between you and Oscar," she told him, "we know you were initially unaware of his age or relationship to Mr. Castro."

In the end, Jimmy learned more than the detective.

Ramon had extensive bruising over his face and body at the time of his death. Was he aware Oscar had been beating him, perhaps for weeks, before the shooting?

No, nothing more than the incident on the stairs.

There were fresh strangulation marks on Ramon's neck. Did he remember anything about the argument he overheard to indicate Ramon was acting in self-defense, that Oscar was attacking him, or that he shot him to save his own life?

"No, I just heard the screaming."

Oscar had a blood-alcohol level higher than Ramon's at the time of his death—had he observed a marked change in his behavior in the last days or weeks before the incident?

He had ended contact almost completely with them both after Ramon attacked him on the stairs, he told her. The one time Oscar had come up, naturally, he had seemed distant, muted, but not obviously upset.

"One last thing," she said. "We doubt you could have known because we suspect even the deceased were unaware: they were not related."

"What?"

"We did DNA tests and found that Mr. Castro was not Oscar's biological father. Based on interviews with family members in Mexico and the Bakersfield area, we believe Mr.

Castro did have a relationship with Oscar's mother, but he was not his biological father. We believe she deceived him. However, as she is also deceased, she was not available for questioning."

Friends and staff attended Jimmy's graduation from the hospital after six weeks of recovery, including physical therapy to help with his new visual impairment, and counseling for both the trauma of the attack and his inadvertent rehabilitation from alcohol dependency.

Dee brought balloons and they raised glasses of sparkling cider in his hospital room. "I'd like to say 'You stopped in time' before you lost the last shred of your virtue, your dignity, your eye—but that's all out the window. The good news is: your transformation into butt pirate is complete! Congratulations!"

Jimmy adjusted his eye patch with his middle finger.

"A song! A song!" Feo and Vic demanded, and Dee strapped on his banjo.

"How about a little Smiths?"

Jimmy protested—he knew what was coming. "I—"

"Girlfriend in a Coma?"

"No—"

"I know! Five, six, seven, eight...! 'Girlfriend in a coma, I know, I know, it's serious...'" Dee launched into his number as several male nurses gathered around the local celebrity.

"You know he was here every day while you were in the coma, right?" Vic asked Jimmy.

"Was that Dee? A voice kept whispering, 'Run to the light, Carol Anne.'"

"Wow, you really can't take him anywhere—OH!" Vic's eyes

popped wide and they grabbed their belly. “Oh, that was a good one.”

“Baby kicking?”

“Yeah, here—feel.” They drew Jimmy’s hand to the spot, and there came a sharp doink that made him jump.

“Wow—feisty, like his Auntie Dee.”

Vic raised their eyebrows. “Are we sure about this ‘he/his’?”

“Do you know?”

“No, they asked if I wanted to know when I got the ultrasound but I didn’t want them to say while you were out of it. Anyway, nothing’s set in stone—maybe we let the kid tell us their pronouns.” Jimmy nodded absently, distracted by Dee’s second song, “Both Sides Now” by Joni Mitchell.

“I’ve looked at life from both sides now...”

Jimmy shouted. “David Dennis Waters! I swear to god...!”

[Interview transcripts edited for clarity.]

Broken Spirits was an enormous success—your paintings got reviewed in some major publications, and all of them mentioned how the artist was recovering from the recent domestic shooting in California.

Yeah. Great publicity right out of the gate—Paul and Dexter knew it—they pushed the schedule up to capitalize on the news cycle, made it a solo pop-up show with a community sponsor, hired a special publicist just for the event. The fact that the artist was not on site meant they could say and do anything they wanted.

Obviously, I wasn't happy once I found out how they exploited the situation, but it did create a mystique. Every one of my paintings sold before I even got out of the hospital. Probably wouldn't have happened if I'd been there or just been part of a group show.

Your life changed dramatically—sudden fame, and notoriety—sudden wealth, but also, a disfiguring injury.

Oh, you noticed the eye patch, huh? (Laughter.)

And there's that other element to this—these were not entirely your own works of art.

Several of them were—seven of them were untouched, of the original ten that I'd sent to meet Dexter—he wouldn't let Paul touch them. Paul wanted to make all of the paintings consistent—Dexter said no—and besides, they were already in New York and had been used for some of the marketing for the group show. He felt they gave more depth—if all of them had the splashes of black on them, they might start to feel conspicuously "matchy-matchy" and he preferred a more complex story. In fact, those seven fetched some of the highest prices in the sale.

Back to Paul's scheme—he went to your apartment and he took the paintings. And did he steal those?
No—taking them was on the up and up, technically. My mother gave him permission to enter the premises while I was incapacitated and he was simply fulfilling the terms of the contract by shipping them out for the show—he convinced her that even my early work would sell. She certainly didn't want to know anything about the state of things in the apartment, forensically speaking. She ended up inadvertently giving Paul permission to clean out my studio of all artwork, and the right to make material changes to the art for the purpose of making them more marketable—in his words, to clean them up, to conserve and restore them after the shooting.

And that's where things got dicey.
What I didn't know, what nobody but the police and Paul knew because no one else actually went to the studio—it was a crime scene for a while, and they were focused on me and Vic—was that most of the paintings were against the wall behind Ramon when he put the rifle in his mouth. As Paul put it so inartfully later—in his own defense—Ramon "shot his wad" all over them, and they were ruined—all more or less covered with a spray of blood, bone and brain matter. The cleaning crew had done the floors and wall but left the artwork mostly untouched for fear of ruining it,

except for the big chunks, of course—ugh. Paul said at first he thought the whole thing would have to be scrapped.

Of course, you were in no condition to produce more work for the foreseeable future, and seven paintings in New York wasn't enough to launch a career.

Exactly. But Paul said he went down to the alley to take out a stinking bag of trash—partly out of curiosity to see the basement, and partly because he saw the dumpster through the window and there were a couple of paintings stacked behind it. He had a hunch. They were mine, the ones I had given to Ramon and Oscar. They were dirty, it had rained, he said someone had put out some cigarettes on them, small round burn marks and black slashes—Ramon obviously, in his last days.

Paul said he started thinking how he might be able to salvage those two, just dirty but not bloodied. He thought: what if he covered the burns with paint, like Jackson Pollock? Splatters and drips and so forth. And from there it wasn't too much to think of sealing in all the dried pieces of Ramon—not to be graphic—under a layer of paint, black, of course. Why not?

So that's how that happened.

Yep. He went to the hardware store for plain old semi-gloss black house paint, and right there in my studio he started dripping and pouring the black over all the dried muck basically. He didn't even use a tarp—the spills and drips are still on the floor. Not a bad gimmick, it turned out—the landscapes and dreamscapes, the impressionist crap Dexter had laughed at suddenly became part of the later series with a compositional technique he used to cover up the unsavory bits, as well as my embarrassing efforts. He pressed some paintings against each other and made, like, inkblots, mirror images, called them diptychs and jacked the prices up for the sets.

Nothing to do with you.

Nope. Not my idea. Clever, but I didn't know about any of it, and by the time I got out of the hospital, the show had happened, the paintings were out the door—and they were hoping the fat check would keep me from asking too many questions. And they were right. I had plenty to think about with my recovery, Vic and the baby, and putting my life back together.

It was a perfect setup in a way, my debut show. The mysterious wounded artist, fighting for his life. They used the pictures JT had done, including some of the ones with the bruise showing. It all had an almost memorial quality to it, like "Get in on the ground floor cuz this guy might not make it." They could say anything. The publicist's assistant leaked a rumor that the work contained actual pieces of the Albany shooter's head, and the artist's blood—some of them did!—and for those people who were horrified by it, Paul and Dexter laughed and said people would believe anything. And for the people who were fascinated by this ghoulish spin on "mixed media," they let them believe it with a lot of "I can neither confirm nor deny."

Anyway, horrified or fascinated, lots of people came to see it, and by the time I was up and out of the hospital, the show had already happened, I had a publicist through Dexter's gallery at my disposal, a string of interview requests—and checks for almost a quarter million dollars, between the proceeds of the sale and GoFundMe campaign.

No shit…
In the end it was the clients who bought those three *Ghosts*-series paintings Paul sold privately, for significant sums, the ones I had abandoned at his apartment that Dexter sneered at, and he did the same black splashes on those. One of the buyers had theirs examined for insurance purposes, and the mixed media on those turned out to be soggy almond granola.

Paul confessed most of that part of the story to me later. What a mess…
Seriously. Luckily, Harold Fisher was able to provide multiple affidavits that I was completely unaware of all their shenanigans. But Paul was pretty much a pariah after that.

He ended up paying a large sum to settle with the three plaintiffs. It ruined him—he had to halt renovations on the duplex, he even considered closing up the stairwell and reselling the upstairs unit. He was never himself again. It was always his ambition to have a proper, beautiful duplex to entertain in, and it was their family home for forty years.
I assume that's why he spent the remainder of his life in a blizzard of cocaine.

Strange. Paul was your first real patron.
I guess so—in the end, the bungalow painting and his portrait were the only two pictures he bought. He made

more money off of my paintings than he ever paid. He was a great promoter if he believed in you, if he thought you were going somewhere. Or if he wanted to fuck you.

He did love the picture of the bungalow—never sold it, even when he was having money troubles. His son had it insured for high five figures.
I noticed the portrait was still in the library.

The agent told Paul Jr. and Blair to leave it while it's on the market, for the ah-ha factor. He was well known, almost as much as his wife, but they didn't want to mention it in the listing to avoid the lookie-loos.
Huh.

In spite of everything, you became a public figure and your work is in some important collections.
And it only cost me an eye.

This is the first time you've talked on the record about your relationship with Ramon and Oscar Castro. Why?
You mean besides the pedophilia, incest, and murder-suicide? Jesus. Technically I told Paul a lot of this, but in the story he wrote at the time, he chose to focus on aspects that had less to do with me and the art—he was too personally and financially involved. His article was about issues of mental health, immigration, substance abuse. And a lot of what I told him was off the record. But here we are, and I assume you can see why I kept a lot of it quiet.

How do you feel, now, looking back on it—on your relationship with a pedophile and murderer—this monster who killed two people, tried to kill you and your friend, and then committed suicide?
He wasn't a monster. He was mentally ill—he was an alcoholic. I'm so tired of having to explain that to people.

That's it? He was mentally ill?
He was—I mean, there is still that stigma, isn't there? To a lot of people addicts and alcoholics are just bums, degenerates—filth. News flash: I'm one of them! I'm an alcoholic. It may be alcohol was the reason I missed all the clues. Ramon was so degraded by his alcoholism that he sexually abused his son for almost ten years. Reprehensible? Absolutely. For the violation of his child's trust and vulnerability, I feel disgust and anger—and I regret not having told someone, the police, the school, anyone. But he was drowning, and I didn't see it.
Paul went down to Mexico to talk to his family, and they said Ramon had been sexually abused by his own father—it was an open secret. Paul also got gonorrhea from a Mexican prostitute while he was down there, but that's another story.

Ha! Of course...
Ramon started drinking at the age of eleven and he committed suicide at thirty-seven—he was basically intoxicated for twenty-five years. After everything that happened, after everything he did, the only thing I have left for him is pity. I grieve the lives he took, of course, but I grieve the life he lived—it was a living hell—I honestly believe that.

And in the end, the family didn't even claim their bodies—they sure stepped right up to take ownership of the apartment building, though. We—mostly Feo—arranged for a burial of their cremains in the cemetery in Albany, and a headstone. We had a funeral after I got out of the hospital. Dee played "Rainbow Connection."

On the banjo?
Jesus Christ, in a cemetery? No. He plays the ukulele too.

And your family…
Amapola Gabriela Garcia-Traywick was born full term, healthy, loud, and hairy as hell. We named her after the Spanish word for poppy.

And you guys have another baby, I think?
Feo and Vic made a baby together—they talked about it for a while—Vic was an only child too and wanted to give Ama a little brother or sister—brother, actually—Ruso. He's already two!

How'd that happen—the old-fashioned way?
Yes. Turkey baster.

And you all live together?
We have a duplex, in Kensington. Me and Feo on one side, and Vic and their boyfriend on the other with an adjoining door—the kids go bombing through all day and night. I kept the studio—we bought the whole building from the family, me and Feo turned it into condos—most of the people renting from Kitty wanted out right away,

and the family wanted a quick cash out. I still spend a fair few nights down there—I love the kids, and I love Feo of course, and Vic, but I need time to myself. I still paint there.

You're still living and painting in the studio where you were shot?
I know! Scene of the crime, right? But you know what, horrible as it was, the shit that goes on in my head is worse, and I get jangled if I don't get away from the commotion at home. Feo and Vic got the kids covered. I've tried painting at home, and it's just too much chaos for me. People ask me if my studio is haunted, but what is a muse but a kind of spirit?

I need to wrap things up here, Jimmy—any last words?
Ugh. Really? That's grim.

Haha. Sorry. Hundred words or less: What's YOUR story of modern art? You've painted a pretty cynical picture of the art world.
You want a soundbite. OK.
Art is like the sea, right? You go to a museum or a gallery, and for most people, I'm talking ninety-five percent, it's like a day at the beach, a nice view from the shore. Beautiful—sunsets and sailboats—placid, calm, serene.
It's not until you become a sailor that you begin to understand all the things you can't see—the treachery, the depths, the chance. You might even say only those lost at sea really understand it.

Good enough, I can work with that—thanks, Jimmy! Gotta go, I have another meeting—hey, talk soon. Ciao!

OK, bye.

A NOTE FROM THE AUTHOR

Thank you for reading *Waterspout*.

If you were moved by this book, leaving a short review wherever you bought it makes a real difference—even a sentence or two helps other readers and the author enormously.

ABOUT THE AUTHOR

Troy Ford is an author, editor, and the publisher of two popular newsletters: the writing-focused Ford Knows Books, and Qstack, an LGBTQIA+ Directory, Platform, and Community of newsletter writers and readers. As a creator and advocate, his mission is to give voice to queer people and issues by promoting their visibility through media projects and collaborations, and through his own fiction and essays.

Troy's writing explores the joy and pain of queerness through the lens of gay men who struggle in a world that views their lives as *other* and *less than.* His themes include love and sex, romance and friendships, community and family, growing up and bullying, substance abuse and self-destructiveness—all with a touch of humor to lighten otherwise difficult topics.

A native Californian, he grew up overseas in the Middle East and eventually settled in the San Francisco/Bay Area where he earned a B.A. in Rhetoric from UC Berkeley. Since 2019, he has lived in Sitges, Spain with his husband and AmStaff Terrier.

Subscribe to his newsletter for updates and insights at: troyford.substack.com

www.ingramcontent.com/pod-product-compliance
Lightning Source LLC
LaVergne TN
LVHW091254150826
845673LV00006B/1418